MEGA 3
WHEN GIANTS COLLIDE
JAKE BIBLE

Chapter One- Paradise Lost

The sun beat down on Ballantine as he paced back and forth across the blindingly bright sand of the unnamed beach. Dressed in his usual khakis and polo shirt, Ballantine felt the sweat trickle from his armpits and down his sides, as the speaker on the other end of the satellite phone he gripped made him more and more frustrated.

"I know that, William!" Ballantine shouted into the sat phone. "What the fuck do you think I've been doing all these months?"

Fit, tan, and muscular, Ballantine may have looked like a golf pro, but he was more than capable of handling himself, when the need arose. No matter his physical skills, or even his intellectual skills, his verbal skills was what he needed and they were failing him at that moment.

"Listen, you pencil pushing piece of rhino dung," Ballantine spat, "you are where you are because of me. I created that division for you. Don't interrupt me! Listen. That's what I'm saying to you, got it? Just listen."

Ballantine took his sunglasses off and pinched the bridge of his nose as the speaker did the opposite of his request. Before putting his sunglasses back on, Ballantine squinted out across the waves at the ship anchored in the deeper waters off the beach. At over 90 meters, the Beowulf III was a triple hulled "research vessel" styled along the lines of the RV Falkor that had been built and financed by Google many years before. Unlike that vessel, the Beowulf III was designed for purposes much more serious.

The B3, as its crew called it, was home to Team Grendel and an additional crew of 10. Ideally it would have had a support crew of 20 persons, but it had become harder and harder to find people willing to sign on to the dangerous, and covert work that Ballantine and Team Grendel were tasked with.

"William, stop," Ballantine sighed as he closed his eyes and raised his face to the blinding sun. "You are preaching to the choir, my boy. I know exactly how deep I am with this situation. I've been running for my life for nearly six months now, so please don't tell me- Fine. Explain it to me, but don't forget who you are talking to."

***

The ocean breeze made the thin drapes flutter as Shane Reynolds sat in the lounge chair, a large cocktail in one hand and an almost as large glass pipe in the other. He placed his lips to the stem of the pipe and sucked, as a beautiful Samoan woman lit the bowl that was filled with sticky, stanky pot. Smoke bubbled into the reservoir of water, curled up into the glass stem then disappeared into Shane's mouth.

"That is amazing," he said when he finally exhaled the smoke and smiled at the woman. "You have the gift of a green thumb, Linny."

"Thank you, Shane," the woman grinned as she took her hit then set the pipe aside.

Blond haired, green eyed, and tan, Shane had rugged good looks made even more rugged by the eyepatch over his right eye. Decorated with a mutli-colored pot leaf, the eye patch covered the reminder of Shane's run in with a Somali pirate gang leader two years earlier. A solid reason why he no longer liked ice picks. While Shane had learned to live with the disability, it took some adjustment since he was an ex-Navy SEAL and trained sniper. As he told everyone on Team Grendel, "You only need one eye to shoot. You know, so I can see. Not that I'd shoot my eye. I didn't mean that."

Linny sat on Shane's lap, dressed in a slight, thin dress, and placed a finger on the eye patch.

2

"My poor Shane," she said, "what a cruel world it is to take the eye of such an accomplished shooter."

She started to lift the eyepatch, but he stopped her as he gently gripped her hand.

"You don't want to see what's under there," Shane said, setting his cocktail down on the table by the side of his lounge chair. "It will ruin the mood pretty quick."

"I doubt that," Linny said as she leaned in and kissed his hand, and then carefully plied it away from hers. "I'm not some weak stomached skirt that can't handle the realities of life."

"Weak stomached skirt?" Shane laughed. "Are we in some Sam Spade movie?"

"Who?" Linny asked.

"The Maltese Falcon?" Shane asked. "Humphrey Bogart?"

"Never saw it," Linny said.

"Too bad," Shane smiled, "it's a great movie. I don't know how many times I've blazed up and watched that flick. Max can care less about it, but I totally dig those old noir mysteries."

"Yeah, I like movies with color," Linny said, plucking the eyepatch off Shane's face. "I prefer reality to style."

Shane sat stock still as the beautiful woman in his lap studied the empty eye socket in his face. He waited for the recoil of horror and disgust, but instead, got a coy smile as she leaned in and kissed the edge of the socket then put the eyepatch back in place.

"Oh, my little sniper," Linny said. "I have seen so much worse than that. Any girl that's afraid of a little hole in the head is not paying attention to the right hole."

"I think I get the innuendo there," Shane sighed as Linny's lips found his neck and started to work their way down to his bare chest. "I guess it doesn't matter since we're well past the innuendo portion of the afternoon it looks like."

"Well past," Linny said as she continued to kiss his chest then worked her way back up his neck and to his lips. "Time to move this to someplace more comfortable."

She got up quickly, her long, brown legs peeking through the sheer skirt. She held out her hand and Shane took it as she led him over to the large bed in the center of the room. Two of the four walls were completely open to the view of the South Pacific Ocean and the warm breeze blew freely into the room, only slightly cooling the sheen of sweat on Shane's body as he lay down on the bed.

Dressed only in a pair of camo cutoffs, Shane soon found himself without even those as Linny straddled him and pulled the dress up over her head. Shane let out a low, slow whistle as he looked at her tone body. His fingers traced the tight muscles of her stomach, her chest, her arms, and the many scars that crisscrossed everywhere.

"He should never have done this to you," Shane said as he leaned up and kissed a large white scar that went from her left breast and down to her navel. "Sick fuck."

"Love is a strange weapon," Linny said as she let Shane's fingers play across her skin. "It props you up even as it beats you down."

"Do you ever miss him?" Shane asked.

"Never," Linny said, "and always."

Shane shook his head.

"He got what he deserved," Shane said. "Every ounce of it."

"Do you know what eighteen slugs weigh?" Linny smiled. "Because I do."

"I bet you do," Shane said. "What made you finally say you had enough?"

"Let's not talk about that right now," Linny said. "If you want something to break the mood, then talking about my late asshole of a husband is going to do it."

"My bad," Shane said as Linny leaned down and pressed her mouth to his. "Mmmmm, now it's my good."

***

"Not good," Ballantine said as he tried not to snap the sat phone in half. "That just won't do, William. We need supplies, we need financing, and we need rest. Most of all, we need sanctuary. There is no way the Beowulf III can just keep running indefinitely. There has to be something the company can do to... Yes, I know that... No, no, of course I take full responsibility, but that is beside the... Yes, yes, I understand. No, I'll wait."

Ballantine sighed and sat down right in the sand. He looked at the tips of his brown loafers and wondered how he'd gotten a thick scratch on the right one. Probably during one of the many firefights the Beowulf III had been in during the last eight months of travel and running.

"I'm guessing they don't want to play along anymore," Commander Vincent Thorne called out as he sat with his back against a palm tree, shaded by the thick tree line that bordered the beach. "Can't exactly blame them. We've got some serious heat on our tails."

Former commander of the Navy SEALs BUD/S training, Vincent Thorne was leader of Team Grendel, the band of ex-SEALs and other Special Forces misfits that Ballantine had brought together to handle less than ordinary situations. In his sixties, but still fit enough to take down men half his age, Thorne was not a man that minced words or wasted his time with pointless pleasantries.

"Commander," Ballantine said without turning to look at the man, "how long have you been listening?"

"The whole time," Thorne said. "I followed you down from the lodge when I saw you leave your room with the sat phone."

"It's not polite to eavesdrop, Commander," Ballantine replied. "I obviously wanted privacy."

"Nothing's private anymore, Ballantine," Thorne said. "Not when we keep having to run for our lives from black ops spooks. I signed on to lead Grendel, and work for you, because it was stated that we'd have the unlimited backing of a company with unlimited resources. These last few months have shown me that there are quite a few limitations."

"We made some enemies," Ballantine said. "It can't be avoided in our line of work."

"No, it can't," Thorne said, "but the whole point of working for a company that doesn't even have a name is so those enemies are kept off our asses. The missions are what matters, right? Hard to focus on missions when we're constantly looking over our shoulders."

"Yes, I know that Vincent," Ballantine said. "That is part of the purpose of this private conversation, so if you... Yes, of course I'm still here! Where...? How do you...?"

Thorne laced his hands behind his head and watched as Ballantine stood up and began to pace the beach once again.

***

"Like a fucking caged tiger," a large man laughed as he watched the five foot tall woman before him.

At six feet and eight inches, the man was not only considerably taller than the woman was, but he also outweighed her by close to two hundred pounds. The bulk of his brown Samoan body stood like a mountain over her as she kept walking back and forth in front of him. He sneered down at the woman, ignoring the fact that she was obviously in great shape. With close cropped black hair and muscles tanned from months out on the open ocean, the woman would have been impressive to anyone that didn't tower over her by almost two full feet.

"She ain't got the balls for it, bra," another man said from behind the first. "Just take the money and let's go."

"Hold on, hold on," the first man replied. "Give the paumuku a chance to make good on her braggin'."

The woman stopped and looked up at the man.

"Who you calling a paumuku, you susu poki?" the woman grinned.

Both men growled low at the insult and the sneer faded quickly from the first man's face, quickly replaced by a deadly snarl.

"Uh, sugar ass? What did you just call the very large man?" Max Reynolds asked as he sat at a long table at the edge of a small cliff overlooking the ocean. "Darby? Baby? I don't think you're making friends here."

The woman, Darby, turned and looked over her shoulder and gave Max a wide grin.

"Let me handle this," she said. "He started it, I finish it."

Max Reynolds looked almost exactly like his brother Shane, and they were often mistaken for twins, even though they were nine months apart. Or they used to be mistaken for twins before Max was wounded by an IED during his time in Afghanistan and ended up without a left ear and half of his face a mass of burn scars. He absentmindedly scratched at the scarring as he watched the woman he loved set herself for what was going to be one hell of a fight.

Trained as a Navy SEAL, Max could easily jump in and help Darby out, but he had more than a couple of reasons not to. First, Darby was ex-Israeli Special Forces, amongst other things, and could handle herself. Second, she'd kick his ass if he tried to step in. Third, his right leg was almost healed from a nasty break that had happened during Team Grendel's previous mission in the deeps of the Amazon jungle, and the Beowulf III's Chief Medical Officer, Gunnar Peterson, would gut him if he hurt it again.

More important than all the reasons, Max loved watching his woman kick the living shit out of people. It was a better high than the large joint he held between his fingers.

"Oh, I was totally going to let you handle it," Max said as he took a drag off the joint. "I'm just saying that name calling isn't the answer to solving conflict."

He took another drag, held it, and then let it out slowly, watching as the smoke drifted in the slight breeze.

"So hurry up and kick this guy's ass so we can go have lunch, will ya?" Max grinned. "I'm fucking starving here."

***

"Fresh fruit!" Kinsey Thorne exclaimed, as the bowl of pineapple, mango, passion fruit, and bananas was set in front of her. She clapped her hands together as she sat at a table on the observation deck of the Beowulf III. "Oh, my fucking god, am I glad to see fresh fruit!"

"One of the perks of anchoring off a tropical paradise," Darren Chambers said as he sat down opposite Kinsey. "Dig in, 'Sey."

"Thank you, 'Ren, I think I will," she replied as she grabbed her fork and started to stuff her mouth full of fruit. "Mmmm!"

Kinsey Thorne, daughter of Vincent Thorne and cousin to the Reynolds boys, once had a shot at being the first woman inducted into the elite ranks of the Navy SEALs. The pressure of the task, and the use of methamphetamines, scuttled that history making chance, and she had found herself in a junkie hell that most people only got out of by way of the morgue. With the help of her father and cousins, she was yanked from her nightmare and recruited into Team Grendel.

The man seated across from her could have been a GQ model, but was instead her ex-husband and semi-co-leader of Team Grendel alongside her father. Darren Chambers had left the Navy SEALs to pursue a mad dream of finding an impossible whale that everyone said couldn't exist. He'd encountered it on a mission and he became obsessed with tracking down the ocean giant, even though everyone around him thought he was insane.

Everyone except for the man that plopped down next Kinsey and shoved her over with his hip so he could snag the bowl of fruit for himself.

"Hey!" Kinsey shouted as she swatted Gunnar Peterson's hand away. "My fruit, bitch! Get your own!"

"No smacksies," Gunnar said. "It's not like you got the fruit yourself!"

Chief Science Officer, as well as Chief Medical Officer of the Beowulf III, and childhood friend of both Kinsey's and Darren's, Gunnar was not muscled and trained to kill like the two people he just joined. His training was as a medical doctor and then doctor of marine biology. He was one of the few people that had believed Darren, and along with a small motley crew, had sailed with him in pursuit of the impossible whale. At least until Ballantine had come along and changed all of their lives.

"I'll get you a bowl of fruit, Gun," Darren sighed, "since you're going to join us anyway."

Gunnar looked at the two ex-spouses and frowned.

"Uh-oh, am I interrupting something special?" he asked.

"No," Kinsey said.

"It would have been our anniversary if we'd stayed married," Darren said.

"Really?" Gunnar and Kinsey said at the same time.

"I don't know why I even try," Darren sighed as he got up and headed to the steps down to the upper deck. "I'll be right back with more fruit."

***

"Seventy-five feet long," Lucretia "Lucy" Durning said as she downed another glass of liquor and slammed it on the table. "I shit you not, folks."

Lucy looked into her glass and frowned, her body swaying slightly from the drink.

"What's this called?" she asked the four men seated across from her in the small bar.

"Pulu," one man said as he filled her glass again from a pitcher. "You like it?"

"Tastes good," Lucy hiccupped. "What's it made from?"

"Little of dis, little of dat," the man smiled. "Drink up and tell us more about this giant snake."

"Titanoboa," Lucy corrected as she picked up her full glass and sloshed some of the home-brewed liquor onto the table, "and not just giant, but prehistoric. Fucking thing shouldn't exist, but it did. Until we got a hold of it."

She grinned then took a long drink. With her other hand, she extended her index finger and then cocked her thumb.

"Bang bang," she said when done drinking. "Snake go dead."

"You sayin' you killed a snake that was seventy-five feet long and six feet wide?" one of the men asked then laughed. "Not possible, bra. Things like dat only in bad movies."

"Snake happens, man," Lucy replied, "and when snake happens, Team Grendel is there to save the day." She waggled a finger in front of the men. "Not just snakes, my bulky, muscly, really, really tan friends, but sharks too. Fucking huge sharks. Bang bang, boom!"

Lucy finished off her glass of pulu and smiled. Then she turned and threw up all over the bar's dirt floor. The men gasped then started to laugh as she wobbled, wobbled, wobbled then fell off her bench and right into her sickness. She lay there, all six feet of her, as the men continued to laugh.

"I think I need a wet wipe," she slurred before her eyes closed.

***

"You gonna let me slap your woman around, bra?" the mountain of a man asked Max. "You just gonna sit there like a pipi elo while I give this kefe a smack down? You pitiful, bra."

"What's a pipi elo?" Max asked Darby.

"Stinky pussy," Darby replied.

"Oh," Max nodded then smoked the rest of his joint. "Now, if anything is stinky around here, it's this dank bud. This is some fine, fine shit, dude. A lady we know grows it and I got more. Now, how about you just apologize to my deadly lady friend and we call it a day?"

"I said I'd handle this, Maxwell," Darby said.

"I know, I know, but I've got this killer buzz on and I hate for violence to ruin it," Max replied. "Don't get me wrong, woman with the hot ass, I love it when you beat the split fuck out of assholes that deserve it, but this is a really small island and once you crush him I have a feeling we won't be welcome anymore."

"That some of Linny's weed?" the man asked.

"Hey, dude, I ain't one to smoke and tell," Max said as he started to roll another joint. "Max Reynolds ain't no snitch."

"Linny's our sister," the man responded as he hooked a thumb over his shoulder at the other man, "and she ain't ever mentioned no scarfaced asshole and a midget dyke before."

The man started to step around Darby towards Max, but Darby placed a hand on his gut and shoved him back. He stumbled a couple of steps and his eyes went wide with surprise.

"Little thing got some solid to her," the man laughed. He looked at Darby and nodded. "I give you that, girl." Then he pointed at Max. "I think you stole some of my sister's stash. Only reason you'd have her good stuff."

"Whoa, whoa, whoa, brown beefcake," Max said as he licked the joint and sealed it tight. "I take my pot karma very seriously and I'd never lift someone's stash. Not ever." He tucked the joint behind his ear. His right one. "Darby, my dearest killing machine, I have tried to help these gentlemen avoid their inevitable ass kicking, but they just won't listen. I think a lesson in manners is now in order."

"Just as I have been saying from the start," Darby said. "You waste too much time, Maxwell."

"Don't you just love how she says Maxwell?" Max asked the men. "Isn't it the cutest thing you've ever heard?"

"Stand up and fight for your woman, bra," the man growled. "Grow some and do what's right."

"Oh, I am, dude," Max grinned. "Trust me. Darby?"

"I don't need your permission," Darby said.

"Well, no, I know that," Max said, frowning. "I was just setting you up for one of those cool moments where I say 'Darby?' and then you punch the guy really hard so he falls to his knees. It was all for effect. A little showmanship doesn't hurt now and again, does it? We can't all be brute force and heavy violence."

"Shut up," Darby said.

"Good idea," Max nodded then gave a thumbs up to the two men.

"Your woman owns your cock," the mountain of a man laughed, "and I'm about to own her."

"Own this," Darby said as she rushed the man and basically climbed right up him so her face was in his. She grabbed the back of his head then slammed her forehead into his nose, crushing it into a pulp instantly. She jumped down and gave the man's knees two swift kicks, sending him to the sandy dirt.

"Own this," Max chuckled. "Okay, that's a good one."

***

A scream from outside the bar diverted the men's attention from the passed out Lucy. They all turned and looked out into the glaring sun.

"That sounded like Levi," one of them said.

There was another scream that was quickly choked off.

"Shit," another man said, "we better go see what's happening."

"What about her?" another asked as he nudged Lucy with his toe.

11

"Roll her over so she doesn't choke if she pukes again."

***

The phone on the bedside table rang shrilly, but Linny and Shane were too busy to get it. Their bodies were intertwined, legs wrapped about legs, arms wrapped about backs, mouths pressed hard together. Linny was on top, then Shane, then Linny, over and over as they never stopped moving.

The phone kept ringing.

"Do you need to get that?" Shane gasped as he came up for air.

"Fuck that," Linny said as she arched her back and ground down on him.

The phone rang on and on.

"Kinda hard to concentrate," Shane said.

"You're doing just fine," Linny smiled as she rocked back and forth on top of him. "Shut up and ignore it."

He grabbed her and brought her mouth down to his. They kissed with a passion that left them gasping once they finally broke away.

The phone did not stop ringing.

"Oh, for fuck's sake!" Linny yelled as she grabbed the handset. "What? What the fuck do you want?"

She listened intently as the person on the other end started shouting. Shane traced his finger from her thigh, up across her belly, and to her left breast. Linny swatted his hand away when he began to roll her nipple between his finger and thumb.

"What do you mean a woman broke both his kneecaps?" Linny exclaimed.

That got Shane's attention.

"She just attacked him? For no reason?" Linny asked. "Where?" She listened then looked Shane in the eye. "The man is American with scars on his face. No left ear. Yeah, I think I know who he is. I'll be right there."

Shane didn't protest when she hung up the phone, got off him, and started to get dressed.

"So… American with scars and no left ear," he stated, "that would be my brother."

"I know," Linny said as she pulled on a t-shirt and then a short cotton skirt. "His girlfriend is beating the shit out of my brothers and cousins."

"Oh, shit," Shane said as he hurried from the bed to find his clothes, "that's not good."

Linny had grabbed her keys and was heading to the door when he said that. She stopped and frowned at him.

"Wait, you weren't worried when you heard your brother was involved, but now that you know his girlfriend is, you panic?" Linny asked. "Who is this woman?"

"First, she's not his girlfriend," Shane said as he pulled his cutoffs on. "More like he's her boyfriend. There's a difference, trust me. Second, my brother can hold his own in a fight, so I never really worry about him. Third, her name is Darby and she will probably kill your brothers and cousins if we don't stop her."

Linny just stared at Shane as he got his shirt on. He found his flip flops and hurried to the door.

"What?" he asked as she kept staring.

"A woman is not going to kill my brothers and cousins," Linny said, "they will kill her."

"Yeah, you just keep thinking that." Shane laughed. "I told you I rolled in with a rough crew."

"Your brother knows she can kill them?"

"Yep," Shane nodded.

"He isn't going to stop her?"

"Nope," Shane replied, "he loves watching her kick ass."

"Even if she kills them," she said.

"Even if she kills them," Shane responded. "I'm sure those two have already justified why your brothers and cousins deserve to die. Max wouldn't let it happen unless there was some reason."

"Fucking Navy SEALs," she said, shaking her head. "Why I get involved with you assholes, I don't know."

"Because we're good in the sack," he said as he kissed her and turned her towards the door. "Now, let's save your family from some serious heartbreak."

***

"You're killing me, William," Ballantine said. "All of this was already sanctioned by the company. We were hired to do a job and we did it. There isn't a single one of those creatures left out there. We've even had time to do side jobs along the way... Yes, I know the Brazilian government protested our mission in the Amazon... What do you mean we were convicted? What the fuck, William? We had immunity! The company was supposed to... Yes, I am aware of that... Well, that's the legal department's problem! How is that? They what? Who bought them? Jesus Christ... No, I know exactly who runs that outfit... That really has no bearing on anything... Say that again... No, the last part... How in the fuck can they press charges? They fucking hired us! No, don't even try that shit with me, William! No... FUCK! Yeah, I'll hold, but hurry the fuck up... Oh, and William? Protocol fifty-four is in effect if you don't come back with an answer I want to hear... Yes, you heard me... Well, too bad. They should have thought of that before."

"This sounds like it's going well," Thorne said from his shady spot under the palm tree.

"Fucking swimmingly," Ballantine replied. "The Team better be enjoying themselves because I don't think we're going to get any off boat R and R again for a long time."

"That bad?" Thorne asked.

"I haven't seen worse," Ballantine nodded.

***

"Left side!" Max shouted. "Right side! Duck! Duck! Yeah! Oh that has to hurt! What?"

Darby rolled to the side just as a foot came down where she'd just been. She sent a quick jab into the man's calf, right into a nerve cluster that sent the huge man to the ground. Without missing a second, she slammed her fist into the man's temple then rolled herself backwards to her feet.

"Stop distracting me, Maxwell," Darby said.

"My bad," Max said as he took the joint from his ear and put it to his lips. "Behind you."

Darby roundhouse kicked the man coming for her in the balls. He squealed then collapsed onto his knees while his hands gripped his crotch. Instead of punching him herself, she stepped to the side and let the man behind her do it as the fist that was meant for the back of her head went flying by.

"Oh, shit, bra," the man said to his friend he'd just punched. He started to say more, but Darby sent a high kick into his throat. He fell to his knees, his hands around his neck as he struggled to breathe through his crushed windpipe.

Two more men rushed her, but she easily avoided their massive bulk and sent one down with three hard shots to his left kidney, and then sent the other one down by stomping on the back of his right foot, snapping his Achilles' tendon in half.

Men, huge men, used to cracking open coconuts with their bare hands, lay on the ground in various forms of agony. Some cried out for help as they clutched broken limbs, while others just moaned and rocked themselves, gripped by a crushing disbelief that they were taken down by a woman and now lying in their own piss and blood.

"Last one, sexy killer," Max said as he pointed to the mountain of a man that started it all. "You gonna beat that apology out of him or has he had enough?"

The mountain man, Levi, lay on the ground, his hands protecting the shattered remains of his kneecaps. He looked up at Darby with pain and fear filled eyes as she stood over him.

"Sorry, lady," Levi said. "I'm so fucking sorry. I shouldn't have hassled you."

"Or my boyfriend," Darby said.

"Right, or your boyfriend," Levi agreed. "I was being rude."

"Dang skippy," Max said as he stood up and walked over by Darby. "Now, let this be a lesson to you, young man. You don't say bad things to people you don't know because sometimes they are highly trained killing machines that have an OCD need to beat the shit out of rude fucks like you. Understood?"

"Yeah, bra," Levi nodded, tears streaming down his cheeks, "understood."

An open top Jeep without a roll cage came skidding to a stop in the gravel and sand a few feet from the aftermath of the fight.

"Hey, it's Shane," Max said as he waved. "Dude! You totally missed it! Darby like fucking crushed these assholes!"

"Those assholes are my family, you stupid..." Linny yelled then stopped as she saw the state her brothers and cousins were in. "Oka... what did you do?"

Max looked from Linny to the broken men that lay in the sand outside the bar.

"Oh, shit," he said. "Family?"

"Family, dude," Shane responded, "brothers and cousins."

"Oh...huh," Max nodded then looked at Linny. "Hey, totally sorry about this. That one there said some shitty things to Darby and then it all went downhill pretty fast."

"You did all this?" Linny asked Darby.

"All he needed to do was apologize," Darby said as she looked up at the woman that was nearly a foot taller than she was. "I gave them more than a few chances."

"She did," Max nodded. "I gave them chances too. They just kept being dicks."

"Oh, I'm sure you did everything in your power to diffuse the situation," Shane scowled.

"*Diffuse the situation?*" Max asked. "What strange words you say, brother. Methinks the Samoan woman has you under her witchcraft."

"You're the last one to talk about being under a woman's witchcraft," Shane said.

"Ain't gonna argue with you there, dude," Max smiled as he took a hit from his joint and handed it to Shane.

Despite the carnage before him, Shane didn't hesitate to take the joint and suck it all the way down.

"Thanks," Shane said as he dropped the roach and crushed it under his flip flop. "Now, how the fuck are you going to make this right?"

"Me?" Max asked.

"You and Darby," Shane said. "Look at them. This island only has around 200 people on it and you just broke like half of them."

"There are only six there," Darby said, "and they'll heal."

"How?" Linny snapped. "This is Olosega, not Ofu. There's no clinic on this island, and the one across the straight is total shit. They are going to have to be taken to Faleasao or even to Pago Pago to get the care they need. You have any idea how much that is going to cost?"

Linny threw up her hands and turned in a circle.

"Why does this shit happen to me?" she yelled. "Why do I get mixed up with these assholes?"

"Lin, come on," Shane said, "we'll make it right."

"Why?" Darby asked. "They started it and I finished it. They should know better than to pick fights they can't win."

"Look at you!" Linny shouted. "What man thinks he can't beat you in a fight?"

Shane and Max both raised their hands.

"That's because you know what she can do!" Linny yelled.

"Now they know what I can do," Darby said. She took a deep breath then let it out. "You are upset because you have to take care of them. I understand and for that I'm sorry. No woman should have to take care of assholes like these. They were the ones that thought insulting a woman and her boyfriend, who were just enjoying the sun and some drinks, was a fun way to spend the afternoon. You should thank me for teaching them a valuable lesson in caution."

"Are you for real?" Linny growled then looked at Shane. "Is she for real?"

Before Shane could respond, Ballantine and Thorne came up a trail from the small cliff that overlooked the beach below.

"Well, someone's been busy," Ballantine said as he looked directly at Darby.

"Boys," Thorne sighed, "what the fuck have you two done now?"

"Us?" Shane asked, looking shocked.

"I didn't touch them, Uncle Vinny," Max said.

"Obviously not," Ballantine nodded. "I'd know Darby's handy work anywhere." he saw the stricken look on Linny's face. "I assume you know these gentlemen, what with it being such a small island."

"They're her family," Shane said. "Brothers and cousins."

"Employed or unemployed?" Ballantine asked as he reached into his pocket and pulled out a roll of 100 dollar bills.

"Excuse me?" Linny asked.

Ballantine started to pull bills from the roll. "Are they employed or unemployed?"

"They work for me," Linny said, "in the family business." She turned and glared at Shane. "Harvest is about to start."

"So employed then," Ballantine said as he looked at the roll and just handed it over. "This will cover their medical expenses and any temp labor you need to hire for your crops, Ms. Taaloga. My apologies for the inconvenience."

"How do you know my name?" Linny asked.

"This is my boss," Shane said. "He makes a point of knowing everyone's name."

"Yes, I do," Ballantine said. "I was hoping to be able to get to know more about all of you, as I do love this little island of yours, but unfortunately, we must leave immediately."

"Whoa! You said we'd have a couple weeks to rest up," Shane said, looking at Linny. "We can trust her, she isn't going to rat out our location to anyone. That's why I suggested this place."

"No, I don't think she will rat us out, even with the current circumstances," Ballantine said, "but that doesn't matter. We have to go."

"We have a mission?" Max asked.

"That's need to know," Thorne said, "and right now all you need to know is that your ass needs to be back on the B3 in two seconds."

"Uncle Vinny, come on, man," Shane said. "We have been running for months. We haven't stopped working. We've killed everything we've been sent after. What the fuck is left in this ocean?"

"Plenty," Ballantine said. "More than you want to know, actually, but all of that is inconsequential. Our priority at the moment is to get back to the Beowulf III and get out into international waters as soon as possible."

The brothers stared at Ballantine then turned to their uncle. Thorne's face was completely blank as he refused to give even the slightest hint away of what was happening.

"Fine," Shane said as he looked at Linny. "I guess this is goodbye. I really am sorry for what happened."

He moved in for a kiss, but Linny took a couple steps back and turned her head.

"Yeah, great," he said as he glared at his brother. "Come on. The Zodiac is down this way. I'll drive."

"Where are we going?" Lucy asked as she stumbled out into the sunlight, her bikini top and shorts coated in vomit. "There a beach party? I love beach parties."

She stopped halfway and hunched over, and then proceeded to empty the contents of her stomach in such a violent way that her head jerked and slammed into the ground, knocking her out cold.

"You get to carry her," Shane said as he walked past his brother and pointed at Lucy. "Maybe your girlfriend will help."

"Yeah, we got it," Max said.

Darby didn't argue as she grabbed Lucy's legs while Max grabbed Lucy's shoulders. They followed Shane to a different trail than the one Ballantine and Thorne had come up. In seconds, they were lost from sight as they made their way down to the beach and the Zodiac raft waiting to take them back out to the Beowulf III.

"Again, my apologies," Ballantine said to Linny. "I hope they have a speedy recovery. At least know that it looks like she took it easy on them."

Linny just stood there as Ballantine gave her a wide smile and followed the brothers and Darby down to the beach.

"What?" Linny snapped as Thorne stood there watching her.

"I know you used to be a SEAL," Thorne said. "Shane told me all about that asshole. You seem tough and obviously know how to be in charge."

"Yeah, so?" she grumbled.

"Normally those qualities are good things," Thorne said, "but when we leave you need to forget about being tough and in charge. If anyone comes here looking for us, you hide. Just hide, and if you can't hide, then you tell them everything you know. Do not try to lie for Shane, got it? You tell them everything and hopefully they'll believe you and go away."

"I don't fucking know anything," Linny said. "Shane didn't tell me shit."

"I think he probably did," Thorne said as he pointed at her skirt. "That's on backwards, by the way."

She looked down and closed her eyes. "Mother fucker."

"Remember what I said," Thorne said one last time as he walked away. "Hide or be honest. Don't fight."

Linny looked up as Thorne stepped onto the trail. "Who's coming after you?"

"Bad people," Thorne said. "Very bad people. It's probably best you take that cash Ballantine gave you and get your people out of here. That'll be safer than hiding or being honest. Best just not to be around."

Thorne gave her a sad smile then was lost from sight as he descended the trail.

Linny looked down at the roll of 100s in her hand.

"Yeah, I think getting the fuck out of here is better," she said. Then she looked at the huge men that lay on the ground. "Great. How the fuck am I supposed to get you assholes to the fucking hospital?"

***

Boatswain Trevor "Popeye" De Bruhl cut the motor to the lift and shook his head as he looked at Lucy lying in the bottom of the Zodiac.

"What the hell happened to her?" Popeye asked as he waved his hand in front of his nose. Short, thin, bald, with massive forearms that were covered in tattoos. De Bruhl even had a one eyed squint like the cartoon Popeye. The main difference between the man and the cartoon character was that the flesh and blood Popeye was missing his right leg and in its place was a segmented, titanium prosthetic with a splayed piece of heavy duty rubber at the bottom. "She got food poisoning or something?"

"Something like that," Max said as he and Darby lifted Lucy out of the Zodiac while Popeye kept it steady. "Where's Gun? He's going to need to pump her stomach and put some fluids in her. Pretty sure she has alcohol poisoning."

"Lightweight," Popeye said.

"Can you have Captain Lake draw anchor and ready the ship?" Ballantine asked Popeye as he stepped onto the deck. "We will need to leave these waters ASAP."

"Sure thing, bossman," Popeye said. "You gonna need to call a meeting? That's your gonna need to call a meeting voice."

"Do I have a gonna need to call a meeting voice?" Ballantine asked.

"Yeah, you do," Shane said as he stepped around Ballantine and headed up to the observation deck. "Sounds just like your constipated voice."

"Stow it, Reynolds," Thorne said.

Shane just raised his hand and gave everyone the finger as he took the stairs up to the observation deck where he heard Kinsey and Darren talking.

"I'll call the meeting," Thorne said to Ballantine.

"Thank you, Commander," Ballantine said, then looked down at the stains on his khakis from where Lucy had puked on him during the ride from the island to the ship. "Give everyone time to clean up. Say, thirty minutes?"

"Will do," Thorne nodded.

***

The briefing room looked more like a corporate boardroom than a meeting room on a ship. The walls were paneled in expensive wood while the long table in the middle was made from a single piece of teak. Monitors lowered from the ceiling along the walls except for one side of the room which was nothing but sliding glass doors that looked out onto the clear blue waters of the South Pacific.

"Everyone take a seat," Thorne said as he sat towards the front of the table. "Lake won't be joining us since we have to get moving into open waters as soon as possible."

Darren, Kinsey, Shane, Max, and Darby, all came in and took their seats. Two of the newer additions to Team Grendel came into the room just after them.

In her late forties, with short, bobbed blonde hair and hazel eyes, Dr. Lisa Morganton was known as calm, cool, and collected.

In charge of the advanced bio-alternatives division of the company Ballantine worked for, Dr. Morganton was presumed dead in order to be protected from retribution by the Colende drug cartel after having her cover blown as an inside operative. Unfortunately for the doctor, that rouse made no difference since the cartel wanted everyone on the B3 dead.

The other newer addition was former Navy SEAL, Mike Pearlman. A double amputee, Mike had been recruited by a man called McCarthy to pilot narco-subs that Dr. Morganton had designed. Team Grendel had thwarted those plans and recruited Mike once the mission was over, not just because of his skills as an ex-SEAL, but because he had a personal relationship with Gunnar.

It was all very complicated for everyone.

"How the legs doing today, Mike?" Kinsey asked as she looked at his robotic prosthetics. "Still no glitches?"

"None," Mike said as he sat down, the gyros and servos in his legs whirring then going silent once he was settled. "Morganton and Gunnar have kept them running beautifully."

"I bet Gunnar has," Max said, nudging his brother. "Wink, wink. Nudge, nudge."

"You ever take them off before you do it with Gunnar?" Shane asked Mike. "I bet you do, huh? Give him a little double stump action."

"What the fuck is double stump action?" Max asked.

"I don't know, I just made it up," Shane replied. "Sounds dirty, though, doesn't it?"

"Totally," Max grinned then looked at Darby. "Maybe you and I could have a little double stump action later, eh, my little assassin of love?"

"Don't be an idiot," Darby frowned, "you have both of your legs."

"Yet, none of his brains," Kinsey said, getting a smile from Darby.

"We are not together," Mike said. "Gunnar has been very clear on that."

"Clear on what?" Gunnar asked as he stepped into the briefing room. "What'd I miss?"

"Apparently you're missing some double stump sexiness," Max said. "Your loss, dude."

Gunnar looked at the brothers then just took his seat. "Okay, I'm going to ignore that. Sorry I was late, had to make sure Lucy was hooked up to an IV."

"She going to be alright?" Darren asked.

"She'll be fine once she's fully hydrated," Gunnar said then looked at Ballantine. "So, what's the hurry that you had me backup all my files and start a satellite transfer?"

"That wasn't supposed to be public knowledge," Ballantine said.

"There's twenty of us on this ship, Ballantine," Gunnar said. "Everything becomes public knowledge at some point."

"Like my amazing sexual prowess," Max said. "I'm sure you hear it echoing through the passageways at night."

"Yet, we never hear Darby," Shane said. "Hmmm, I'm thinking this may be a one sided love affair."

"She's a pillow biter," Max whispered loudly. Darby just sighed.

"Boys?" Thorne asked.

"Shutting the fuck up, Uncle Vinny," Shane said.

"Zippity zoo," Max added as he pretended to zip his lips.

"Now that is out of your systems," Ballantine said as he stood up from his chair at the head of the table, "I'm now going to jump right in with both feet first. I hate to be the one to tell all of you, but as of this morning, every person on this ship, as well as the ship itself, has been disavowed by the government of the United States Of America."

They all stared at him for a minute.

"Does that mean we aren't citizens anymore?" Max finally asked.

"That means that those of us that were citizens are now considered nonexistent and those that weren't citizens are considered to be foreign aggressors and added to every watch list on the planet."

No one said a word.

"It's nothing special," Darby said. "You get used to it."

"You what?" Max asked, whipping his head around to look at Darby. "Whoa, what haven't you told me about yourself?"

"Almost everything," Darby said.

"Well, yeah, I knew we had secrets, but being thought of as a foreign aggressor is something you tell your boyfriend," Max said. "I mean, come on, Darby, I put my penis in you every night. I like to know when my penis is going into an enemy of the United States, because I'm just old school that way."

"Now I'm going to be sick like Lucy," Kinsey said.

"You've been on US soil lots of times since I've known you," Darren said to Darby.

"See?" she said casually. "Not a big deal."

"You're a traitor fucker," Shane said to Max. "It's like I don't even know who you are."

"Knock it off!" Thorne shouted. "This shit is very fucking serious!"

The brothers were about to respond, but their uncle's glare stopped them and they kept their mouth shut.

"I have Captain Lake taking us out into international waters since these waters are considered United States territory because of their proximity to American Samoa," Ballantine said. "He is then plotting a course to someplace that I believe we can be safe from our pursuers."

"They're still after us?" Darren asked. "We didn't lose them after that dust up in Chile?"

"No, unfortunately, we did not lose them," Ballantine said.

"Do we know for sure they're cartel?" Kinsey asked.

"We know they are connected," Ballantine replied. "They may not be cartel themselves, but they have certainly been set on the chase by the cartels."

"Why are more than one after us?" Shane asked. "Why not just the Colende cartel?"

"Apparently by killing Espanoza, we have upset the balance of power in Mexico," Ballantine replied. "He had made several alliances with other cartels to fund his creation of the cocaine additive. When we destroyed that, we angered more than just the Colende operation."

"Dudes need to chill and get over it," Max said. "They have to be wasting all kinds of money coming after us. Not like they can take us anyway. We fucking kill monster sharks and giant fucking snakes and whatever the hell that thing in Chile was. In the dictionary you'll find a group picture of Team Grendel under badass."

"Hooyah," Shane said and fist bumped his brother.

"Tell them," Thorne said to Ballantine.

"I am not sure now is the time, Commander," Ballantine said. "I would like to gather more information."

"Yeah, and I'd like to retire to a quiet condo in San Diego and watch sports, drink beer, and die happy," Thorne growled, "and that ain't gonna happen either."

"Very well," Ballantine said, as he slowly made sure to look everyone in the eye that was seated at the table. "I have received some alarming news today."

"More alarming than the fact that we are all now citizens in limbo?" Shane asked.

"Limbo contest," Max said. "After the meeting we'll mix some drinks, non-alcoholic for Kinsey, of course, and then have a limbo contest. It'll begin the healing process." He held up his hand as his uncle was about to snap. "Shutting up now, Uncle Vinny."

"The client that hired the company to dispose of their shark problem has been purchased by an outside entity," Ballantine said, "and it is believed that outside entity has employed a specific resource of the former client for the explicit purpose of hunting us down."

"Is it a zeppelin?" Shane asked. "It would be pretty cool to be chased by a fucking blimp."

"No, Mr. Reynolds, it is not a zeppelin," Ballantine sighed. "Anyone care to guess what it is?"

"Just tell them," Thorne snarled.

Ballantine glared at the commander, but let it go.

"They have released another shark," Ballantine said. "This one is considerably more dangerous than the previous sharks we've encountered."

"Considerably?" Shane asked.

"More dangerous?" Max finished.

"How so?" Gunnar asked, leaning forward in his chair. "Is it larger? Stronger? Better senses? More equipped to track us? Able to get through the triple hull? Be specific, Ballantine."

"Yes to all of those," Ballantine said, "and more."

Gunnar leaned back and his face went white at the prospect. Ballantine looked at everyone else and saw that they were just as pale as Gunnar was.

"There, now we are all up to speed," Ballantine said as he sat back down. "Let's open the table to suggestions, shall we?"

Chapter Two- Bigger Problems

The small fishing boat bobbed in the subtle waves that lapped at its sides. Weighed down by a bountiful catch of a mix of mahi mahi, skipjacks, and a couple swordfish, the captain started the engine and carefully steered his boat back towards home, ready to unload and reap the benefits of his catch.

The two hired deck hands were busy folding and stowing nets, packing up lines and hooks, and making sure that everything was strapped down as it should be. The sky didn't show any hint of a storm or problems with weather, but out on the open ocean, in a boat as small as the one they were on, they knew not to take chances.

"We get quarter split?" one deck hand named Peter asked. A short thick man, he looked like a brown barrel with stubby arms and legs. "That right? We each get a quarter?"

"Nah, bra," the second hand replied. His name was Hekali, but everyone just called him Hek the Neck because of his long, skinny neck. He shook his head on that neck and glanced towards the captain in the wheelhouse. "We split a quarter. He keeps three quarters."

"Ain't right, bra," Peter said. "We did most of the work. We should get at least half."

"His boat," Hek shrugged. "We'd get nothing if we didn't have his boat."

"He'd get nothing if we didn't do it all for him," Peter complained.

"Is what it is," Hek shrugged. "Good haul today, so even splitting a quarter will be worth it."

"Splitting half would be more worth it," Peter grumbled as he finished folding a net. He arched his back and stretched his sore, tired muscles. "Next time we ask for half."

"Next time he may not hire us," Hek said as he wound a rope about his hand and forearm, making sure it was tight and not kinked. He was about to say more to Peter about being careful he doesn't ruin a good thing, but the words became stuck in his throat as he saw movement far off across the water.

"You okay, bra?" Peter asked him.

Hek still couldn't answer as he watched the impossible come towards them. Peter turned and followed Hek's gaze.

"What is that?" Peter asked. "That can't be what I think it is, bra."

"Tell the captain," Hek nearly whispered. "Tell him now."

Peter nodded and then hurried his short bulk over to the wheelhouse. "Captain! We have a problem!"

***

"Do we have a problem, gentlemen?" Linny asked as the Land Cruiser pulled up to the bar just as she was loading boxes into her Jeep. "You look like you're in a hurry."

Four men stepped from the Land Cruiser and Linny's eyes instantly focused on the weapons they held.

"Tavor SAR series," Linny nodded as she put her hands on her hips. "Nice guns. Those converted to 9mm or still .223?"

The driver, a large man wearing a black tank top and khaki shorts, smiled at Linny, and then looked down at the semi-automatic rifle he held.

"Good eye," the man said as he patted his weapon. "9mm conversion it is. That way I don't have to worry about switching up ammo." He patted the 9mm pistol on his hip. "Keep it simple, stupid, right?"

Linny just smiled back while she slowly moved her right hand from her hip to the small of her back.

"What are you packing?" the man asked, taking a few steps closer while the other three men stayed close to the Land Cruiser. "No, let me guess. Hmmm. A Walther PPK? Powerful, but fits a woman's hand well. Not too much of a kick to it either."

Linny froze, her hand still behind her back.

"Can I see?" the man asked. "I love small arms. Sometimes, I wish I could get rid of these bulky things and just use pistols."

"Lin? You good?" the bartender asked as he came outside to check on her.

Tank Top's rifle barked and the man fell, his chest torn open by several rounds.

"No!" Linny screamed as she pulled the pistol from behind her back.

She took two slugs to her right shoulder before she could even get the pistol raised. The impacts spun her about and she slammed into the hood of her Jeep. The pistol fell from her hand and went off as it hit the gravel at her feet. There was a grunt of pain by the Land Cruiser, but Linny barely noticed as she dealt with her pain and slowly slumped to the ground.

"Damn," Tank Top said as he walked up to Linny. "You nailed Slaps in the foot. Looks like he's done for a while."

Tank Top squatted next to Linny and pushed some stray hairs from her forehead. Linny started to spit in his face, but he slammed his right fist into her mouth before she could even get the lugee formed. Teeth cracked and her lips split wide open as he pulled back for another shot.

"Stop," Linny said as blood poured down her chin. "I don't know where they went."

"So, you know why I'm here," Tank Top said. "Good, good, this'll go much faster."

"Are you going to kill me?" Linny asked.

"If I tell you the answer to that then you'd have no incentive to talk," Tank Top replied.

"I think you already answered my question," Linny said.

"Far from it," Tank Top replied as he stood up and kicked Linny's pistol across the parking lot. "You're still going to talk in the hopes that I don't kill you."

"I already said I don't know where they're going," Linny said. "They left here yesterday afternoon. They could be halfway to Australia by now."

"Could be," Tank Top nodded, "but I don't think that's where they're going. Too public. Too much red tape. They're going to find a place to hole up and hide for a while. Certainly a better place than this. I have to get to them before they do that."

"Who are you?" Linny asked.

"When you ask a question like that, then I know you expect me to kill you," Tank Top chuckled. "You'd never ask if you thought you were going to live."

"They'll kill you," Linny said. "You better have an army with you, because that's what you'll need."

Tank Top looked over his shoulder at the two men that were helping Slaps into the Land Cruiser.

"I have an army," Tank Top said, "of a sorts, and I'm about to have a Navy."

"Who hired you?" Linny asked.

"Well, aren't you just the inquisitor," Tank Top laughed. "Here I thought I'd interrogate you, but you have totally flipped it around on me."

He pulled the trigger and put a round in Linny's left leg. She screamed and clutched at her thigh then screamed more as the motion pulled at the wounds in her shoulder.

"I don't like to be interrogated," Tank Top said, "brings up bad memories."

He placed his foot on her thigh and pressed down.

"Your memories, I don't mind bringing up," he said as he ground down on the bullet wound. Linny's scream built until it was only a squeak in her throat. "So, let's start from the beginning and see what we can dredge up, shall we?"

***

The B3's engines were pushed to full capacity. Thorne and Kinsey sat on the observation deck and listened to the dull thrum of the engines far below. They watched as the ship cut through the water, slicing the waves in half as if they never existed.

"This place we're headed?" Kinsey asked. "What has Ballantine told you about it?"

"Research facility," Thorne said. "Off books."

"Off what books? The company's?" Kinsey asked.

"Yes," Thorne replied. "Ballantine has assured me that only a couple of people know it exists and one of those people is Dr. Morganton."

"It isn't a full secret," Kinsey says, "which means others know and there could be a trail to follow."

"I mentioned that to Ballantine," Thorne said. "He says we'll worry about that when we get there."

"Where is this place?" Kinsey asked.

"The middle of nowhere. Some uncharted island."

"Great," Kinsey said. "Let's hope it's not Gilligan's Island."

"With Ballantine, it's more like the Island of Dr. Moreau."

Kinsey laughed and stretched in her seat. Thorne looked over at his daughter and tried to smile, but what was on his mind wouldn't let him. He looked back out at the water.

"What were you up to when you were deep in your addiction?" Thorne asked.

"Daddy, you don't want to know," Kinsey sighed.

"No, no, I probably don't," Thorne sighed with her, "but as commander of this Team, I may need to. I know you lied, cheated, and did whatever you had to in order to stay high. That's common, I get that."

"You can pretty much write a script of how a junkie's life will play out," Kinsey said.

"A regular junkie, yes," Thorne responded, "but you aren't regular, Kinsey. You are a trained Marine and were almost a trained Navy SEAL. You have skills and ways of looking at the world that very few others do."

Kinsey sat there silent and Thorne tore his eyes from the bright blue horizon and looked at her. He could see the fear on her face, the tension in her neck, the way she gripped the armrests of her chair.

"Time to spill it all, Kins," Thorne said softly, "because I think who you were, who you became back in that nightmare, has bearing on what is happening to us now."

"I...I don't remember it all," Kinsey said after a few moments. "I have dreams sometimes..."

"I don't think that's true," Thorne said. "I think you do remember what you did. Darren is under the impression you do. He mentioned something you told him a while back. It bugged him and when he told me, it bugged me."

"He what?" Kinsey snapped. "What the fuck did that ass tell you?"

"Don't blame him," Thorne said. "You know he loves you and only wants you to be safe."

"Maybe," Kinsey said.

"Well, I'll let you two work that out," Thorne said dismissively, "not my deal. What is my deal is what you did while you were strung out. I need to know how you got a hold of all your drugs. Where'd you get the money to live? How'd you survive that long without being taken down?"

"Taken down?" Kinsey asked. "You're talking like I was part of the business. I wasn't, Daddy. I was just a junkie like a million others."

"Don't go backwards," Thorne said. "We've established you are not like others. Just tell me the truth. We are going to need all the information we can get to fight these guys coming after us."

"Team Grendel, Ballantine, and the company have nothing to do with my days as a junkie," Kinsey stated then crossed her arms over her chest like the conversations was done.

"Is that so?" Thorne laughed. "Then why are more than one cartel sending people after us? Why not just the Colende cartel? Espanoza was leader of the Colende cartel. There's no reason the others should want us dead no matter what bullshit Ballantine spews about cocaine additives."

He let the words hang there for a minute, but Kinsey didn't bite.

***

The captain of the fishing vessel had the ship's throttle pushed to full, but what pursued it kept gaining.

"Has to be a submarine," Peter said, as he gripped the edge of the doorframe that led into the wheelhouse, his eyes locked onto the shape in the water far behind them. "Look at it. It's huge. Nothing that big can move like that. Nothing."

"You ever see a sub with a dorsal fin?" Hek asked. "I haven't."

"US Navy," Peter nodded. "Some government secret. Wasn't there something on the internet about subs looking like whales off the coast of Mexico a few months back?"

"Just internet bullshit," the captain said. "Can't believe anything on the internet. Believe only what you see with your eyes."

"I see that thing," Hek said, "but I ain't believing it."

"How fast are we going?" Peter asked.

"Twenty knots," the captain said, "and the engine is going to give out if I keep pushing it."

"Twenty knots," Hek whistled. "Still ain't fast enough. That thing is going at least twice that, maybe more."

Peter and Hek looked out past the stern of the boat and watched in horror as the thing that chased them suddenly dipped all the way into the water and was lost from sight.

"Captain," Hek said, "it dove."

The captain looked over his shoulder and glanced at the empty water behind them.

"What you say? The thing is sixty, maybe seventy feet long?" the captain asked.

"Longer," Peter said.

"A lot longer," Hek agreed.

"Eighty? Ninety?" the captain asked. "Can't be a hundred. Nothing is that big. Not a whale and certainly no shark."

"It looked longer," Peter said.

"Bullshit," the captain replied. "Let's say it's eighty feet. That means we need the 30-gauge line. I want you to drop it all. Then get the nets ready."

Peter and Hek looked at the captain as if he'd just said they were going to fly the boat to the moon.

"What are you standing around for?" the captain asked. "We can't outrun the son of a bitch, so let's tangle it up. Get those lines in the water and get ready to toss all of the nets. It can be fifty feet or a hundred feet, for all I care. Doesn't matter how long it is if it can't swim and push water through those gills."

"We're going to drown it?" Hek asked.

"We're going to try," the captain said. "Ain't nothing else we can do."

***

"So there were the twins," Tank Top said as he wiped the blood from his knuckles, "the crazy bitch and the drunk chick. Then the golf pro and the old man showed up, is that right?"

"They aren't twins," Linny said through swollen lips. Her face was a patchy, puffy mess of bruises and cuts from Tank Top's fist. "Just brothers."

Tank Top popped her again right between the eyes. Linny gasped, but didn't cry out, as her crying out days was done.

"You see what I'm doing?" Tank Top grinned. "I learned this technique from an ex-general in the Chinese military. Now, those guys know how to interrogate someone. The trick is to randomize your hits, keep the subject off balance and always guessing when and where the pain is going to come from next."

"Fuck you," Linny spat.

"That would have been an option at one time or another," Tank Top said, "unfortunately, I don't have the equipment for it anymore. Still got my balls, which helps keep my aggression up, but I have to piss through a prosthetic and fuck with my mouth. You have no idea how good I am at giving head, lady."

"You sick fuck," Linny grunted as she tried to shift her weight. Another pop from Tank Top then another and another made her give up on trying to get more comfortable.

"How many back on the ship?" Tank Top asked. "Your boyfriend ever mention any numbers?"

"Just the number one," Linny said as she raised her middle finger.

Tank Top grabbed it and snapped it off her hand, then jammed the digit into her right eye.

"He's missing his right eye, yes?" Tank Top smiled as he watched Linny claw at the finger and try to pull it free from her orbital socket. "Now you two match."

Tank Top stood up and walked over to the Land Cruiser. He looked into the cargo area at the man that sat there bleeding from his foot.

"You good, Slaps?" Tank Top asked the man.

"I'll live," Slaps replied, a hairy beast of a man with a full, bushy beard and tufts of dark black hair peeking out from everywhere. "Can I kill the cunt when you're done?"

"Sure," Tank Top said, "be my guest."

"What? Now?" Slaps asked.

"Yeah, I think so," Tank Top said.

"We get to have some fun with her first?" one of the other men asked.

Tank Top turned and studied the man for a second then smiled wide.

"You bet, Took," Tank Top replied. "If that's your thing."

Took was a skinny man held together with wiry muscles and bone. His face nearly split from his head when he smiled back at Tank Top and hopped out of the Land Cruiser. He walked with a strutting swagger as he moved towards the broken form of Linny lying against the tire of her Jeep.

"Let me help you out," Tank Top said to Slaps as he went around and opened the back hatch. "Just lean on me. Got your pistol?"

"Right here," Slaps said.

Tank Top helped Slaps out then assisted him while he hobbled over to Linny. The woman lay there cursing up at Took as the man took off his belt and unzipped his pants. He pulled out his cock and waved it in front of Linny's face.

"You're gonna be nice," Took said. "I haven't had a hot piece like you in a while."

"You like to rape 'em, Took?" Tank Top asked.

"Yeah, man," Took laughed, "ain't no fun when they give it up."

"No fun for whom?" Tank Top asked.

Took looked over at his boss and frowned, his cock still out and in his hand.

"Whom? What is this? English class?" Took asked.

He screamed as Tank Top reached out and grabbed him by his hard cock then twisted with all of his strength.

"More like anatomy class," Tank Top said, "and physics."

Tank Top dug his nails into Took's flesh and yanked back as hard as possible. Took's cock shredded into nothing but loose strips of bloody meat.

"Slaps," Tank Top said.

Slaps pulled his 9mm from his hip and put two slugs right between Took's eyes, then turned the pistol on Linny and did the same to her.

"Sorry about that," Slaps said as he looked down at Took's dead body. "Didn't know he was a rapist. I wouldn't have recommended him for the job."

"All cool, Slaps," Tank Top said. "That shit isn't always on the resume." He looked down at Slaps' foot and frowned. "Let's get you back to the ship and patched up before the rest of the ships arrive."

"You think we're going to need that kind of backup?" Slaps asked as he hobbled back to the Land Cruiser and Tank Top helped him up into the cargo area.

"Not really," Tank Top said, "but hard to enjoy profits when you're dead. I'd rather catch these fucks with help than end up at the bottom of the ocean like the rest of the dumb shits that let their egos and greed get in the way."

"That's why you're the boss," Slaps smiled then grimaced. "Fuck. Getting shot in the foot hurts."

"First time?" Tank Top asked.

"Getting shot?"

"No, stupid, in the foot," Tank Top grimaced. "I know you've been shot before."

"Yeah, first time in the foot," Slaps nodded.

"All those fucking little bones," Tank Top said then grabbed the hatch. "Look out. Coming down."

He slammed the back hatch closed then moved around the Land Cruiser and jumped into the driver's seat. The man in the passenger's seat looked a little green. He was young and bulked up like a body builder. Tank Top started up the SUV then glanced at the young man.

"You aren't a rapist, are you, Lug?" Tank Top asked him.

"No, sir," Lug replied, his voice a little shaky.

"You sure?" Tank Top asked.

"Yeah, I'm sure," Lug said, "but I do pay for it. I don't mind the whores. Just want to be honest about that."

"I appreciate that," Tank Top smiled as he put the Land Cruiser into drive. "Honesty is always the best policy."

***

"Here's my theory, and you can take it for what you will," Thorne continued. "I think word spread that a certain Kinsey Thorne is part of Team Grendel. That word has gotten to the other cartels and they have joined forces to take us out because the junkie Kinsey Thorne spent a good deal of time taking them out while she was strung out on everything known to man."

Kinsey still didn't respond.

"Fine," Thorne said. "I tried to get you to tell me in your own words."

He reached under his chair and picked up a stack of files then plopped them onto Kinsey's lap.

"Have a read," Thorne said. "It's everything Ballantine has on you. It's probably more than what the cartels have on you, but I don't know that for certain. Considering how intertwined they are with the Mexican government, there's no reason to think they don't have duplicates of these files as well."

Kinsey looked down at the files then looked back out at the ocean.

"Open them," Thorne said.

Kinsey didn't move.

"Kinsey Thorne, you will open those files and look at what's inside," Thorne ordered.

"Or what?" Kinsey snapped.

"Or you're off the Team," Thorne said.

37

Kinsey turned and stared at her father then looked down at the files. She opened the first one and studied the photographs inside. There were some written files, but Kinsey ignored those and only focused on the photos. Once she was done with the first file, she moved onto the next, and the next, and the next. She tossed each finished one onto the deck by her chair until she was through and her lap was empty once again.

"There're a lot of blood and bodies in those files," Thorne said. "My count is close to three dozen dead."

"They were all criminals," Kinsey said coldly.

"They were, true," Thorne said, "but does that give you the right to execute them?"

"Who says I did that?" Kinsey shrugged. "I don't remember doing that."

"I think you do," Thorne said. "I think the reason you spiraled so low, but never died of an overdose is because you gave yourself a cause. You got to kill bad guys and feed your habit. You murdered those men then stole their drugs. That's not really what is getting to me, though."

"Oh? What is getting to you, Daddy?" Kinsey sneered. "Please tell me."

"It's the level of violence," Thorne said. "There is a rage in those photos that scares me, Kins. You are a trained killer, but the person that did that was a wild animal. There was no training, just butchery."

"They deserved it," Kinsey said. "*They* were the animals."

"Maybe," Thorne nodded, "but those animals had friends and now their friends are coming to put you down. Ballantine has confirmed that some of the ships pursuing us are being financed by several cartels. You are a demon in their circles and they mean to exorcise you."

"Why?" Kinsey asked. "Why spend the money for one person? Why go to all of this trouble for just me?"

"It's not just you," Thorne said. "They are coming for us because of what we've done. They are coming for Ballantine because of God knows what he's done, and they are coming for you because of what you've done. These people have many reasons to kill us, and it just happens that one of those reasons is my own daughter, because she got a taste for warped justice."

"I got a taste for high quality heroin and cocaine," Kinsey laughed. "The justice was just a perk."

"See," Thorne smiled. "That is the honesty I need from you."

"Honesty?" Ballantine asked as he climbed the stairs up to the observation deck. "Be careful, that's a dangerous game to play. Trust me, I've never been honest a day in my life."

***

"I don't think this is a good idea, Captain!" Peter yelled as he helped Hek throw the last net off the stern of the fishing boat. "That thing is big enough to take us under!"

"Nonsense!" the captain yelled back as he finished baiting a thick fishing hook and tossed the line out into the water. "This baby is 15 meters long! No shark can pull this under!"

Hek watched as the net sank below the boat's wake. He shook his head and pulled a long knife from his boot. Peter looked at the blade then pulled his own.

"We cut loose the second this goes to hell," Hek said. "I don't know what the captain is thinking."

"He wants to catch it," Peter replied. "The crazy bastard wants to catch the fucking thing."

Hek's eyes grew wide and he looked back at the captain. The man stood on the deck and grinned from ear to ear as he studied the water all around them.

"This ain't good," Hek said just as the boat lurched. "What was that?"

Before Peter could answer, the whole boat came to a full stop as the aft end was ripped from the rest of the boat.

"Fuck!" Hek yelled as he scrambled across the deck towards the wheelhouse. "Fuck!"

He looked over his shoulder and saw the captain gripping onto the side rail while he watched Peter slide down the deck and into the open water.

"Grab him!" Hek yelled at the captain. "Stop being a coward and grab him!"

Peter screamed then was lost in the churning water behind the boat. The captain just stood there, nothing but pure terror on his face.

A well of anger built in Hek's stomach and he was about to shout at the captain again when in the blink of an eye, the man was no longer there. Neither was that part of the boat.

Hek felt warm piss run down his leg as the world around him was turned up on end and he was suddenly face to jaws with a shark that was bigger than any prehistoric nightmare the Discovery Channel could come up with.

***

Ballantine looked at the stack of files on the deck then frowned at Thorne.

"I don't remember giving those to you," Ballantine said.

"Good, because if you did, then we'd have to have your head checked," Thorne grinned. "I took them."

Ballantine studied the Thornes for a good few seconds then laughed.

"Vincent and Kinsey Thorne," he smiled, "a formidable duo."

"What brings you up here, Ballantine?" Thorne asked. "Any new intel?"

"Yes, unfortunately," Ballantine said. "Darby and I have been going over reports of ships missing or damaged. Once we filtered out obvious weather related incidents, we found a bit of a pattern."

"Let me guess," Thorne said. "There's a path of destruction heading our way."

"There is," Ballantine said. "The pattern suggests that we have perhaps a day or possibly two before it catches up."

"What about our other pursuers?" Thorne asked. "Have you found them on the satellite images?"

"Yes, about that," Ballantine said as he pulled up a chair next to Thorne. "That was what I was coming up here to speak to you about."

Thorne leaned forward and rested his forearms on his knees. It made his biceps bulge against his t-shirt, showing that even at his age he held some serious walloping power.

"Spill it," Thorne said to Ballantine. He removed his sunglasses and squinted against the bright sun. "Take yours off. I want to see your eyes."

"I'm not going to lie to you, Commander," Ballantine said, but took his sunglasses off anyway. "I'm up here to be perfectly frank."

"That your first name?" Kinsey chuckled. "Frank?"

Ballantine gave her a small grin then put his focus back on Thorne.

"We've lost access to military satellite imaging," Ballantine said. "I have Carlos working on a hack, but I'm pretty sure we've been flagged and there's no way to get that resource back."

"What about the company?" Thorne asked.

"Occupied," Ballantine said. "We are not their number one priority at the moment."

"Occupied? The whole company?" Kinsey asked. "That seems like a stretch."

"You have no idea," Ballantine replied. "I said the same thing to Darby. She suggested I forget about the company and focus solely on the Beowulf III and the people on board."

"Uncharacteristically empathetic," Thorne said as he put his sunglasses back on. Ballantine did the same.

"Yes, well, Mr. Reynolds seems to be having a softening effect on Darby," Ballantine frowned.

"You don't like that," Kinsey stated.

"One reason Darby has been so effective in her career is because she roughed up all her soft spots," Ballantine said. "It could put us at risk if she cares too much for your cousin."

"Or it could save our lives," Kinsey said, "because she actually cares whether we live or die."

"Oh, she's always cared about that," Ballantine laughed. "She has had a fondness for Team Grendel from day one."

"It's just you are worried she'll make a mistake trying to protect Max instead of making the right choice when needed," Thorne said. "Welcome to human nature, Ballantine. It's something I've dealt with for decades leading SEALs. At some point you just have to trust your operators to do their job *and* save their comrades."

"Well, Thorne, if you haven't guessed by now, trust isn't my dominant personality trait," Ballantine said as he stood up and looked out to the water.

"So, no idea when we're going to get hit by the hired guns?" Thorne asked as he stood as well.

"None, I'm afraid," Ballantine said. "I have put the feelers out to contacts at dozens of different ports as well as my contacts in the shipping companies. If anyone spots them then we'll get a heads up."

"If your contacts are still loyal and haven't been scared off," Thorne said.

"Yes, well that's a good point," Ballantine said. "Self-preservation is a part of human nature that I am well acquainted with."

"I bet," Kinsey said. She looked at the two men and frowned. "Carlos have anything new for us to use if we get in the shit?"

That got a huge smile from Ballantine and all the worry and fears fled from his features.

"Why, yes, Ms. Thorne," Ballantine beamed, "I believe he has exactly what you and the rest of Team Grendel will need if you indeed get in the shit."

***

The smell of shit joined the smell of piss and fuel as Hek clung to the top of the bow of the fishing boat. He looked down at his pants and saw the dark stain spreading down the insides of his thighs. Then he looked past his legs at the last six feet of the boat still above water.

All it took was two chomps from the giant shark and the boat was obliterated. Hek had seen those jaws up close and knew that the shark could have destroyed the boat in one bite if it had wanted to. The beast's mouth was enormous, like a baleen whales, but full of thousands and thousands of teeth instead of a natural krill filter.

He said a prayer repeatedly, it was something his grandmother had taught him to say when he was small and afraid of the dark. The sun may have been beating down on him, but there was certainly the darkness of death all around and not just because the water was clouded with blood.

Hek felt a jolt and cried out as the bow shook and started to tip to the side. If it turned all the way over, it would fill with water and sink in seconds, then he'd have nothing to cling to. That's when he realized that he still gripped the knife he normally kept in his boot. He was more than surprised he hadn't dropped it in all of the chaos. Not that a ten inch blade would do much against a hundred foot predator.

The blade glinted in the sun and Hek looked down at it and his reflection in the metal. He turned it this way and that and squinted every time the reflection hit his eyes. Then he focused past the knife and into the water. There was a darkness below that hadn't been there seconds before. Hek knew exactly what the darkness was.

Death was coming to get him.

Just as the shark burst from the water, taking the rest of the ship and Hek entirely into its mouth, Hek put his knife to his own throat and dragged it across as fast as possible. He had no desire to be swallowed whole and digested alive. His life was his to take, not some creature from a monster movie.

***

Tank Top waited until the Zodiac was locked in place and lines secured before he attempted to help get Slaps' bulk onto the deck of the SS Monkey Balls, a 50 meter cutter outfitted to be ready for almost any contingency. Although he was pretty sure the next couple days would test the MB to its limits. Not that it hadn't been tested before plenty of times.

"Ready to go see an old friend, girl?" he said to himself.

"What?" Slaps grunted. "What the fuck you saying?"

"Nothing. You good, Slaps?" Tank Top asked. "Need me to carry your baby ass down to the infirmary?"

"Fuck you, Tank," Slaps grimaced as he tried to put weight on his wounded foot. "I can handle myself."

"Then go for it, big guy," Tank Top grinned as he let go of Slaps and watched the man try to hobble his way across the deck, leaving a trail of bloody one-sided footprints.

Slaps made it about six feet before he teetered and then toppled over, his head hitting the metal deck with a loud thunk that sent the seagulls resting up on the communications array screeching and flying into the air.

"Yeah, that's what I thought," Tank Top laughed then pointed at Lug. "Go get some help and have Shabby Paul ready for a transfusion. I think our friend has lost a little blood."

Lug nodded and took off quickly across the deck and into the first hatch he came to.

"What the fuck did you do to Slaps?" a huge black man shouted from the hatchway of the bridge. "You try to shave the fucking ape and he give you shit for it?"

"The weed bitch shot him," Tank Top said as he jogged to the ladder and climbed up to the bridge. "Actually, she dropped her pistol and it went off."

"An accidental bullet?" the black man laughed. He was tall, more than half a foot taller than Tank Top, and wore a spotless white t-shirt that had to be a size too small as it hugged the layers of muscle that made up his arms and torso. "Figures it would be an accident to take down that sasquatch."

"Don't let him hear you call him that, Bokeem," Tank Top laughed. "He'll fucking kill you in your sleep."

"I don't sleep," Bokeem replied, "you know that."

Tank Top looked out at the five other ships following behind the MB and growled. "They didn't waste any time getting to us."

"Can't be helped," Bokeem said. "The cartels and Somalis are paying our employer. They want to come, then that's their deal."

"As long as they stay out of our way and just act as muscle when we need them," Tank Top said, "and they don't forget that this is a job and not just a revenge mission."

Bokeem only shrugged in reply.

"Didn't really learn much from the weed bitch," Tank Top said, "except that they know we're after them."

"Ballantine wouldn't be Ballantine if we caught them by surprise," Bokeem replied then nodded to the five other ships. "The real question is whether or not he knows we have backup."

"Lady didn't say," Tank Top said, "but it would have been good information to get from her."

"You leave her alive?" Bokeem asked.

"You fucking kidding me?" Tank Top laughed. "After she shot Slaps?"

"You said that was an accident."

"Accident or not, it was her gun," Tank Top said. "Oh, and Took is dead."

"I was wondering where he was," Bokeem responded.

"Turned out he was a rapist," Tank Top frowned. "Even after all that vetting, a perv still got through."

"Can't always know what's inside a man sometimes," Bokeem said. "Slaps take it hard? He vouched for the skinny fuck."

"He was the one that put the bullets between the sick fuck's eyes," Tank Top replied. "It was cathartic."

"Look at you and your big words," Bokeem laughed.

"I graduated high school," Tank Top said.

"I have a fucking Master's degree and don't know when the last time I used the word cathartic," Bokeem said then slapped his hands on the railing and turned back to the bridge. "Thirsty? I have some beers on ice in here."

"I'm fucking dying," Tank Top said. "We killed the bitch outside a bar and I didn't even think to grab a drink before leaving."

"You're slipping," Bokeem said as they stepped into the cool dark of the bridge.

Tank Top smiled at the sight of the bridge equipment. All of it was next generation technology and part of the upfront payment for taking the job to hunt down Ballantine. Bokeem cracked open a beer and handed it to Tank Top before he opened his and sat down in the Captain's chair in the middle of the bridge.

Tank Top took a long swallow from his beer, belched, then pointed at a screen that showed a satellite image of the ocean surrounding them.

"The Beowulf is about a day ahead of us," Tank Top said. "If we push it, we should be able to catch up to them."

"Weird hearing that name after all this time," Bokeem said. "I thought we were done with that."

"Me too," Tank Top said as he reached out and patted the wall, "but sometimes, you can't whitewash the past even if you do give it a new name."

"That new boat of his has some heavy steam in those engines," Bokeem said. "We may not make much headway if they are pushing it as well."

"Ace up our sleeve," Tank Top winked, "don't forget."

"That ace could just do us a favor and blow that ship up," Bokeem said. "That would save us a lot of time and effort."

"It would also lose us a good amount of money," Tank Top said. "They want Ballantine alive. The cartels want the junkie and the Somali's want the junkie's dad. We let the ace blow up that ship and we no get paid, partner."

"I know, I know," Bokeem nodded. "The ace could at least turn on the beacon so we could pinpoint where they're at."

"Not yet. Not with the fucking techies they have on that ship," Tank Top said. "If the ace turns it on too soon, then they'd find the beacon and know they have a traitor on board. Too risky."

"Are you going to shoot down everything I say today?" Bokeem asked.

"Just the stupid stuff," Tank Top smiled and took another drink from his beer.

Tank Top swiped at the screen in front of him and widened the view until their ship was nothing but an almost imperceptible dot.

"If they are a day ahead then they have to be within this radius," Tank Top said as he drew a circle with his finger. "My guess is they are heading that way. Our employers believe Ballantine has some secret asset in that direction, but that's all they know."

"Ballantine must be slipping if our employers know that much," Bokeem said.

Tank Top studied the image for a long while before he turned and fixed his gaze on Bokeem.

"Where's our competition at?" he asked.

"The shark?" Bokeem replied.

"No, the fucking US Navy," Tank Top grumbled. "Yes, the fucking shark."

"You need a nap," Bokeem laughed. "You are one grumpy mother fucker. The shark is two days behind us."

"Two days?" Tank Top exclaimed, almost spitting beer across the bridge. "How the fuck did it catch up so fast? That's not going to give us much time."

"No, it isn't," Bokeem said, "but we'll have to. We were warned that the fucking thing doesn't discriminate. It'll eat the Monkey Balls just as happily as it will eat the Beowulf."

"We should have fought harder against them releasing that thing," Tank Top said as he shook his head. "They didn't need to do that. We know how to clean up after ourselves."

"My contact said some type of protocol had been executed. They couldn't have stopped it if they had wanted to," Bokeem said. He leaned forward and looked out the side window at the bow of one of the companion ships. "I have a feeling the shark is for cleaning up loose ends."

Tank Top looked out the window as well. "As long as we aren't one of the loose ends too."

***

With hunks of the fishing boat still stuck in its teeth, the giant shark dove deeper and deeper, sending itself down into the ocean's depths and darkness so it could move faster with the cold current below. Its senses told it that there were more targets above that it needed to take care of, but the call of its main target was too strong. If it got hungry enough, it would surface again and eat, but until then, it needed to close the distance on its true prey.

Other ocean creatures fled the area as fast as possible. Natural enemies that would have never stayed in close proximity to each other were forced to school in numbers that would have made marine biologists shit themselves. Fish of all sizes, from tiny, to what anglers called big game, hurried as fast as their fins and tails would take them to get away from the eating machine that had intruded upon their delicate ecosystem.

The current surrounded the massive beast and it whipped its tail back and forth to add to the force and speed that drove it on. The lesser creatures that escaped before it, were inconsequential distractions and barely registered in its focused brain. The monster cared nothing for the animals of the ocean, it was made to find and feast on the human intruders that continued to pollute its water and home, but was it home?

No matter how natural it felt to the shark to be swimming free in the open ocean, a small part of it longed for the sheltered bay that it had spent its short life in. It wanted to circle, circle, circle, over and over again, and wait for the screams from above the surface that signaled a meal was being thrown in. That was the focus and simplicity it truly craved.

Circle, circle, circle, wait, listen, and then eat.

That tiny part of its brain was overridden by the artificial need programmed into it to hunt down prey it had never seen, never known, and until a couple days before, had never wanted. The great monster could do nothing to stop its relentless drive to find the Beowulf III and devour it whole.

Chapter Three- All In This Alone

Carlos stood before Team Grendel, his arms crossed over his less than tone chest, and glared. He hated having to give demonstrations on equipment that any six year old could figure out.

"The channel guns have been modified so they have more stopping power and no longer need to be submerged to be effective," he said as his fellow weapon smith, Ingrid, held the large rifle in her hands. "The slugs are now aerodynamic as well as hydrodynamic."

"They fly and swim!" Max said.

"It's a bird! It's a fish! It's gonna kill the fuck outta some giant sharks!" Shane added.

"Did you add the disco ball effect I suggested?" Max asked.

"That was a great suggestion, by the way," Shane said.

"I know," Max smiled. "I'm full of all kinds of great suggestions."

"You're full of something," Kinsey said.

"Lame, Sis," Max replied.

"Yeah, that was not a burn worthy of our ears," Shane said. "I say good day to you!"

"Good day to you" Max echoed.

"That's my line, you just shake your fist and look offended," Shane responded.

"Like this?" Max asked as he shook his fist at Kinsey then arched an eyebrow.

"That makes you look like a constipated chimpanzee," Darby said.

"Which makes me wonder how you know what a constipated chimpanzee looks like," Shane said as he started to stroke his chin in an exaggeratedly thoughtful manner.

"I lived with a troop for six months," Darby shrugged.

"You used to not encourage them," Darren said to her. "I miss those days."

"I'll still put my boot up either of their rectums if needed," Darby replied.

"Shhh, baby, now is not the time for sexy talk," Max whispered loudly. "We'll save that move for later."

"I want nothing to do with that," Shane said as he held up his hands. "Let that be on the record that I-"

"SHUT UP!" Carlos yelled then looked at the bored face of Thorne. "Aren't you going to stop them from prattling on?"

"I could," Thorne said, "but this is your show, Carlos. You shut them up."

"Yes, Carlos," Shane grinned as he politely took the channel gun from Ingrid's hands. "Shut us up."

Ingrid giggled and rolled her eyes at Carlos.

"Tell them the cool part," she said.

"There are many cool parts to our-" Carlos began.

"You can remote detonate the channel gun rounds," Ingrid said, her face lit up by an enthusiastic smile. "That means you can blow them up before they make contact with the target or you can let them pierce the target like a normal slug, but delay their detonation until the exact moment you desire."

"I like how you talk, lady," Shane said, winking at Ingrid. "Nothing hotter than a gunsmith saying delayed detonation desire."

"That was a little misogynistic," Ingrid said and frowned at Shane.

"What? No, it was a joke," Shane protested and looked at the others. "Tell her it was a joke."

"Your grave," Lucy responded, "you sleep in it."

"No, stop, I didn't mean anything by it," Shane said. "I was just riffing with what she said."

"Gotcha!" Ingrid laughed. "You're too easy."

"That's what the chimpanzees said," Max replied.

"Okay, high-five on that one," Shane said as he raised his hand and high-fived his brother then looked at his cousin. "See, Sis? That's a burn."

"What else is there?" Lucy asked. "Let's hurry this up so I can go take a nap."

"Dude, you've been asleep for like two days," Shane said.

"Your point?" Lucy replied.

"Rarely does he have one," Max said.

"Again with the wit!" Shane laughed.

"Ah, I hope I'm not too late and have missed the big reveal," Ballantine said as he joined Team Grendel in the Toyshop. "I've obviously missed many jokes, though."

"Many jokes," Max said.

"So many jokes," Shane added.

"I hate them," Carlos snarled.

"Yes, well, they are a necessary evil," Ballantine replied. "Where are we in the tech breakdown?"

"Channel guns go boom when we want," Max said.

"Something important hold you up?" Thorne asked Ballantine.

"Let's table that for later," Ballantine said. "I'd like Carlos to finish his presentation first."

"It's not a presentation," Carlos snapped. "I do not present. I'm not an emcee at a roast or a model at a car show."

Shane looked at Ingrid and started to open his mouth then closed it quickly.

"He's learning," Darren said.

"Oh, god, will you all be quiet?" Carlos yelled. "I want to go through this and get back to work!"

Team Grendel all stood there and glared at the master weapon smith.

"I believe you have the floor, Carlos," Ballantine said, "go ahead."

"Channel guns you know, mustache rebreathers you know, compression suits you know," Carlos said as he checked off a list of equipment the Team had used to fight off the cloned sharks before. "This thing, this technological marvel, is something totally new."

He stood there and looked about as smug as any human being could look. Then continued to stand there, and stand there, until he looked over at Ingrid who was standing and smiling as well, but not in a smug way.

"Ingrid?" Carlos asked.

"What?" she replied.

"The sensory concussion grenade, please," Carlos said.

"The what?" Ingrid asked.

"The sensory concussion grenade," Carlos repeated.

"Don't know what you're talking about," Ingrid replied.

Carlos sighed heavily. "The pineapple."

"Oh, that," Ingrid grinned. "I'll be right back."

"She totally set you up, dude," Shane said as Ingrid hurried through the shelves of the Toyshop.

"Yes, I know," Carlos said.

"Here!" Ingrid announced as she held out a small, bright yellow grenade in front of everyone. "It's called the pineapple because regular fragmentation grenades are green and look like avocados, while this one is bright yellow and looks like a mini pineapple."

"It looks nothing like a pineapple," Carlos muttered.

"How does it work?" Ballantine prompted.

"Triggering mechanism is here," Ingrid said as she pointed at a recessed button on the side. "Don't worry, it can't accidentally go off. You have to push in so the button pops out then press again and the button locks back into place. Once it's locked back in place, then you have about thirty seconds to get clear of the blast."

"Or your eyes, ears, and sense of smell will be overloaded," Carlos added. "While that may not sound like much danger to you macho people, it is a hundred times worse than standing over a flash-bang."

"Who are you calling macho?" Kinsey asked. "Do these tits look macho to you?"

"Too easy," Max said, shaking his head. "You just make it too easy."

"We worry about you, Sis," Shane added, "setting yourself up like that. It's careless."

"Reckless," Max nodded.

"Senseless," Shane added.

"Not until a pineapple goes off," Max replied.

"Good one," Shane winked.

"Anyway, the shark that has been released after us is 115 feet long, so it's not like one of those will stop it," Ballantine announced. "It will take a coordinated effort to stun the creature so you can kill it."

All eyes turned to Ballantine and more than a few jaws dropped.

"I'm sorry, but did you say 115 feet?" Darren asked. "That's nearly double the size of the other sharks we've dealt with."

"Good to see arithmetic is alive and well with Team Grendel," Ballantine responded.

"Don't be a dick, Ballantine," Thorne grumbled, "tell it to them straight."

"It is a very large shark," Ballantine said, "is that straight enough?"

"Uh, a shark that big is going to require heavier ordinance than just some channel guns," Darren stated. "Please tell me we have bigger guns."

"We do," Carlos responded, "Moshi?"

The diminutive woman stepped out from one of the shelving units and gave a shy wave.

"Hey, Moshi," Lucy smiled.

"Moshi, my boshi!" Max said.

"Dude, you can't just make up words," Shane responded.

"Blerby blop," Max said.

"That's better," Shane grinned.

Moshi walked forward and held out a three foot long steel rod. Team Grendel stared at it for a second then turned as one and looked at Ingrid.

"Why are you looking at her?" Carlos asked. "I developed it."

"Yeah, but she's not an asshole," Shane said.

"Exactly," Max agreed.

Ingrid didn't bother to hide her grin as she took the rod from Moshi. "This is completely next gen tech," she announced. "In fact, it could even be called *next* next gen."

"We are impressed, Ingrid," Ballantine said. "Let's move along."

"Yes, sir, of course," Ingrid nodded. "Stand back for a second."

No one argued and they all took a couple steps back.

Ingrid waved the rod back and forth and in seconds the air lit up with blue sparks and strange green lines.

"This is the particle field," Ingrid said, "and anything that crosses this field will basically be evaporated."

"That is not technically accurate," Carlos said. "A liquid would be evaporated, but a solid would be-"

"I think she was dumbing it down for us," Thorne interrupted. "How about you let her?"

"I really wasn't trying to dumb it down," Ingrid said. "I just know you are in a hurry and didn't want to bore you with detailed explanations that have no bearing on how it works."

"I believe all the details have bearing on how it works," Carlos snapped.

"Continue. Please," Ballantine growled.

Ingrid stopped waving the rod and the blue sparks and green lines disappeared almost immediately.

"Let me demonstrate in the tank," she said and walked back into the Toyshop. "Follow me."

"Will this be worth our time?" Ballantine asked Carlos. Carlos just shrugged. "Wonderful."

Team Grendel followed Ingrid through the shelves until they came to an open space about ten feet square. She tapped at a tablet and a large tank of clear liquid lifted from the floor.

"We just keep those hanging around?" Max asked.

"You know there's like a ton of water outside the ship, right?" Shane said.

"This isn't water," Ingrid smiled. "It's a containment gel we use to keep projectiles and explosives from damaging the ship when we test them."

"Oh," Max smiled, "cool."

"Can we come down here and play with it sometime?" Shane asked.

"No," everyone said at once.

"Well, fuck you too," Shane pouted.

Ingrid grabbed a step ladder and climbed up so she could dip her hand and the rod into the gel. She started waving it again and the blue sparks and green lines reappeared. Then she flicked her wrist and the sparks and lines shot away from the rod.

Everyone stared in disbelief as the gel in the sparks and lines' path was vaporized, leaving a completely empty space. Then the gel above the space crashed down and the concussion rocked the sides of the vat, making everyone cover their ears as a loud bang echoed through the Toyshop.

"Sorry," Ingrid winced, "I should have suggested ear protection."

"That was a sonic boom," Darren said. "How the hell…?"

"The particle field," Carlos began then cringed. "*Evaporated* every atom in its path, leaving a swathe of dead space."

"True dead space," Ingrid smiled. "For a split second, there was nothing there. Absolutely nothing."

"Why isn't Gunnar here?" Kinsey asked.

"Not now, Ms. Thorne," Ballantine smiled, "let them finish."

Kinsey glared at Ballantine, but let it go and nodded to Ingrid.

"So that was a sonic boom?" Max asked.

"More like thunder," Ingrid answered, "but, to be honest, it's actually like nothing else ever done before."

"You two didn't come up with this, did you?" Thorne asked.

Carlos frowned, Ingrid smiled, and they both looked around until they found Moshi peeking at them from behind a shelf.

"Our very own Moshi developed this technology," Ballantine said. "She has been working on it for some time now, well before her tenure on the Beowulfs."

"So we just have to wave a rod and flick our wrist and it wipes out everything in its path?" Shane asked. "Cool."

"How many do we have?" Darren asked. "Will we each get one?"

"This is the only working model," Carlos admitted, "and it is a prototype. We do not have any ready for the field."

"Tease," Max said.

"I was all hot and bothered and now I'm just bothered," Shane said. "You, sir, have bothered me."

"The elves are working hard on duplicating the technology," Ballantine said. "Hopefully we will have more very soon." He glowered at Carlos. "Or at least one that's field ready."

"Don't call us elves," Carlos whispered through gritted teeth.

"Okay, so no heavy ordinance to kill the giant shark?" Shane asked.

"They give us hope then take that hope away!" Max exclaimed. "Why? WHY?"

"Are we finished here?" Ballantine asked as his phone rang. "Carlos?"

"Yes, please," Carols answered.

"Good, then we should adjourn to the briefing room for today's update," Ballantine said, "and someone let Gunnar know, please." He answered the phone. "William? Good, good... Protocol Fifty-four? Excellent... They know? Even more excellent..."

Ballantine turned and left. Everyone focused on Ingrid.

"Show us that again," Thorne said.

"Ballantine said there was an update in the briefing room," Ingrid replied.

"Show us again," Thorne said, "this time don't dumb it down. We need details and we need to know the pros and the cons of this weapon for when we can use it. Educate us."

Carlos snorted then pretended he stifled a sneeze when he received a roomful of glares.

"Go ahead," he said to Ingrid, "I have something else to do, uh, somewhere else."

He hurried through the shelves, leaving Ingrid alone with Team Grendel.

"Phew," Max said, "I thought he'd never leave."

"Let's kill some atoms," Shane almost giggled.

***

"I should be down there with them," Mike said as he sat on a stool in the corner of Gunnar's lab. "Technically, I'm part of Team Grendel."

"So am I," Gunnar replied as he stood in front of a counter, a tablet in his hand, "but we have work to do."

"You have work to do," Mike said as he rapped his knuckles on one of his robotic prosthetic legs. "I'm just here for maintenance."

"Which you wouldn't need so often if you'd listen to me and keep your legs from getting wet," Dr. Morganton said as she rolled a cart of equipment into the lab. "I am getting tired of telling you that, Michael."

"We live on a ship," Mike replied. "It's a little hard to keep my legs dry."

"Which is why I am trying to develop a prophylactic that will do the job for you," Dr. Morganton said as she stopped the cart next to Mike and opened a large case on top. "This should be the answer."

"Prophylactic?" Mike asked. "You want to put rubbers on my legs?"

"Yes, Michael, I want to put rubbers on your legs," Dr. Morganton replied.

She pulled out a long piece of skin tone rubber and smiled at him.

Gunnar looked over his shoulder and laughed. "I heard the sarcasm in your voice, Lisa, but that does look suspiciously like a leg rubber."

"It's synthetic skin," Dr. Morganton replied. "If you'll extend your left leg, Michael."

He looked at Gunnar, but all he got was a shrug.

"Fine," Mike said, "rubber me up."

Dr. Morganton rolled the synthetic skin then proceeded to slide it up and over Mike's left leg. It extended past the prosthetic by several inches and bunched around Mike's thigh. He looked down at the wrinkled skin and frowned.

"I look like I have elephant skin," he said.

"That will be fixed shortly," Dr. Morganton stated as she grabbed what looked like a basic taser.

"Whoa!" Mike exclaimed. "You are not going to tase me!"

"Actually, I am," Dr. Morganton replied, "but the current will be set to a low level and you shouldn't feel much discomfort."

"Much?" Mike asked.

"Shouldn't?" Gunnar smirked.

"I haven't had a chance to try it on a living person," Dr. Morganton said.

"That sentence brings up so many more questions," Gunnar said as he turned and leaned back against the counter, his arms folded across his chest. "First being, so have you tried it on a non-living person?"

"Yes, of course," Dr. Morganton replied. "Ballantine has been very forthcoming in procuring cadavers as I need them when we have been in port."

"Right," Gunnar laughed, "of course he has."

"We have cadavers on board?" Mike asked. "Where?"

"My lab," Dr. Morganton said, "or the less than adequate space Ballantine has given me to use as my lab."

"I told you we can share," Gunnar shrugged, "but Ballantine wants you working alone."

"Yes, I am painfully aware of that," Dr. Morganton said then smiled at Mike. "Ready?"

Before Mike could answer, she activated the taser and the synthetic skin on Mike's leg began to contract. In seconds, the skin had fitted itself around the prosthetic and looked completely real. Except that, it was a different shade than Mike's true skin color.

"Yes, I can see the issue," Dr. Morganton said before either Mike or Gunnar could point out the color discrepancy. "I'll have to incorporate a skin tone matching element."

"Hey, that actually looks like skin," Mike grinned. "Gun? Look at this!"

"I see it, Mike," Gunnar said. "You are almost a real boy."

"You are already a real asshole," Mike said. Then he frowned. "Hey, Doc? Should my leg hurt?"

"How do you mean hurt?" Dr. Morganton asked.

"Like with pain," Mike replied as he winced. "That kind of hurt. Ow. It burns. Ow! Hey! Shit!"

The leg started to twitch and then kicked out uncontrollably. Mike's foot hit Dr. Morganton in the hip, causing her to bend over, then nailed her in the forehead, sending her falling backwards onto the floor.

"Shit," Gunnar snapped as he rushed over.

He grabbed a screwdriver from Dr. Morganton's cart, and jammed it into Mike's knee while also dodging the flailing leg. He ripped the skin free, inserted the screwdriver into a small slot on the inside of the knee, gave it a couple twists, and then slammed the end of it with his hand. Mike's leg froze in mid-kick.

"Thanks," Mike said, sweat dotting his brow. "That fucking hurt like hell."

"You alright?" Gunnar asked as he knelt next to Dr. Morganton.

"I'm fine," she said. "The electrical charge must have shorted something in his prosthetic. I'll need to work on the insulation levels in the skin so that doesn't happen again."

"Good idea," Gunnar said as he helped her to her feet.

"Everything okay in here?" Kinsey asked as she walked into the lab. She gave Gunnar and Dr. Morganton a concerned look. "What happened?"

"My rubber broke," Mike said.

"Never mind," Kinsey said, "I don't want to know."

"What's up, Kins?" Gunnar asked as he assisted Dr. Morganton with stripping the rest of the synthetic skin off Mike's leg.

"Ballantine is calling a briefing," Kinsey said. "I was sent to fetch you." She nodded to Dr. Morganton and Mike. "All of you, actually, so it's a good thing you're all right here."

"We'll be up in a minute," Dr. Morganton said. "Just let me recalibrate Michael's prosthetic."

"Don't take too long," Kinsey said. "We've already kept Ballantine waiting while we played with the elves' new toy."

"They hate it when they're called that," Gunnar said.

"Carlos hates it," Kinsey replied, "and fuck him."

"Can't argue with that," Gunnar smiled. "We won't be longer than five minutes."

"Cool," Kinsey smiled. "I'll let big bossman know."

As soon as she was gone, Dr. Morganton looked at Mike. "So much for the leg rubber," she sighed. "You'll just have to promise me you'll make sure your compression suit is sealed before you get in the water, and then dry before you get out of it, okay?"

"Okay," Mike nodded.

***

Everyone filed into the briefing room, chatting and laughing as usual. At least until they saw the look on Ballantine's face, and the shattered sat phone on the table.

"That wasn't a good phone call," Thorne stated.

"No, Commander, it was not," Ballantine replied then waved towards everyone. "Don't bother sitting, the briefing is postponed for now. We have a bigger task at hand."

"Such as?" Thorne asked.

"We have to double check this ship to make sure there are no tracking devices or locating beacons," Ballantine said.

"I thought that had been done," Thorne said.

"As had I," Ballantine replied, "but the information I just received proves otherwise. Apparently, while I was conversing with my acquaintance, something began to broadcast our location."

"Just now?" Darren asked. "How?"

"I don't know, Mr. Chambers," Ballantine sneered. "If I did, then this wouldn't be so distressing, would it?"

"Back off, Ballantine," Kinsey said. "Same team, asshole."

"Yes, yes, I'm sorry," Ballantine said then sighed and leaned back in his chair as Carlos, Ingrid, and Moshi arrived at the briefing room's doorway. "What can you tell me?"

All three of the techs held modified tablets in their hands. Moshi looked at Ingrid and Ingrid looked at Carlos.

"The armory is clear," Carlos said.

"Toyshop," Max said under his breath.

"As I knew it would be," Carlos glared. "All company tech has been removed from every single device. There isn't a piece of hardware down there that is connected to the company in any way.

They'd have better luck tracking a single drop of seawater than tracking us."

"Do you have more scanners?" Ballantine asked.

"As many as needed," Ingrid said.

"Good, then assign one to each member of the crew and break the ship up into grids," Ballantine ordered. "We shut down the power until we find what is giving off the signal."

"Shut down the power?" Darren asked.

"That way we don't have any interference from the B3," Ingrid said. "If our scanners pick anything up, then we'll know it's not tied into the ship and could be the tracking device."

"You want us to be sitting ducks while we have ships on our ass and a giant shark hunting for us?" Thorne growled. "At what fucking point does that make sense?"

"It makes sense because where we are going, no one can know about," Ballantine said. "I would rather risk those ships and that shark catching up to us than exposing our destination."

"Is it a secret clubhouse?" Max asked.

"No girls allowed?" Shane asked.

"There better be girls allowed," Kinsey said.

"How about no little dicks allowed?" Lucy asked.

"Max will be fine then," Darby said.

Everyone turned and looked at the Reynolds brother. He just winked and gave a thumbs up.

"GODDAMMIT!" Ballantine roared as he slammed his fists down on the table. "This is fucking serious! I am tired of the constant jokes and sarcasm! From now on you act like fucking professionals or I throw you off my ship!"

"Marty is captain of the B3," Darren said, "it's his ship, not yours."

"Don't test me, Mr. Chambers," Ballantine snapped.

"Don't test the chain of command on a ship at sea, Ballantine," Thorne said as he stepped in front of the group, taking Ballantine's focus all on himself. "Things fall apart very quickly when that chain of command is fucked with. It's there for a reason."

"Captain Lake works for me," Ballantine replied. "There's your chain of command."

"Everyone out," Thorne said.

"Yes, everyone out," Ballantine said. "You have scanning to do."

Carlos, Ingrid, and Moshi left immediately, but no one else moved until Thorne looked over his shoulder and nodded. They were reluctant, and made sure Ballantine was very aware of that, but they departed and left Thorne and Ballantine alone in the briefing room.

"This isn't all about a tracking device," Thorne said. "We've always known we'd get caught at some point, so tell me what really has you pissed off."

Ballantine opened his mouth, closed it, opened it again, closed it, then sighed and shook his head.

"We've been let go," Ballantine said. "Officially."

"Let go?" Thorne asked as he took a seat at the table. "By the company?"

"Yes," Ballantine said. "As of an hour ago, the Beowulf III, its crew, and Team Grendel are officially free agents. We have no country and we have no company to fall back on. We are alone."

"Good," Thorne said.

"I'm sorry?" Ballantine asked. "Did you just say that's good?"

"I did," Thorne said. "I never liked working for your company, and since I'm disavowed by the country I have spent my life protecting and bleeding for, then I'd rather we were cut loose and on our own. Simplifies things."

Ballantine studied Thorne for a long time then took a deep breath.

"Simplifies things," Ballantine smiled sadly. "If only that were true. Without the company's protection, we are now open game for every enemy we've made. Plus every enemy I've made."

"Every enemy I've made and every enemy Darren has made and every enemy my daughter and nephews have made," Thorne laughed. "I am pretty fucking confident Darby's made some enemies too. We all have enemies, Ballantine. So fucking what?"

"So fucking what?" Ballantine barked.

"So fucking what," Thorne stated.

"So fucking what..." Ballantine muttered then smiled. "Yes. So fucking what? We have some of the most capable people on the planet on this ship. We've proven ourselves as a unit that can't be taken down. We've fought governments and impossible monsters. We've dealt with cartels, traitors, and pirates."

"Plus cannibal tribes," Thorne grinned.

"Yes, those too!" Ballantine laughed. "That was something, wasn't it?"

"It was," Thorne said, "and we're still here."

"We've also lost team members," Ballantine said, "and some of us have been wounded permanently."

"Company didn't really help prevent any of that, did it?" Thorne asked.

"No, the company did not," Ballantine agreed. "We probably *are* safer on our own."

"Less variables."

"Yes, less variables," Ballantine said then slapped the table, but not in anger that time. "Thank you, Vincent. You have cleared the fog from my mind and shown me what we need to do."

The lights in the briefing room went out and the constant hum of the ship died.

"Let's clean house and begin our next chapter as rogues and malcontents," Ballantine said as he stood and extended his hand.

Thorne stood as well and grasped Ballantine's hand tightly.

"I think we've always had the malcontent part covered," Thorne said. "You've met my nephews."

***

"So we sit here and wait for the ships and the shark to catch us," Lake said as he leaned against the dark control console on the B3's bridge. "Just hang out in the ocean until we find a tracking device that we should have found a long time ago. What could possibly go wrong?"

"Not my call, Marty," Darren said as he systematically waved the scanner over every inch of the bridge. "Carlos says we need the power off and Ballantine does what Carlos says when it comes to tech."

"Anyone think to ask me or Cougher or Popeye?" Lake asked. "We're the fucking professional sailors. Maybe we could have come up with a way to scan without stopping the ship."

"Is there a way?" Darren asked, looking up from his work.

"Fuck if I know," Lake shrugged. "What the fuck do I know about tracking devices?"

Darren grinned and got back to scanning.

"I hear ya," Darren said. "You have to vent."

"Fucking A right I do," Lake grumbled. "I'm captain of this ship, not just a fucking chauffeur."

"No one thinks you are," Darren said. "Trust me. We all had your back when Ballantine broke the news."

"There's more to it than he's telling us," Lake stated.

"I know," Darren agreed, "but Ballantine is used to juggling secrets. He'll tell us when he's good and ready."

"He better," Lake said, "or I'm turning this thing around and going home."

"We don't have a home anymore, Marty," Darren said.

"Fuck!"

***

"There they are," Bokeem smiled as he pointed at the satellite image on the screen by his chair. "Just where we were told they'd be."

"Beacon is still working?" Tank Top asked as he moved around behind Bokeem for a better view.

"Still working," Bokeem said. "Even though they've powered down the entire ship. Look at this reading. They don't even have a coffee maker going."

"Then what's that?" Tank Top asked as he zoomed in on the image of the B3. "That looks like something has power."

"That's where the beacon is hidden," Bokeem smiled. "What I want to know is why it took our ace so long to activate it?"

"Being a traitor on that ship can't be easy," Tank Top said. "You know how it is. The real question is how they don't know the power source is active? That ship has tech we have wet dreams over at night, even with all our new gear."

"I haven't got a fucking clue," Bokeem replied, "and I don't really care. As long as we can catch up to them, then I'm happy."

"Me too," Tank Top said. "John Bill?"

"Yeah, Tank?" a short Indonesian man replied from the helm.

"How far out are we?" Tank Top asked.

"Eight hours at the most," John Bill grinned. "They keep their engines down and it'll be shorter than that."

"Eight hours," Tank Top sighed. "It's like knowing you have a winning lottery ticket and 7 p.m. can't come fast enough."

"7 p.m.?" Bokeem asked.

"Yeah, you know, when they draw the lottery numbers," Tank Top replied.

"They draw those at 11 in Kentucky," Bokeem said.

"Kentucky?" John Bill asked. "I thought you were from Nigeria."

"Do I fucking sound like I'm from Nigeria?" Bokeem snapped. "Who the fuck are you to talk? You're Indonesian with an Irish accent."

"I grew up in a Catholic orphanage," John Bill shrugged. "It's how I learned English."

"A Catholic orphanage in the largest Muslim country in the world?" Tank Top laughed. "That had to be fun."

"Loads," John Bill frowned.

"How did we start talking about this?" Bokeem asked.

"The lottery," Tank Top replied.

"Right," Bokeem nodded, "the lottery."

"A cool half a billion dollars," Tank Top grinned. "Doesn't get better than that."

"Makes you wonder how much those dipshits are paying our employer if that's our cut," Bokeem said as he switched the view on his screen to the ships following behind the Monkey Balls. "Too bad we couldn't cut out the middle man."

"Not how we play the game," Tank Top said. "The middle man keeps things honest."

"Yeah, right," Bokeem laughed deeply. "Honest!"

***

"We've been at this for hours," Gunnar said as he walked down the passageway with Dr. Morganton, each with a scanner in their hands. "We have to have covered the whole ship at least twice."

"We haven't found the tracking device," Dr. Morganton said. "Until we do, Ballantine won't be satisfied. Not to mention Thorne."

"It's weird that Ballantine just found out there was a tracking device at all," Gunnar said.

"He said it had just been activated," Dr. Morganton replied.

"Yeah, but why now? And how?" Gunnar wondered. "Does that mean we have a traitor on the ship? Is someone working for the people coming after us?"

"I don't know," Dr. Morganton said.

"Hey!" Mike called as he turned a corner and hobbled up to them.

"How's the leg?" Dr. Morganton asked. "Still glitching?"

"A little," Mike said as he got up to them. "It's like it has a skip in it."

"A skip?" Gunnar asked.

"Yeah, every few seconds it just kicks out for no reason," Mike replied. "It's starting to piss me off."

Mike's leg twitched and he had to brace himself to keep his balance.

Both Gunnar's and Dr. Morganton's scanners beeped.

"Did you see that?" Gunnar asked as he checked the reading on his tablet. "We had the tracking device for a second there!"

"Yeah," Dr. Morganton replied. "My scanner shows the same thing. It's a weak signal, like it's shielded."

"How could a tracking device be shielded?" Mike asked. "Wouldn't that defeat the purpose since someone wants the signal to get out?"

"No, actually," Dr. Morganton replied, "if the device is shielded and only reveals itself when it transmits, then it wouldn't need much power at all to send a signal, especially if it's using some type of frequency other than radio waves."

"High intensity microwaves?" Gunnar asked. "If it's dialed in right to a receiving satellite then it'd have less of a footprint than a digital watch."

"If that," Dr. Morganton said. She turned around in a circle then started to walk up and down the passageway. "It's gone."

"Let's check the rooms," Gunnar said.

"I'll go tell Thorne," Mike said as he started to hobble away. His leg twitched again and he put his hand out against the wall to steady himself. "Fucking piece of crap!"

Gunnar's and Dr. Morganton's scanners beeped once more.

"Mike," Gunnar said, "stop right there." He looked over at Dr. Morganton and then down the passageway at Mike. "Actually, how about both of you stop right where you are."

"Me? What for?" Dr. Morganton asked.

"Just stay there," Gunnar said as he held his scanner up, his eyes going from Mike to the scanner to Dr. Morganton and back to the scanner.

Over and over again he watched the two other people in the passageway while also trying to keep his attention on the scanner. Then Mike's leg twitched and the scanners beeped.

"You mother fucker," Gunnar said as he looked right at Dr. Morganton. "You fucking traitorous piece of shit."

"Excuse me?" Dr. Morganton snapped. "How dare you speak to me that way, Dr. Peterson!"

"How dare me?" Gunnar shouted. "How fucking dare *me*? Oh, right, because I'm the one that has been working and tweaking Mike's prosthetics! In fact, it must have been me that decided today would be the day to put synthetic skin on his leg and jolt it with a taser. Was that really a taser, Doctor? Or was it what you needed to activate the tracking device?"

"Oh, shit," Mike said as he looked down at his leg, "the fucking thing is in my leg?"

"Stay right there," Gunnar snarled at Dr. Morganton then he sidestepped over to Mike. "Hold still."

Gunnar knelt by Mike's leg and waited. In just a couple of seconds, the leg twitched and the scanner beeped.

"Gunnar, listen, you can't possibly think I had anything to do with that," Dr. Morganton said. "I'm part of this team, part of this ship and crew. I've given up my life for Ballantine and the company! I died for them!"

"Bullshit," Gunnar said. "I don't know you for shit, lady. I know everyone else on this ship, but you. You're a stranger that hitched a ride."

"You really think you know everyone on this ship?" Dr. Morganton laughed. "You may know the crew, you may know the Thornes, the Reynolds, Darren Chambers, but do you really know Ballantine? Or Darby? Or Ingrid? Or Moshi? Or...Carlos?"

Her eyes went wide.

Gunnar started to argue, but he saw the disbelief and then realization dawn in her eyes.

"Shit," Gunnar said, "you didn't build those legs."

"Carlos did," Dr. Morganton responded.

"We have to get Thorne and Ballantine and the Team down to the Toyshop," Gunnar said. "Carlos has all the weapons. He can take this ship at any time, if he wants."

They both took off running, leaving Mike to hobble after them.

"Hey! Wait up, you fucks!" Mike shouted as his leg twitched. "I still have the fucking tracking device in my leg, morons!"

***

Thorne and Darren took point as they stepped into the pitch dark Toyshop, their M4 carbines to their shoulders and their game faces on. Kinsey and Darby were next with Lucy right behind. They stepped past the counter with the metal cage that was the entrance to the storage area of the armory and quietly made their way past each row of shelves until they came to a long work bench. Sweeping their heads back and forth, their NVGs turned the Toyshop into a glowing landscape in their eyes.

"Where is he?" Thorne snarled as Moshi looked up from the circuit board she was working on, a headlamp lit up on her forehead to make up for the lack of power to the lights.

The headlamp blinded Thorne and Darren rushed forward and yanked it from Moshi's head. The small woman squeaked and fell off her stool then tried to crawl under the work bench, but Darren grabbed her by the ankle and pulled her out.

"Where is he?" Darren snapped.

"What the fuck is this?" Carlos asked as he came out from between two shelves, his own headlamp blindingly bright. "What the hell are you guys doing? Moshi? Are you all right? What the fuck, guys?"

"Get on the fucking ground!" Thorne yelled and rushed forward. "Get down now, you fucking traitor!"

Thorne grabbed Carlos by the shoulder then swept his legs out from under him. Carlos's back hit the ground hard, knocking the wind out of him. He lay there gasping, his hands up, his eyes wide with shock and terror.

"You think we wouldn't figure it out?" Darren asked. "This ship is filled with trained minds, you idiot! How the fuck could you possibly think you'd get away with it?"

"Get away with what?" Carlos gasped. "I haven't fucking done anything!"

"We found the tracking device in Mike's leg," Thorne said as he dropped quickly and planted his knee in Carlo's solar plexus, making the man gasp even harder. "It was clever, I'll give you that."

"I...don't know...what...the...fuck...you are...talking about," Carlos wheezed. "Get...the fuck...off me."

"Carlos? Moshi?" Ingrid asked as she moved slowly towards the work bench. She didn't have a headlamp and was feeling blindly in the dim light given off by Moshi's and Carlos's. "What's going on?"

"Get over there with her," Darren ordered as he swung his carbine towards Moshi.

Then the power came on and Ingrid stopped in her tracks. She looked down at Carlos, looked over at Moshi, and then looked at Team Grendel with their carbines to their shoulders. She stood stock still for a second then turned and bolted.

"Oh, you have got to be kidding me!" Kinsey shouted as she slung her carbine and pulled out her pistol then took off after the woman. "It's not those two!"

Ingrid sprinted between the shelves, dodging this way and that so Kinsey couldn't get a bead on her. She yanked gear off the shelves and tossed it to the floor forcing Kinsey to jump and leap over random pieces of equipment and weaponry.

"Goddammit, Ingrid!" Kinsey yelled. "Don't make me shoot you!"

Ingrid didn't stop. She just kept winding back through the maze of shelves that made up the Toyshop.

"Ingrid! If you stop now, I promise nothing will happen to you! We just need to talk!" Kinsey yelled.

"Yeah, right!" Ingrid shouted back.

Kinsey zeroed in on the voice and changed directions. She backtracked two rows of shelves and then ran as fast as she could down the aisle between them. Ingrid crossed her path and then bolted towards the wall at the far end of the aisle. Just before getting to the wall, Ingrid tapped at her wrist and suddenly there was nothing but passageway in front of them.

Well, almost nothing but passageway.

"Hey, there," Max said as he slammed the butt of his rifle into Ingrid's face just as she reached the secret entrance/exit to the Toyshop. "Forget about us?"

Ingrid hit the floor in an unconscious heap.

"I think she did," Shane said as he stepped up next to his brother.

"I would have preferred if she was awake, boys," Ballantine said from behind them. "Pick her up and bring her below."

"Below?" Kinsey asked as she skidded to a stop and tried to catch her breath. "Why below?"

"Because that's where my interrogation room is," Ballantine grinned. "I think it's the appropriate venue for what is about to happen to our dear, sweet Ingrid."

"Dude, dial back the scary, will ya?" Shane said.

"Yeah, I think I peed a little," Max said.

"Just pick her up," Ballantine frowned. "We don't have much time."

***

The door opened and Ballantine stepped out, wiping his hands on a hand towel as he looked up to see Thorne, Darren, Darby, and Carlos standing in the passageway.

"What?" Ballantine asked. "I didn't have to lay a finger on her, if that's what you're worried about. She confessed to everything."

"You want to fill us in?" Thorne asked.

"Walk with me," Ballantine said. "I need some fresh air."

"Can I see her?" Carlos asked, his eyes flitting from Ballantine to the interrogation room door.

"Not a chance in Hell," Ballantine said. "You are the one that let this happen."

For once, Carlos kept his mouth shut and just nodded.

"I'll wait here," Darby said as she stepped next to the door. She looked at Carlos. "You can wait with me."

"Okay," he nodded and gave a weak smile. "I'm sorry, Ballantine. I didn't know she was-"

"None of us did," Ballantine said, "but your apology still means nothing. Part of your job is to know what those under you are up to. You failed with this one, Carlos. It'll be a long time before you can make that up to me. Especially considering what damage you've already caused in the past."

"Don't," Darby snarled, "just don't, Ballantine. That was never his fault, despite how you want to spin your web of lies."

"We'll have to permanently agree to disagree on that one, Darby," Ballantine said. "Commander? Mr. Chambers?"

"Knock off the Mr. Chambers shit," Darren said, "it doesn't impress me."

"I never intended it to," Ballantine smiled. "Quite the opposite, in fact."

He walked down the passageway and Thorne and Darren hurried to catch up.

"She's been in the company's pocket for quite some time," Ballantine said. "Apparently her mother has been sick and the company has paid for all of her medical bills as well as hospice care once she took a turn for the worse."

"Why would the company want her in their pocket?" Darren asked.

"Because they haven't trusted you since the first Beowulf was lost," Thorne stated.

Ballantine stopped and fixed his gaze on the commander.

"That's very perceptive of you, Vincent," Ballantine said. "You figured that out quickly."

"I don't know what went down with that ship," Thorne said. "Especially since you don't talk about it."

"Never," Ballantine nodded.

"Whatever happened, it was bad enough to put Darby on edge and defend that tech against you," Thorne said. "I think I know Darby well enough to say that her actions speak volumes on your culpability in the accident."

"It was far from an accident," Ballantine said as he started walking again.

"Then what was it?" Darren asked as they took a set of stairs then another up past the next couple of decks. "What the fuck happened on the Beowulf I?"

"Darren," Ballantine sighed, "I just stated that I never talk about that."

"I don't fucking care," Darren replied. "I just stated that."

They took more stairs until they were walking onto the upper deck and out into the sunlight and ocean breeze.

"Hey! You guys better come look at this!" Lake yelled down from the bridge.

"In a moment, Captain," Ballantine said as he waved up at Lake. "We are having a discussion right-"

"Oh, shut the fuck up, Ballantine!" Lake snapped. "Get your high and mighty ass up here now!"

"I think we had better do as he says," Thorne said.

"Apparently," Ballantine frowned.

They climbed up to the bridge and Ballantine was about to lay into Lake when he was handed a set of binoculars.

"Due east," Lake said, "just off the horizon."

Ballantine reluctantly took the binoculars and turned in the direction Lake had indicated. He focused the binoculars and studied the ocean for a few seconds.

"Monkey Balls," he said as he gave the binoculars to Thorne.

"I'm guessing that's not good," Darren said.

"Monkey Balls," Thorne said as well.

"Hardly original," Darren responded as the binoculars were handed to him. He put them to his eyes then focused. "Oh, shit. Monkey Balls."

Just in front of the horizon was a group of ships heading towards them quickly. On the bow of the lead ship were the words "SS Monkey Balls."

"Those are the people tracking us, right?" Lake asked.

"Yes, Captain, they are," Ballantine answered.

"That's a lot of ships," Lake said.

"It's not the amount of ships that worries me," Ballantine said, "but the one leading the charge."

"I count five ships following the Monkey Balls," Thorne said then sighed at the stupid name before continuing. "Three are cutter class while two are destroyers. Destroyers, Ballantine. Do you see the flag they are flying?"

"Mexican," Darren said. "Fucking cartels bought out two Mexican naval destroyers. This is great."

"The cutters have Somali clan flags," Lake said. "Fucking pirates again."

"Tell me, Ballantine," Thorne said, "if there are three cutters with Somali clan flags and two destroyers flying the Mexican colors, then why are you afraid of the one ship in front with the stupid name Monkey Balls?"

"Because the other ships we can handle," Ballantine said. "I have faith in the Beowulf and its crew, and more importantly, I have faith in Team Grendel, but the Monkey Balls? If who I think is on that ship is actually on that ship, then I am not sure we can handle them."

Lake pulled out a Desert Eagle pistol and set it by the wheel. "Can I shoot him if he doesn't tell us what the fuck is going on?"

"He's going to tell us," Darren said, "but you're the Captain, Marty, you can shoot whomever you want on this ship."

"There is a Team of men on that ship," Ballantine continued as if Lake and Darren hadn't just threatened his life. "A very dangerous Team."

"A Team?" Thorne asked. "What kind of Team?"

"My first Team, Commander," Ballantine said as he turned and looked Thorne directly in the eye. "What? You didn't think Grendel was the first, did you?"

"Son of a bitch," Darren said.

"You're saying there are SEALs on that ship coming to kill us?" Lake asked.

"SEALs? Not even close, Captain," Ballantine replied. "No, they are nothing but cold blooded mercenaries. That's why when I put Grendel together, and I chose Commander Thorne and his expertise. I knew he'd pick people with integrity and loyalty, as SEALs are trained."

"So, your first Team didn't work out and did what?" Thorne asked. "Bit the hand that fed it?"

"Far worse," Ballantine sighed. "You want to know what happened to the Beowulf I?" Ballantine pointed out at the horizon and the quickly approaching ships. "They happened, Commander, and it is all about to happen again if we don't prepare ourselves."

"They are the ones that sunk the Beowulf I?" Darren asked.

Ballantine laughed. "The Beowulf I was never sunk."

"But you said…?" Darren trailed off.

"Never honest a day in your life, right Ballantine?" Thorne sneered.

"You got me, Commander," Ballantine shrugged.

"Sound general quarters," Thorne said to Lake. "Everyone to battle stations."

"Jesus, Mary, Mother of God," Lake said.

"Yes, Captain," Ballantine said, "prayer is a very good idea right now."

Chapter Four- The Prodigal Is Home

Tank Top was about to depress the button on the handset and hail the Beowulf III when Bokeem cleared his throat.

"What?" Tank Top asked.

"I'm the fucking captain of the Monkey Balls," Bokeem said. "I get to do the hailing."

Tank Top looked at the handset and then at the man in the captain's chair.

"Fuck that," he grinned as he pressed the button. "Hello, Ballantine! Guess who this is?"

"Those are the first words you are going to say?" Bokeem laughed. "You'll really have that psychopath quaking in his leather loafers."

"Hello, Mr. Lodensheim," Ballantine replied. "It has been a while since we have had the pleasure of conversing, you murderous fucking asshole of a man."

"Wow," Tank Top chuckled, "and here I thought you may not remember me. How ya been, you polo shirt wearing fuck nut?"

"Better than average, but less than great," Ballantine responded. "Is Bokeem with you? How about the rest of the old Berserker team?"

"We dropped that Team Berserker bullshit years ago, Ballantine," Tank Top said, "and no one calls me Lodensheim, you know that."

"They don't? What do they call you?" Ballantine asked. "Turncoat? Deceitful cunt? Dead man, if I get my hands on you?"

"You know what my handle is, Ballantine, so say it," Tank Top said then whispered to Bokeem. "He's always hated my name."

"Tank Top," Ballantine sighed. "It's not a name so much as a description."

"All good nicknames are," Tank Top said, "and to answer your earlier question, yes, Bokeem is here. He's the captain of the Monkey Balls, in fact."

"Bokeem is?" Ballantine asked. "Well, that's a surprise. Tell him congratulations for me. The man is a better leader than you could ever be. Not that any of you are worth a shit."

"I hear your hate, Ballantine, but I think it masks your true feelings," Tank Top said. "You know you love us. We're your first born, your first Team."

"One that should have been aborted," Ballantine said.

"You tried, but it didn't take," Tank Top replied. "Abortion aborted."

"Get to the point," Bokeem said. "We have a schedule to keep if we want to avoid the abomination coming behind us."

"Bokeem has already reminded me that we're on the clock today, Ballantine," Tank Top said. "We're steaming to you and plan on boarding without incident. You make this easy for us and we spare the crew."

"That's a worthless lie, if I ever heard one," Ballantine said. "You'll butcher us all, just like before."

"I didn't butcher all of you, now did I?" Tank Top said. "You're still breathing, unfortunately. Those weapons nerds are still breathing, even though you sent that loser Carlos to try to trap and blow us up. I count his escape as one of my greatest failures as a soldier of fortune."

"That's what you call yourself? A soldier of fortune?" Ballantine laughed. "That's like a fresh turd calling itself a diamond."

"You are just full of insults today," Tank Top exclaimed. "Certainly not the polished gentleman I remember from before. I guess living with those SEAL pussies has rubbed off on you."

"You'd be a fool to consider my new Team pussies, Lodensheim," Ballantine said.

"Tank Top," Tank Top insisted.

"*Jason,*" Ballantine mocked.

"Whatever," Tank Top shrugged. "Hey, is Darby still with you?"

Ballantine didn't respond.

"I'll take that as a yes," Tank Top smirked. "She ever tell you that we fucked on your desk? You know that sweet dark mahogany number you had in your office? Yeah, all over that. Man, we slicked the top of that thing up so much you could see the reflection of our asses as we went at it. That Darby sure gets wet when she's excited."

"It would be wise to close your mouth now, Jason," Ballantine whispered. "It would be very wise."

"She there by your side as always?" Tank Top asked. "Put her on, if she is. I'd love to reminisce about old times. Hell, if she's nice, I'll even let her fuck me on that desk again. Yep, I still have it. I left your office exactly the same. I go in there for a morale boost when I'm feeling down. Beating you and taking your ship was one of the high points of my career."

"I have a new ship, Jason," Ballantine said, "and it can blow yours out of the water."

"Maybe," Tank Top replied, "but, I doubt it can blow the Mexican destroyers out of the water. At least not before they unload every missile they have on you."

"If that was the plan, Jason, then they would have done it by now," Ballantine said. "So that means you need at least one person from this ship alive. Which person is it? Is it me?"

"Oh, there's that ego I've missed so much!" Tank Top exclaimed. "You just can't believe that someone else might be more important to our employers than you."

"Who?" Ballantine pressed.

"Okay, full disclosure, yes, we need you alive," Tank Top admitted. "We also need the Thorne twat and her daddy. If we get all three of you, then your crew and the ship can go free. Scout's honor."

"You have no honor and I'm fairly certain you were never a Boy Scout," Ballantine said.

"Not true, not true," Tank Top said, "I was. I even got the cock up the anus by a troupe leader badge. Probably why I have issues with authority and lack any sense of rage control. I'm deeply scarred."

"No shit," Bokeem laughed.

"Bokeem agrees with my self-diagnosis," Tank Top continued. "His input has saved me thousands of dollars in therapy fees."

"I can understand why the company wants me, but why would they want the Thornes?" Ballantine asked.

"Who said anything about the company wanting the Thornes?" Tank Top asked.

***

The smell of oil and grease permeated the water, despite there not being any ships within fifty miles of the creature. It was an offensive smell, but one that drove the shark towards its target.

Not that it needed the smells to hone in on its prey. Even from its far off distance, the shark knew how many ships were in the ocean ahead, their sizes, their weights, and even the amount of people that made up their individual crews. The monster was a feat of science and engineering that transcended almost all breakthroughs during the past century.

It was a killing machine of impossible size with an intellectual capacity that one of its long dead species should never have been capable of. It could reason, plot, plan, and out maneuver most humans, and it perfectly intended to once it caught up with its target, even if it had to destroy the other ships that its mind quickly realized were its competition, not its allies.

***

"We are not fucking around here!" Thorne shouted. "You are getting in the fucking water with Team Grendel!"

"That's stupid," Kinsey snapped as the two Thornes hurried down the passageway to Gunnar's lab. "As soon as they realize I'm not on board, they'll start torturing or shooting crewmembers."

"That's why I'm staying behind," Thorne said, skidding to a stop as he entered Gunnar's lab. "What the fuck is she doing in here?"

Everyone looked at Ingrid who was busy working on Mike's left prosthetic with Dr. Morganton, as the man lay back on a lab table.

"I needed her assistance," Dr. Morganton said as she stepped away from the lab table and approached Thorne with her hands out in a pacifying gesture. "I couldn't disengage the tracker without frying out the main junction of the leg's brain."

Thorne was less than pacified.

"Legs don't fucking have brains" he yelled, "and she is an admitted traitor! Get her back in the fucking brig right now!"

"Daddy, I think-" Kinsey began.

"Not one more word from anyone!" Thorne roared. "Ballantine and I have given orders and we expect them to be carried out! The life of everyone onboard depends on the chain of command right now!"

"Chill, Vinny," Gunnar said as he stepped up next to Dr. Morganton. "We need Mike in the fight. We also need to get the tracker off this ship. The shark is zeroed in on it and that means it's zeroed in on the B3."

"What the fuck do you mean it's zeroed in on it?" Thorne asked. "I thought it had been disabled."

"It has," Carlos said, "for the most part. There is a sub-frequency signal still transmitting from the device. I can't figure it out, Moshi can't figure it out, and Ingrid didn't know it was capable of transmitting that kind of signal. Technically, it's a theoretical signal and nothing should be able to transmit using a sub-frequency like that. As annoying as it is, it is fascinating to see it in action."

"You know what's fascinating to see in action?" Thorne growled. "My boot-"

"Up our asses," Gunnar and Kinsey said in unison.

"Let it go, Daddy," Kinsey said, "and let it go that I'm getting off this ship."

"Darby is already suited up, so are the boys and Darren," Thorne said. "You are going with Grendel and you are going to help take these ships down before they surround us."

"I'm on that list," Mike said, looking at Ingrid, "right?"

"If everyone will please be quiet so I can work on this," Ingrid said. "Then yes, you will be able to suit up as well."

"I'll be below getting ready," Kinsey said as she turned her attention to Carlos. "Gear all ready for me?"

"Suit, mustache, and channel guns," Carlos nodded. "Checked and ready."

"Good," Kinsey smiled. "Thanks."

She kissed her father on the cheek and took off out of the lab. Thorne started to follow, but a cry from Ingrid made him turn his attention back to the lab table.

Ingrid was holding her hand to her chest as a small square of metal shivered on a tray next to the table. Small blue sparks emanated from the square as tendrils of smoke wafted away from it.

"What the hell was that?" Mike asked as he flexed his leg.

"Stop that," Carlos grumbled. He took over Ingrid and checked Mike's leg for damage. "Systems are in the green. I'm closing it up. You're ready for duty."

"The thing bit me," Ingrid said.

"Bit you?" Gunnar asked.

"Well, it shocked me," Ingrid said. "I don't think it wanted to be pulled free."

"Who would?" Mike smiled as he looked to Carlos for the okay to start flexing his leg again. He got the nod and eased himself off the table. "I'm a sexy hunk of SEAL. No one wants to leave this bod."

"Careful there, stud," Gunnar said, "that ego isn't very sexy."

The square sparked more, then began to bounce up and down on the tray. Moshi pushed past everyone and looked at the wiggling hunk of tech. She glanced around the lab then hurried over to a counter and grabbed a pair of rubber gloves. When she got back to the tray, she carefully picked up the tracker then smiled as she met everyone's eyes.

"I'm not sure what you want, Moshi," Ingrid said.

The silent woman held out her hands, but not to the techs or the scientists.

"What the hell would I want with that thing?" Thorne asked.

Moshi smiled and looked around the lab then back at the commander.

"Someone help me here," Thorne said.

"Duh," Carlos said as he slapped his forehead. "She's right. We can use this against them. The shark is tracking this device, not this ship."

Thorne got it immediately then.

"Get me some gloves," he said. "I have to get this down to Grendel."

***

"Incoming Zodiac," Lake said over the com as Lucy laid prone in the crow's nest, her .50 cal rifle tucked against her shoulder. "You got it, Lucy?"

"I got it," Lucy said.

Lucy watched through her scope as the Zodiac bounced across the waves towards the B3. Three men were in the Zodiac and all of them heavily armed. The one that rode at the fore of the raft wore a pair of khaki shorts and a black tank top; Lucy guessed he was the leader that Ballantine had told her to watch for.

The other two men were both large, muscled, and armed with M4s that looked heavily modified. Lucy doubted that the men would be easy to take down once they were on the B3 and her finger itched to fire as it rested next to her trigger guard. She could take all three men out in less than three seconds, but Ballantine had said to hold her fire unless she was fired on.

She turned her scope from the Zodiac and lifted it towards the shop that was steaming closer by the second. Monkey Balls. She laughed at the name, but the laugh caught in her throat as she saw that she wasn't the only one playing sniper.

"Lake? We have three shooters with eyes on us," Lucy said as she studied one man in the Monkey Balls' crow's nest, then one on the observation deck and another standing on the bow. The one on the bow waved to her as he waggled his .300 Win Mag back and forth. She glanced at the other two and they were doing the same thing. "The shooters are smart asses."

"That isn't good," Lake said. "Smart ass shooters tend to hit what they aim for."

"Yes, we do," Max said over the com.

"We'd hit our targets anyway," Shane added, "because we're that good, but being smart asses doesn't hurt."

"Guys, shut the fuck up and get prepped," Darren said. "Sorry, Lake, I'll keep them off the channel."

"Switch to Team channel," Thorne ordered. "Ballantine?"

"I'm here, Commander," Ballantine responded, "what can I do for you?"

"I'm going with the Team," Thorne said. "Sorry, but they will need me. The plan has changed."

"Has it?" Ballantine asked. "I wasn't aware we'd decided to change the plan."

"Don't worry," Thorne said, "we have it all under control."

"I am sure you do, Commander," Ballantine said.

"What channel do you want me on?" Lucy asked. "Grendel or Beowulf?"

"I get an Anglo-Saxon woody when you say things like that," Max said. "Ow! No hitting, Darby! Ow! Okay...I"ll shut up."

"Stay on the Beowulf channel," Thorne said. "Coordinate with Ballantine and Lake. If I need you I'll switch over."

"Got it," Lucy replied as she continued to move her scope from one sniper to the next and back.

They weren't waggling anymore and Lucy shivered knowing she had three sniper rifles all pointed at her.

***

The hatch to Specimen Bay One opened and Team Grendel hurried through, hustling across the deck to the open water. They each slipped off the deck and into the water without saying a word. Their compression suits adjusted automatically to the pressure of the water and each member of the Team winced as the mesh tightened then loosened.

"It's like a hug from a creepy uncle," Shane said.

"Not you, Uncle Vinny," Max said as he placed his mustache rebreather under his nose and pulled the tabs at each side. Tubes slid up his nose, into his sinuses then down his trachea and into his lungs. He choked and gagged for a second then shook his head. "That's just gross."

The rest of the Team did the same with their rebreathers, all agreeing silently.

"I'm pretty sure all you have to do is place this on the hull," Carlos said as he knelt by the edge of the deck and handed a small box to Thorne. "The tracker is still active and should send the shark right for the other ship."

"You're pretty sure?" Thorne frowned, his voice a little off putting as it was amplified by the mustache instead of coming directly from his mouth. Due to the rebreather sealing off the airway at the back of his throat, as it did for all the Team members, there was no way for him to speak normally, although the facsimile the rebreather produced was fairly accurate.

"I haven't had time to study the tech," Carlos said. "I'm only making educated guesses here. If you want, I can take it back and spend the next few hours dissecting it. Will that work on your precious time table?"

"Thanks, Carlos," Kinsey said, "you did what you could."

"I'm here!" Mike said as he rushed into the bay. "Sorry I'm late."

"You're not late because you're not coming," Thorne said.

"What?" Mike protested. "Why? Because of my legs? Max broke his only a few weeks ago and you're sending him out."

"The water helps," Max said. "It's physical therapy with guns."

"I need you on this ship as backup," Thorne said to Mike. "You make yourself scarce and keep your eyes and ears open. I want to hear regular updates in my ear on the Team channel, got it? If things go south, you shout 'Monkey Nuts'."

"Monkey Nuts?" Max asked.

"It's Monkey Balls," Shane added.

"I know what the fucking name of the ship is," Thorne growled.

"Uncle Vinny isn't in a funny mood, is he?" Max whispered.

"See? What'd I tell you about the creepy uncle hugs?" Shane whispered back.

"Oh, for fuck's sake," Thorne muttered.

"You want me to stay below decks?" Mike asked.

"Below decks and out of sight," Thorne ordered. "The Toyshop might be a good place. Get in there with the techs and lock it down. They have the equipment to monitor the whole ship."

"We have the equipment to control the whole ship," Carlos said. The Team all turned their attention on the man. "What?"

"You can pilot the ship from the Toyshop?" Darren asked.

"Yeah. So?" Carlos replied.

"If we live through this then we're having a sit down where I learn every single thing about every aspect of this ship and crew," Thorne snapped. "So fucking tired of learning about things just as I'm getting in the shit."

"What Uncle Vinny said," Max nodded.

"I second that emotion," Shane said.

"So now probably isn't a good time to tell you that I modified your compression suits so that the nanotech can magnetize, allowing you to scale the hulls of ships, then should I?" Carlos smirked.

"I get to shoot him," Max said.

"No way, I'm calling that one," Shane said.

"Get to the Toyshop," Thorne said to Mike, ignoring his nephews and Carlos, "and have this asshole fill you in on any other need to know information he's been holding back."

"Hey," Carlos protested, "I didn't hold that back, I just forgot until now, and as for the controls in the armory, I just thought Ballantine would have told you. Or at least told Darren."

"He didn't," Darren said.

"Well, that's your problem, not mine," Carlos shrugged.

"Come on," Mike said, "time to tear you away from all the friend making."

"Not my fault these Jarheads don't know how to ask the right questions," Carlos grumbled.

"Hey!" Thorne, Max, Shane, Mike, and Darren snapped.

"I'm the only Jarhead," Kinsey said as she raised her hand. "Jarhead refers to a Marine, not Navy SEALs."

"Who fucking cares?" Carlos shrugged as Mike dragged him back to the hatch.

"The guy with the channel gun pointed at your crotch," Max glared.

Mike got Carlos through the hatch and slammed it shut. He peered through the porthole them gave a thumbs up. Claxons and flashing red lights filled the bay as the pressure changed and the space began to fill with water.

Having used the mustaches before, none of Team Grendel panicked when the water completely filled the bay. They all just took deep breaths through their rebreathers then gave each other the thumbs up that things were working right.

Below and in front of them, the bottom of the bay split open to reveal the ocean outside. Thorne locked eyes with each member of the Team then pointed at the opening and started to swim.

Team Grendel was through the doors and on its way to the Monkey Balls.

***

"We should have brought more men," a thick-necked man said as he steadied the Zodiac by a ladder that had been dropped from the B3's railing above. "Three of us won't hold long if their whole Team decides to start wailing on us."

The thick-necked man was in his mid-forties with a deep brown sailor's tan and a shaved head. Across his head, was a tattoo of a mermaid holding an M16 machine gun and smoking a cigar. The tattoo was marred by a long, white scar that ran from the top of the man's skull and all the way down to his ear.

"Gil, you need to relax," Tank Top said as he grabbed the ladder. "They aren't going to do shit, not with two Mexican destroyers pointing all guns at them. Trust me, Ballantine won't come at us head on. That sneaky bastard like's his attacks to be unseen."

Tank Top tapped at his ear.

"Bokeem? You read me?"

"Loud and clear," Bokeem replied over their com system.

"How's it looking from Shabby Paul, Wonkers, and Bub's angles?" Tank Top asked.

"They have the chick sniper clocked and see the ship's captain standing on the bridge with a pair of binoculars pointed right at us."

"You pointing your eyes at them?" Tank Top asked.

"Nope," Bokeem said, "that'd be too clichéd. John Bill and I are having some tea right now. You just give us a shout when you need us."

"Is he fucking joking?" the third man, Lug, nearly shouted. "Tea? They're up there drinking tea while we do all the work?"

While large like Tank Top and Gil, Lug had a nervousness about him that made him look smaller than the other two. He had the vibe of a fourth grader that had missed his last three doses of Ritalin.

"You think we're doing all the work?" Tank Top asked the man then looked over at Gil. "Gil? Would you say that we're doing all the work?"

"Our fair share," Gil shrugged.

"Exactly," Tank Top smiled. "Our fair share. You hear those words, Lug? We're all doing our fair share. It's all good, so calm down. I need you calm, Lug. Are you calm?"

The man twitched and ticked, but nodded.

"I'm calm," Lug said.

"You don't look calm," Tank Top said then punched the man right between the eyes.

Lug didn't even flinch or stumble back. He shook his head and his whole body seemed to relax instantly.

"Thanks," he said to Tank Top, "I needed that."

"You punch him?" Bokeem asked.

"Right between the eyes," Tank Top replied then looked at the ladder and the man that peered down at them from the railing above. "Let's go meet Ballantine's new Team, shall we?"

***

The shark rocketed through the water, ignoring the small fishing vessels above it as it sped towards its target. It wanted to stop and devour the boats, rip them apart plank by plank, and swallow the crews whole as they screamed their way to their ends.

Even the desire for blood, food, and carnage couldn't tear it away from its path. The target was so close and every nerve ending in the beast was alive with the thought of the final catch. All of its existence had built up to the last chase, the end game.

The massive shark swam closer to the surface of the water and let its dorsal fin nudge the hull of one of the fishing boats. Even from under the water, it could hear the men above cry out in alarm. Marine biologists would have dismissed the grin on its face as anthropomorphizing since sharks don't smile.

Those marine biologists would have been wrong. Very, very wrong.

***

Ballantine stood on the upper deck of the Beowulf III and watched as a ghost from his past climbed over the railing and gave him a huge smile.

"Jason," Ballantine said as he walked forward and offered his hand.

"Fuck you and your mother, Ballantine," Tank Top said, ignoring the offered hand. "This isn't a reunion, so don't get cute."

"Two more coming up, Ballantine," Popeye said from the railing as he looked down at the side of the B3.

"Thank you, Popeye," Ballantine said.

"Popeye?" Tank Top asked as he turned and looked at the smaller man as if he'd just noticed him. "Yeah, I can see the resemblance, but the cartoon guy had both his legs."

"You can have both of these," Popeye said as he turned and raised the middle fingers of each of his hands.

"Now, that's cute," Tank Top laughed. He turned his attention back to Ballantine. "Where're the Thornes?"

"They won't be joining me," Ballantine said.

"Really?" Tank Top asked, folding his arms across his chest. "That is kind of the opposite of my instructions."

"Yes, I am aware of that," Ballantine replied.

Tank Top waited for more then laughed. "Jesus tits, Ballantine, you haven't changed one bit."

"I like to think I have," Ballantine replied. "What is the point of life if we don't achieve growth?"

"Oh, go fuck yourself with your cock sucking wisdom," Tank Top said. "It was all just words when I worked for you and it's all just words now. Go get the fucking Thornes so I can get back to my ship."

"Like I said, Jason," Ballantine sighed, "the Thornes will not be joining me."

Tank Top closed on Ballantine in a blink, his hands clutching at Ballantine's shirt collar.

"This is not a negotiation, Ballantine," he snarled, "call the Thornes up here or I'll have the Mexican Navy blast this ship out of the fucking water."

"Then give the order," Ballantine said. "Be my guest."

"I'll do it," Tank Top warned, "as soon as I have you down in that raft and we're halfway back to the MB, I'll have every gun open up on this tin can and send it to the bottom of the ocean forever."

"Ooh, not forever," Ballantine grinned. "Forever IS such a long time."

Tank Top gave Ballantine a hard shake, and then shoved him away as he turned to the two men that climbed up after him.

"Lug? Gil? Search below deck," Tank Top ordered, "be thorough. I want every corner and shadow checked and double checked."

"I know how to search a ship," Gil said as he pushed past Tank Top and Ballantine to the main hatch. "Come on, Lug."

Lug was busy looking Popeye up and down. "Is this guy for real?" he asked as he reached out and pressed a finger to Popeye's shoulder. "What happened to your leg?"

"Big fucking shark is what happened," Popeye said.

"Bummer," Lug nodded then turned and followed Gil through the hatch.

"That one with Gil is new," Ballantine said, nodding after Lug and Gil. "How'd you sucker him into joining your rag tag crew of miscreants?"

"Miscreants?" Tank Top sighed. "Are you going to use that high and mighty affectation the whole time? It gets old, Ballantine. Everyone knows your mother was a street whore and your father was a random john. Don't even pretend to be above any of us."

"Bokeem is still alive," Ballantine said, ignoring the insult. "John Bill? Shabby Paul? Wonkers?"

"All still breathing," Tank Top said.

"Morningside?"

"Nah, he died a year or so ago," Tank Top said. "Took a knife to his belly and bled out in my arms."

"How poetic," Ballantine replied, "he wasn't worth that end."

"I kind of agree with you," Tank Top said. "The guy was a bit of a creep, but damn if he didn't know how to blow shit up."

"Slaps? Is the man still hairier than a mountain gorilla?"

"Hairier than that," Tank Top laughed. "I think his hair is growing hair."

"That all?" Ballantine asked. "Any more new names I should know about?"

"None you should know about," Tank Top said. He shielded his eyes and looked up at the bridge. "Obviously, we are going to have to do this the hard way. So how about you take me up to the bridge and introduce me to the captain of this little tug of yours. Lake's his name, right?"

"It is," Ballantine said, "but I'd rather not. You came for me and you have me. No need to involve Captain Lake or any of the crew."

"There's all the need in the world," Tank Top replied. "Leverage. You know about leverage, right Ballantine? Isn't that the entire backbone of how you operate? Find the leverage and use it against your marks?"

Tank Top motioned towards the stairs leading up to the bridge.

"Coming?" he asked.

Ballantine didn't move.

"Listen, Ballantine," Tank Top sighed, "I don't have all day here. We both know what's coming for you. You cooperate, bring me the Thornes, and all of you come with me to the MB without resisting or trying anything and I can call off the big, scary shark.

If you make trouble then I let it sink this ship like it's made of paper."

"The Beowulf III is not the same as the Beowulf I, Jason," Ballantine replied. "It can withstand a lot more than you think."

"So can the Monkey Balls," Tank Top said. "Which is its new name, okay? We don't use the B-word anymore. The MB has been modified to avoid a repeat of the last time we saw each other. My ship can take whatever that giant fish wants to give out. Up to a point, of course. I think we both know that what's coming for us wins eventually, right?"

Ballantine looked past Tank Top to the MB and frowned.

"I'm still not sure how you survived," Ballantine said. "That ship should be in an undersea canyon right now."

"Long story," Tank Top grimaced, "and not one I like to think about. Let's just say that physics was on our side that day, which is more than I can say for you."

"I was always on your side, Jason," Ballantine said. "You just decided not to be on mine."

"You know what?" Tank Top responded, aiming his M4 at Popeye. "I'm done with the tête-à-tête."

He pulled the trigger and Popeye screamed before tumbling over the side of the railing.

"No!" Ballantine yelled as he rushed forward, but was quickly stopped by a rifle butt to the side of the head.

Ballantine collapsed to the deck and tried to get back up, but another blow between his shoulder blades sent him sprawling.

"Stay down and listen," Tank Top said as he pressed the hot barrel against the back of Ballantine's neck. "From this second forward, you will do as I say, when I say it. No more banter. No more misdirection. I've already guessed you have people in the water. Guess what? So do I. That sniper you have in the crow's nest is outnumbered and nowhere near as fast as my folks are. She may be good, but my guys are great and you know it. What we are going to do now is you are going to get up, walk me to the bridge then make a general announcement to the rest of the crew that they have five minutes to come out of their hidey holes and show their faces on deck or I order Lug and Gil to shoot anyone on sight."

Tank Top pressed the barrel harder.

"Are you with me, Ballantine?"

"I'm with you," Ballantine said. "May I pull a handkerchief from my pocket? I'm bleeding a little."

"You're bleeding a lot, asshole," Tank Top said as he stepped back and kicked Ballantine in the leg. "Get up and pull out your handkerchief. Fuck, pull out your cock. I don't care, as long as you start doing what I say."

"To the bridge?" Ballantine asked as he looked at Tank Top then the stairs.

"To the bridge," Tank Top nodded.

Ballantine summoned all his strength and pushed aside the dizziness that wanted to drag him down. He walked slowly to the stairs then took hold of the railing, but before he started to climb he looked at the patters of blood by the railing where Popeye had stood just seconds before.

"Should have had his spinach," Tank Top said then jabbed Ballantine in the ass with his carbine. "Move." He tapped at his com. "Bokeem?"

"Yeah?" Bokeem replied over the com.

"Get some guns in the water," Tank Top said. "I think I know where the Thornes are."

"Copy that."

***

Carlos, Moshi, Ingrid, Gunnar, and Dr. Morganton all turned and looked at Mike as they stood in front of a bank of monitors that showed nearly every angle of the B3.

"Yeah, I know," Mike said as he tapped at the com in his ear. "Monkey Nuts."

"Are they there in front of you?" Thorne asked over the com.

"No," Mike replied. "We're all still in the Toyshop. They just killed Popeye."

There was silence over the com for a second.

"Copy that," Thorne responded finally. "We're almost to the ship. We'll plant the tracker then get back to you ASAP. We can't risk you guys exposing yourselves, so don't bother opening the specimen bay back up. We'll find our own way back aboard."

"Be careful," Mike said. "From what we heard, they are about to have people in the water with you. Watch your backs."

"We always do," Thorne said.

***

The dark bulk of the Monkey Balls loomed over Team Grendel as they pressed their hands to the hull. The magnetic feature of their suits kicked in and they all grinned around their mustaches as the ship pulled them along. Thorne took out the tracker box from a bag at his hip and placed it on the hull. It magnetized as well and clung to the Monkey Balls, sending out its never-ending sub-frequency signal.

"They're tagged," Thorne said. "Now we get back and help our people."

"Doesn't look like it's going to be that easy," Max said as he put his channel gun to his shoulder.

Shane, Darby, and Darren did the same while Kinsey pulled two channel pistols from her hips and aimed them at the divers that were swimming right at them.

Team Grendel almost laughed when they saw the old school, bulky rebreathers the men wore, but the idea of laughing was quickly forgotten as guns started to fire and bullets whizzed at them through the water.

"Looks like they have their own modified firearms!" Darren yelled. "Split up and divide their fire!"

Slugs hit the hull of the Monkey Balls and slow motion ricocheted this way and that. Max felt one clip his elbow, sending his first shot wide of its mark. It hurt like hell, but when he looked down he didn't see any blood and the compression suit was still fully intact.

"Remind me to thank Carlos for adding bulletproof to the list of features these suits have," Max said. "That would have been good to know, too."

"Remind yourself!" Shane yelled as he kicked out and ducked his body under a line of bullets that ripped right past him. "A little busy here, bro!"

"Didn't I just say these were bulletproof?" Max said. "That means we can- Ah, fuck!"

"Max!" Darby shouted as she looked over and saw blood billowing out of a wound in Max's right leg. "Max!"

"Not bulletproof! Not bulletproof!" Max cried out. "This leg was almost fully healed! Fuck!"

"No, shit, moron!" Kinsey yelled as she squeezed the triggers on both her channel pistols and swept them to the side. A diver was kicking past her, but the resistance of the water slowed her aim and all of the slugs missed the man by inches. "Fuck!"

"Close combat," Darby said suddenly as she slung her channel gun to her back and tightened the strap. She pulled two knives from her belt and kicked her legs towards the closest attacker. "Take it to them."

The man closest to her fired round after round, but Darby dove down, avoiding the bullets, then came up fast with a turn of her torso and a few hard kicks from her legs. The man was ready for her and instead of firing again, he turned his rifle to the side and brought it down towards Darby's arms.

The rifle stock caught Darby in the left forearm, but she was able to twist her body so it missed her right arm. That arm she brought up fast and plunged one of the knives into the man's thigh. Bubbles exploded from his mouth as Darby buried the blade to the hilt and gave it a couple quick turns.

The water turned dark red as arterial blood poured from the man. Before Darby could pull the knife free, the man was dead, the pressure of the water making him bleed out twice as fast as if he'd been above the surface.

"Darby! Drop!" Max yelled.

Darby didn't hesitate and shoved her hands upward so her body moved deeper. She watched as three bullets left a trail of bubbles above her, right where her head had been. She kept going deeper and deeper then turned about to see another blood shrouded diver several feet behind and above her.

"Got him," Max said. "I may be bleeding, but I can still shoot. Thank god these dipshits don't know that the rounds for the channel guns actually pick up speed as they move through water."

"They're catching on," Shane said as he fired shot after shot towards two men that whirled and dodged each round.

Darby started to swim to Shane's aid, but something caught her eye. She steadied herself by waving her arms and kicking her legs so she could focus better. At first, she thought she was seeing a shadow of one of the other cutters, but then she realized the shadow was moving much faster than the ship above.

"People," Darby said, "we have company."

"Sugar, we've had company for a little while now," Max replied. "Did you bump your head?"

"Shark company," Darby said, "coming fast on our eight, and it's big."

***

"Nice and easy, Captain," Tank Top said as he leaned against the wall, his M4 covering Lake and Ballantine as they stood next to each other by the wheel. "Just bring us around slowly. I think what this ship could use is a good old-fashioned boarding party. I'm sure you have the skills to get us close enough without playing bumper cars, right Captain Lake?"

"I could park this ship right between your mother's legs, if I wanted," Lake said. "The problem would be getting it out since I'm sure the suction of her gaping hole is stronger than any whirlpool in this ocean."

"That was mean, man," Tank Top said. "My mom is actually a very nice woman. She volunteers at the local animal shelter back home and takes cookies to her friends in the nursing home. I'd ask you to apologize, but I know you were just letting off steam. I'd probably say the same thing if I was in your position."

A loud beeping filled the bridge and all eyes turned to the sonar screen.

"Shit," Tank Top said as he hurried over to the console, "if that's what I think it is, it's way too early."

"It can swim a lot faster than you think," Ballantine said.

"You'd know," Tank Top replied. "Fuck, it'll be right on us in seconds."

"What does he mean by you'd know?" Lake asked Ballantine.

"Not the time, Captain," Ballantine replied. "Focus on piloting the ship. What we don't need now is a collision."

Ballantine gave Lake a hard look and the Captain nodded.

"What the hell?" Tank Top said as he studied the sonar screen. "Why is it going to the MB? What's it doing? Shit! Without the tracker on, the stupid thing doesn't know what ship to attack!"

"That isn't quite true," Ballantine said, "but, there's no need to go into that now."

Tank Top whirled on the man.

"Where's the Toyshop?" he barked.

Ballantine was about to play dumb, but he closed his mouth quickly.

"Ingrid," he said.

"Exactly," Tank Top nodded. "I know you have a new Toyshop. Even if the woman hadn't given that intel to my employers, I would have guessed. You've always loved your tech toys."

"Why should I show you the Toyshop?" Ballantine asked.

"Because I'm going to turn on that tracker you found and get that shark pointed in the right direction," Tank Top replied. "So let's move."

He jammed his carbine into Ballantine's ribs and the man grunted, but didn't move.

"There's no need, Jason," Ballantine said, "the tracker isn't onboard the Beowulf III. Just like the Thornes aren't onboard, either."

Tank Top took a step back and narrowed his eyes. He watched Ballantine closely then looked out the bridge windows at the crew that had started to gather on the upper deck outside.

"The tracker is with the Thornes," Tank Top said, "that's why the shark is heading for my ship."

"You may be dumb, but you certainly aren't stupid," Ballantine said.

"No, I'm not," Tank Top said. "Know what else I'm not? Patient."

He walked to the door of the bridge and stepped out onto the landing, and aimed his M4 at the crew below then glanced back at Ballantine.

"How about you call your Team?" Tank Top said. "You get on your com and have them swim ass back here with that tracker. However they were going to place it on my ship, have them do that to the Beowulf."

"Beowulf III," Ballantine said.

"Beowulf III," Tank Top sighed. "Whatever. Just get on the horn and make it happen. If that shark even scratches the MB, I'll cut your crew in half."

Lake started to reach for the Desert Eagle he had tucked away on a small shelf under the wheel, but Ballantine put a steady hand on his shoulder and squeezed.

"You sure you want me to recall my Team?" Ballantine asked.

"I want my employers to recall that fucking shark," Tank Top said.

"They can't do that," Ballantine replied.

"You don't know that," Tank Top argued.

"Like you said, Jason, I'm the one that *would* know," Ballantine replied.

"No more talking," Tank Top said. "I've already told you what to do. Call your Team."

"Very well," Ballantine replied.

***

"Grendel?" Ballantine's voice called out over the com. "Abort mission. We've hit a snag. Return the tracker, and yourselves, to the Beowulf III immediately. No time to explain, just do it."

"That was an open channel," Darren said, "he didn't switch to the Team channel."

"Which means he has no desire for us to do what he says," Thorne said as he fired nonstop at a diver that was coming right for him. The man got about five feet away then stopped as the rounds pierced his wetsuit and then detonated, ripping him to shreds. "Pull the tracker and drop it."

"What?" Kinsey asked, as she followed Darby's lead and her knife blades ripped open another diver. "What the hell for?"

"We need that shark to follow it," Thorne said. "That'll give us some time to work things out and take this ship."

"Take this ship?" Shane asked, as he checked his brother's leg. "What the fuck are you talking about?"

"Ballantine contacted us over an open channel," Darby said as she swam towards the small box magnetically stuck to the Monkey Balls' hull. "That means that the B3's crew is in jeopardy. They're probably being held at gunpoint on the upper deck, ready to be executed one by one until Ballantine gives in."

"Jesus," Max asked as he pushed his brother away and looked down at the wound in his leg. The compression suit had closed over it and the pressure kept the wound from bleeding more, but as soon as the suit came off he'd need serious medical help or he'd probably bleed to death. "How do you know that's what's going to happen?"

"That's what I'd do if I had taken our ship," Darby said, her hand closing on the small box. She yanked it free from the hull then held it out. "We take their ship and get us some leverage."

"Get us some?" Kinsey laughed. "You're starting to sound like Max."

"Is that a bad thing?" Max asked.

"Depends," Darby said as she opened her hand and let the small box fall. It descended quickly and was lost from sight in seconds. "There. Now we climb."

"Hold on!" Darren shouted as he wrestled with a diver.

The two men twisted and turned in the water, thrashing about each other as they threw punches and tried to rip at each other's rebreathers. The diver got his fingers up underneath Darren's mustache and pulled hard, tearing the thing off Darren's face.

Everyone heard Darren cry out then turned to see Darren holding his breath as he ripped the diver's face mask off and jammed his thumbs into the man's eyes. Blood and milky white fluid poofed out from the collapsed eyes. Darren yanked off the man's rebreather and slammed a fist into the diver's throat. The man's mouth opened wide and a deluge of bubbles poured forth.

"Damn, Ditcher," Shane said, knowing Darren could hear him, even though he couldn't respond anymore. "You really fucked him up."

The diver reached for Darren blindly, but he found only open water as Darren kicked away then slid the man's rebreather up over his shoulders and placed the mouthpiece between his lips. He took a couple of deep breaths and got himself under control before he swam around behind the man, grabbed both sides of his head, and twisted as hard as he could.

The man's neck snapped and Darren let the body float down and away from him before he turned and gave everyone a thumbs up.

"Now, he really fucked him up," Shane said.

"We need to get out of this water," Darby said and pointed to the deep darkness below them. "I believe the thing went that way."

"It's probably not going to be happy that it's chasing a tiny box that isn't food," Max said.

"Can you climb?" Thorne asked as he swam up to his nephew.

"Do I have a fucking choice?" Max replied.

"Not in the slightest," Thorne said.

"Then yeah, I can fucking climb," Max nodded.

Team Grendel all placed their hands and feet on the hull of the Monkey Balls and let the magnetic feature take hold again. Once they were sure they were affixed properly, they started to climb up the hull, hand over hand, foot over foot.

***

The small box was swallowed up like a tiny grain of rice in a black hole.

The massive shark immediately sensed that something was wrong. The signal told it that it had found its target, but there was no satisfaction to the completion of its task. It had been sent out before, and it knew there should be satisfaction.

There should be the crushing of metal and the screaming of men. There should be taste of blood and bone, engine oil and diesel fuel, fear and terror.

None of that happened when the signal in the box finally cut off, having been caught by its seeker.

The shark whipped its gigantic tail and turned its body back towards the surface of the ocean. It was a thing of beauty and a marvel to behold if anyone had been deep enough to behold it. Nothing in the history of the world had moved with such speed and grace. At least, nothing the size of the shark that rocketed up towards the many shadows that it now considered its new targets.

The thing intended to have its taste of blood and bone, engine oil and diesel fuel, fear and terror. It intended to feel the crushing of metal and hear the screams of dying men.

As far as the shark was concerned, its mission was completed and now it was on its own to wreak as much havoc as it desired, and it intended to feed that desire for as long as it could.

Chapter Five- Water Red Is Desire Fed

Seven shapes were above.

Seven shapes for it to choose from.

Targets all.

No need to worry about where to start, the shark planned to get to each and every one of them in short order. In very short order.

The first shape was three times its length, but the massive beast did not care. Three times, five times, twenty times- the shark feared nothing other than not fulfilling its desire to hunt and kill, seek and destroy.

It swam under the shape, circling around as it studied the hull and keel with its black eyes. First one direction, then a quick whip of its tail and it was swimming in the opposite direction. It circled, circled, circled, taking in as much information as it could about its prey.

Then it dove.

Deeper than it had been during its entire journey, the shark swam until the light was nearly gone and the water so cold that it felt itself beginning to slow involuntarily. The temperature was how it knew when to stop and bring itself back around so it was pointed at the surface once again.

It left the frigid, muscle slowing cold behind as its tail pumped back and forth, using the resistance of the deep water to drive it on, ever upwards to its goal. Faster and faster it went, never slowing once, never taking its eyes off the target, never letting its senses get distracted by the other shapes, the other sounds, the other smells. Those would wait, would still be there when it was done with what was getting closer and closer with every second.

Then it struck.

Its mouth wide open, a thousand sets of teeth gleaming in the filtered light above, the shark hit the first Mexican destroyer about fifteen feet from the rear propeller. It tore into the drive shaft as it clamped down with all its strength.

Steel and iron were treated like paper and cloth as the gigantic teeth sawed from side to side until a massive chunk of the ship tore free and fell past the shark, destined to spend centuries on the ocean floor.

The shark didn't slow, wasn't satisfied by the one attack, needed more to quench its unquenchable desire for destruction.

It raced along the length of the hull, again its black eyes sizing up its prey. It could smell the oil and fuel it had released into the water and it knew the loud sounds would begin soon. In seconds, were the sounds of emergency claxons ringing out far above the water's surface. The noise reverberated down to the shark and drove it on since it knew the prey would want to fight back.

In seconds, the water's surface was pierced by large barrels, which to the shark's nose, smelled of death.

The first explosion was meters from the monster, well out of range to do any damage other than hurt its fine tuned senses. The second explosion was closer and the third was closer still. The fourth hurt as fire and heat burst against the shark, sending it back to the deep for another run.

The creature knew to wait, wait for the attack to stop before making its rocket ascent again. It couldn't quite keep track of how many explosions there were, but it could keep track of the time between them and then the long silence that filled the water when the last barrel had detonated.

Up it went.

With the drive shaft ripped apart, the destroyer leaked fluid like a wounded fish leaked blood, and just like blood, the smell of the shaft fluid drove the beast on. It pushed the monster to an even faster speed than its first attack so that when teeth met metal once more, a huge portion of the bottom of the destroyer was in turn *destroyed*.

Through the hull, the abomination tore. Its head thrashed back and forth as it pushed itself up into the guts of the ship. Terrified men, men that thought they would be safe below decks, screamed and tried to flee, but they were no match for the teeth of the beast or the pull of the grand ocean.

Arms, legs, heads, all floated through the blood filled seawater, having been separated from their previous owners. The shark slammed from side to side to widen the hole it had made, wanting to get farther up into the belly of the ship and to the poor souls that still clung to the thought that if they only made it to the upper deck they would be safe. They would be able to hail the other destroyer and find rescue.

Even if they did escape the quickly sinking ship, there would be no rescue waiting for them as the shark withdrew from its mortally wounded prey and turned its attention to the slightly larger shape that was steaming quickly away.

As powerful as the second destroyer's engines were, they needed time to get up to speed. The shark did not. With only a couple thrusts of its tail, the shark was rocketing towards the destroyer at three times the ship's current speed. The beast didn't bother with the rush up from the deep tactic and instead rammed the destroyer close to the bow, knocking it off course, and tearing a hunk of steel plating right from the hull.

Again, the sound of annoying claxons rang out over the water and filtered down to the shark's ears. The monster knew that was the sound of panic, and it brought its bulk around for another run. More steel fell away as it slammed into the hull again and again until the first third of the bottom of the ship looked more like a crumpled wad of paper than the front of an ocean war machine.

With the hydrodynamics of the ship compromised, the ship started to list starboard while the bow began to dip down. The shark saw how its prey was wounded and calculated the many angles of attack it could take.

It could keep hammering at the same spot or it could try to weaken a different area. It could come up at it and pierce the hull as it did the first destroyer, or it could simply bite off the propeller and bring the ship to a dead stop. Even with the engines still going the monster knew it could crush the propeller before the blades did any real damage to its mouth; it had no doubt.

The shark knew that the more time it spent on the destroyer, the more time it allowed the five other targets to escape. Its desire was torn between wounding the destroyer pitifully until the last blow was nothing short of mercy, or taking the ship down quickly so it could move on to the next target, and the next and the next and the next and the next.

It shoved all thoughts from its mind then shoved all metal from its way as it shredded the middle of the hull. There was a shriek of gears and a small explosion as the engine room was pierced. The fire and flames surprised the shark enough that it withdrew quickly for a final attack, but as it swam out and then back, it saw the destroyer begin to split in half and knew the prey was dead.

While the second and last destroyer separated and sank to the ocean floor, the shark sized up the five remaining ships. Two were close together and presented easy targets, but three were trying to flee in different directions, and that infuriated the shark, sending it into a rage it had no idea it was capable of. To have three targets think they could escape was an insult to the shark's sense of supremacy in the ocean.

It knew, on some level that nothing else on the planet could match its ferocity, its size, and its death dealing drive to kill.

The three fleeing ships needed to be taught what it meant to be in the presence of greatness.

***

The first ship was a cutter not quite twice the length of the shark. It sped its way east, the crew giving the engines everything they had despite the risk they'd snap a shaft and end up dead in the water. The alternative was to be cautious and most certainly end up dead in the water.

The captain of the ship announced over the PA how proud he was to serve with the fine men and women that made up his crew. Many he knew from their days as children, years before they were recruited into the same pirate gang.

Being from the same clan made them one family, even if they did not share blood with each other. The captain knew his First Mate's brothers and sisters as if they were his own brothers and sisters. He knew his Chief Engineer's mother as if she was his mother, the man's uncle as if he was his uncle. The captain had spent many afternoons watching his children play with the children of the crew, just as he had played when he was younger.

As he stood on the bridge and stared at the horizon that never grew closer, he realized that his twenty-eight years on Earth had not been enough. He had spent half of those years on the sea with his mates, hunting and taking what they wanted from whomever they wanted. He'd spent so much time capturing shipping vessels that he couldn't remember when he'd last been with brothers and sisters, mothers and uncles, his children and the children of his crew.

The sea had been his home, his work, his salvation, his prison.

As the first impact hit the cutter dead on, the captain knew the sea would be his grave.

***

Like a tuna's belly, the cutter was ripped open.

The shark had barely hit the side of the ship, but the cutter wasn't double hulled and designed for battle like the destroyers, so all it took was a glancing blow to cripple it. From the belly of the crippled ship came candy. Small, person shaped nuggets of flavor and fear.

The shark opened its mouth and swallowed eight men whole, their screams never heard as their mouths gaped and their lungs filled with water. Into the gargantuan maw they went, hands scrambling to paddle them out of the giant toothed nightmare they found themselves in.

Then chomp, they were gone, and crushed by a jaw that barely felt their soft, malleable bodies. What was flesh to a monster built to shred steel? It was almost like air, as it had less substance than the water that flowed through its gills and breathed oxygen into its bloodstream, but flesh was delicious.

The shark wanted more. It wanted to eat all of the flailing nuggets of candy that floated this way and that, caught in the pull of the ship that had started to sink quickly. The flesh morsels, the not even close to bite sized treats, filled the water, but the shark ignored them, knowing they weren't going anywhere without its permission.

Its senses could hear and feel the screams and movements of the people still trapped inside the ship. It wanted to taste their panic and fear, to devour it all in huge, gulping bites.

The shark came about and rammed the cutter once more, taking most of the bow off. The seawater rushed in to fill the open hold and more men were flushed from the gash in the ship's side. The beast ignored the men that were forced out into the open water, it wanted the ones that refused to come meet it, and it wanted the ones that hid and fled from its might.

Men scrambled to climb above the water level that was quickly filling the ship. They grabbed at ladders and the extended hands of their shipmates, but it made no difference as the shark wedged its way inside the torn open bow. The monster was relentless, its hunger insatiable. Men were cut in half; their bodies almost pinched shut from the incredible force of the shark's jaws. Torn into bits by sawing teeth or crushed completely by more than ten tons of pressure per square inch, the men that could not escape the beast were turned into bloody flesh confetti.

In minutes, the cutter was sunk. The shark withdrew and let the steel carcass slip into the dark waters below. It had grown bored with the dead and dying men. It wanted to hunt, to find, to feed on fresh terror.

It turned its attention to the next fleeing ship and rocketed through the water towards a new target for its bloodlust.

***

Men fought each other for space on the few, and feeble, lifeboats that the pirate cutter had. Two lifeboats that held eight men each, with a crew of twenty-four, did not make for good survival math. Words were exchanged, then blows, and then weapons were drawn.

Gunfire punctuated the humid South Pacific air as men that had been friends and allies just minutes before turned into bitter enemies. AK-47s, 9mm, .45s, and even .22s were emptied above deck, and below, sending blood across the sun warped boards and dripping off the sides of the ship, down into the water that held nothing but certain death.

The captain tried to get order restored as he shouted down at the fighting men from the hatch of the bridge, but a stray bullet hit his temple and he fell back, unconscious. The First Mate took the captain's incapacitation as a chance to abandon ship himself and he wasted no time stepping over the bleeding and dazed man to get to the ladder that led down to the deck below.

The First Mate only made it a couple of rungs before his legs were shredded by automatic gunfire. The slugs ripped into his calves and thighs, tearing flesh and shattering bone. He screamed as he lost his grip on the ladder and fell fifteen feet towards a pile of corpses below. His spine snapped as he hit and all the breath was knocked out of him. His scream was choked off as everything from his chest down went numb.

The First Mate could hear the crew battling each other, but he couldn't turn his head to see the chaos and bloodshed. All he could do was stare straight up at the blue sky above and pray that the shark would pass them by.

As the ship began to jolt and shudder, the First Mate knew his prayer had fallen on deaf ears. No deity above was looking down on his plight, ready to offer a holy hand of saving grace. There was no heavenly salvation coming for him or any of the crew.

The ship was lost to a demon. A devil of the sea that he had laughed at when he'd been told it was part of the plan to chase down and dispose of the vessel called Beowulf III. Who would believe that a monster shark of such proportions could be real? What fool would buy into an obvious fear tactic designed to keep the Somalis and Mexicans in line? He hadn't considered himself a fool then and had scoffed at the idea of such a thing, but as he lay paralyzed on a pile of dead bodies, he knew how wrong he had been.

More gunfire, more screaming, more shouting. All about the First Mate, men killed and men died. Blood and brains splattered his face and he tried to cry out, but he didn't have the strength to do even that. A body collapsed across him and the little strength he did have was crushed from him. With the weight of the dead man on his chest, the small amount of air he had been able to take in was slowly squeezed from his lungs.

He gasped and tried to fight against the slow suffocation, but neither his arms nor legs would obey. All he could do was shake his head from side to side in a futile effort of his defiance of death, but death was inevitable. There was no escaping the fate that the sea had brought him.

His mouth opened and closed, opened and closed, in a pitiful imitation of a fish out of water. His last thought was how sad it was he would die like a worthless fish, instead of a proud man.

***

The captain of the second cutter put his hand to his head then pulled it away and stared dumbly at the blood that coated his palm. He knew he was in trouble, and that there was something horrifying happening to his ship, but he couldn't pull his thoughts together to figure out what it was.

He tried standing, but his legs were wobbly and he only managed to get to his hands and knees and crawl to the bridge's hatch. The far off sounds of panic and cruelty filtered into his dazed mind and he reached for the thought that would tell him what the trouble was.

Gunfire. Were they under attack?

The ship rocked to port and he gripped the edge of the hatch to keep from collapsing. The world outside the bridge tilted at an angle that he knew wasn't right. To be tilted that way there would need to be a storm and high seas, but he could tell there was barely a cloud in the sky, even if the sky was listing to the side.

A man climbed the ladder to the bridge and saw the captain there in his confused and bloody state, then disappeared back down the ladder.

"Wait!" the captain yelled. "You! Man! Come back here!"

He knew the face he had seen, but he couldn't place the name. He tried to think, but he realized he couldn't remember any names at that moment. His mind was a clump of pained fuzz and he struggled to reach through that fuzz for something solid to hang onto.

His ship. He was captain of his ship. The ship he was on, the ship that was tilted, the ship that was under attack.

There! The ship *was* under attack!

That truth stuck with him and he forced his legs to obey and pulled himself up until he was standing once again in the hatch of the bridge. His eyes focused on the brutality on the deck below. Men were killing each other without thought. He could see them lash out with their fists, with knives, with machetes. They turned in a bloody dance of pure animal violence, slashing into anyone that came near them.

"Stop!" the captain shouted. "Stop this!"

If the ship was under attack then the men needed to be at their stations, ready to defend it. They shouldn't have been fighting amongst themselves like hyenas approaching carrion.

"STOP!" he roared then winced at the daggers of pain that pierced his brain.

There was a loud splash and he turned his attention to the port side of the ship. Because of the way the ship was listing, he had a perfect view of one of the lifeboats as it floated on the small waves, filled with angry, shouting men that continued to fight even though they had escaped the sinking ship and found safety.

Safety from what? From what were they fleeing and why was the ship sinking?

The captain stepped from the bridge, stumbled, and slid his way to the railing. He held on tight, using all of his strength to keep from tumbling over as the ship continued to tilt. Far off, he saw other ships and memories started to come back to him slowly. Those ships were his allies, he knew that. They were part of a flotilla that had been in pursuit of another ship.

Was that where the attack came from? Was the ship they pursued firing on them?

He listened, but other than the gunfire from down on the deck which had slackened to almost nothing, he didn't hear any sounds of artillery or battle. If there was a ship attacking then it was no longer firing on them.

His eyes were drawn back to the lifeboat and the squabbling men that filled it. Then it all changed. Everything came back in a rush of horrendous violence as the lifeboat was lifted into the air by jaws that should not have existed.

The captain screamed and lost his grip on the railing as he watched the lifeboat crushed completely in one bite. The men in the boat no longer screamed at each other, but screamed at what held them in its teeth.

Without his grip on the railing, the captain slipped between the bars and tumbled to the tilted deck. He landed hard, but didn't feel anything break. He would have been thankful for that if his mind had had room for thoughts beyond the nightmare that was before him. He watched as the lifeboat was crushed with such violence that men and vessel joined together into one homogenous bite of wood and bone. Blood sprayed from the creature's mouth as it turned in the air and fell back into the water. Over a hundred feet of massive shark slammed into the small waves and then was lost below the surface.

The monster's impact created a massive wave that washed up over the side of the sinking ship's deck. The captain struggled to keep ahold of anything he could, almost thinking he'd succeeded until he realized he held a severed arm and not someone offering him safety. The wave took him over the side of the ship and out into the open water. He screamed for help, screamed for someone to throw him a lifeline, screamed for someone to have the sense to drop the other lifeboat and rescue him.

He had thought his cries had been answered when he looked past the stern of his doomed ship and saw the last lifeboat there, filled with men paddling as hard and fast as they could towards another cutter far in the distance.

"Here!" the captain shouted. "I'm here!"

It made no difference. With a blink of his eye it was all over. The lifeboat met the same fate as the first. The captain stared in fear and awe as the men and boat were lifted even higher than the first. The jaws nearly swallowed them whole, only having to open one more time for a second bite before all were lost.

"No," the captain whispered, "no."

He treaded water, surrounded by shattered wood and broken bodies. Corpses bobbed up and down, some like face down logs, others like buoys, upright and stoic against the waves. The ocean was no longer a bright blue, but a deep crimson. The small waves splashed against his face and he spat the salty water from his mouth, knowing that the taste was doubly so because of all the blood.

So much blood.

Realization hit him and he panicked, his head turning this way and that as he tried to catch sight of the beast that he knew had to be below him somewhere. Where there was blood, there were sharks, or at least one shark. The captain had no illusions that any other sea creature was anywhere even remotely close to the carnage. They would have fled before the beast like rats from a, well, *sinking ship*.

The ship. The sinking ship next to him. That energized his stunned mind and body. If he was caught in the pull of the ship he'd be sucked underwater and there would be nothing he could do about it. His only hope for escape was to swim as hard and fast as he could.

He could hear the sound of men screaming as they fell from the ship and were plunged into the deadly water, but he ignored the sounds and kept swimming. No longer was he captain, but just a man trying to survive. He thought that maybe, just maybe, if he put distance between himself, the blood, and corpses that the shark would forget about him and instead focus on easy pickings.

The impact against his legs told him he was stupid for having any hope in the face of such horror. There was a brief flash of pain then nothing. He stopped swimming and reached below the water to feel what the problem was. It became quickly apparent that the problem was he no longer had legs.

His eyes went wide as he saw the giant shark swimming past him. It rose slightly and its back raked against the stumps of his thighs. The pain was excruciating. The shark's barbed, sandpaper skin shredded the open wounds of his legs and the captain could see his life smear across the monster's back before it was washed free by the animal's passage.

"Go away!" was all he could think to shout. "Leave me to die!"

The shark would not. Its dorsal fin slammed into the captain's back and he cried out as his shirt was basically torn from his body. He spun about, his arms still trying to keep him above the surface, and saw the tail coming right for him. He had no time to react as the tail fin whipped one way then back, crushing his face and chest.

He flew backwards, lifted out of the water from the impact, and then came crashing down so hard that every rib in his body broke free from his spine. His shoulders separated from their sockets and his neck snapped. Agony filled his body and the captain despaired that he hadn't been granted the mercy of a swift death from the horrible break. Instead, he was forced to endure pain that no man could withstand without succumbing to madness.

Madness was where he went.

The laughter bubbled up from his throat, barely above a whisper since he had no strength to produce much more. He rasped out a cackle and his eyes looked up to see wisps of clouds floating by. It had been such a beautiful day.

He had no last thoughts before the horrible mouth closed around him. He had no time to think any before he was crushed between the teeth that were as large as his head.

***

Lake tried to get the Desert Eagle out and up in time, but he barely had a hold on the grip before the fist connected with his face. He crashed against the B3's wheel and felt the ship start to turn to starboard.

Ballantine grabbed Tank Top from behind and pulled him away from Lake. He was able to duck as the mercenary whipped about and sent a fist flying at his head. Ballantine did not waste the opportunity and dropped to a knee then landed a solid shot to Tank Top's groin. The man grunted and fell to his knee so that he and Ballantine were eye to eye.

"Good thing you only lost your cock and not your balls," Ballantine grinned.

"Fuck you," Tank Top hissed.

"This is bigger than us," Ballantine said just before slamming his forehead into Tank Top's nose. "We won't survive that monster if we don't band together. It's too late for it to be called off."

Tank Top collapsed backwards, but used the momentum to roll his legs up over his head and come up on his knees a few feet away. He jumped to his feet, glanced at the M4 that lay between himself and Ballantine, then dove.

Ballantine dove as well and covered the carbine with his body. Tank Top landed on top of him then pushed up and started to hammer at the back of his head. Ballantine tried to get his hands underneath him so he could get some leverage to get free from the man, but each blow sapped more and more strength form his body.

"Hey!" Lake yelled. "Get off my boss!"

Tank Top turned his head just in time to see the sole of Lake's boot come crashing against his face. His already broken nose was turned into a shattered pulp and he choked and gagged as he fell off Ballantine. Blood filled his throat and he struggled to breathe.

"Yeah," Lake sneered, "how's that feel?"

He closed on the man and kicked out again, but Tank Top grabbed his foot and twisted as hard as he could. Lake was spun about and was sent falling to the floor with a cry escaping his lips as he felt the cartilage in his knee tear and tendons snap. Then he was silent as his head slammed into the floor.

Tank Top scurried backwards like a crab until his back hit a wall then he reached up and pulled himself to his feet. He stood there, a wobbly, bloody mess, and raised his fists.

"Get up, you fuck," he slurred at Ballantine. "Come on. We finish this."

"There's nothing to finish, idiot," Ballantine said as he gripped one of the control consoles and slowly got himself to his feet. "The danger has just begun. Did you think I was really running from you?"

Ballantine pointed out the windows of the bridge at the insanity and destruction being rained down on the flotilla.

"You think a bunch of jackass mercs like you scare me when there's that thing in the water?" Ballantine laughed. "Not now. You are nothing compared to Protocol Fifty-four."

"Protocol Fifty-four? You did this? " Tank Top said. "Then you brought this on yourself. That is your end out there, not mine."

"It's all of our ends!" Ballantine shouted. "That creature could give ten shits who or what it eats now! It has no way to know friend from foe because it has no friends! You think because the company is paying you that the beast sees you as a co-worker? Are you completely out of fucking your mind?"

Tank Top started to reply then closed his mouth and turned his attention to the destruction that surrounded the B3 and Monkey Balls. All that was left out there was a sinking cutter and a fleeing one. If the ship that fled managed to get away then that left only the B3 and Monkey Balls as targets.

"I was told that the thing wouldn't attack my ship," Tank Top said. "That the MB gave off a signal that shielded it from the shark, telling the thing to pass us by."

Ballantine just stared at the muscled man.

"My god, you're stupid. How did I miss that when I first hired you?" Ballantine said finally. "How in God's name could you believe that? You're a professional, Jason, so think like one. Put the pieces together."

Ballantine watched the thoughts flit across the man's face and sighed.

"Okay, we don't have time for you to work it all out," he said, "this is how it is, alright? The company hired you to track me down. They let the Somalis and the cartels follow. Why? So when it all went down it would look like it was a battle between criminals. An easy explanation that maritime and governmental authorities wouldn't think much of. None of us, including you, were meant to survive."

"I was sent to capture you and the Thornes," Tank Top said. "The money is in my account right now."

"Is it? When was the last time you checked your account?" Ballantine laughed. "What the company gives, the company takes away. Even if you did manage to capture the Thornes and me, it would have made no difference. The shark was designed to devour everything, and you Jason, are part of that everything."

Ballantine could see Tank Top make the last connection.

"They didn't hire me and my crew because we knew you better than any other guns for hire, but because we just plain knew you," Tank Top said. "We were your first Team and that meant we needed to be taken out as well if there was going to be a full erasure."

"Exactly," Ballantine said, "you were never the predator in this job, you were the prey along with the rest of us."

"So what is Protocol Fifty-four?" Tank Top asked.

"My pre-emptive strike which included the release of that beast from its containment," Ballantine said. "That's all you need to know, but it was never supposed to have caught up to us so fast. Your fucking tracking device made that happen. Good job, as always, Jason."

Tank Top's eyes went to the bridge windows again. "So the company didn't send the shark after us?"

"No," Ballantine said, "I did."

"They expected you to do that, and that's why they extorted the ace and had the beacon placed on board," Tank Top said.

"The ace?" Ballantine asked.

"Your traitor," Tank Top replied. "If they knew the shark would track and kill us all, then who did they think would kill the shark? They couldn't just let it stay free in the ocean."

"That's a very good question," Ballantine said, "and one I don't have an answer to."

A gunshot echoed up from the ship below.

"Shit," Tank Top slurred, "Gil and Lug."

"Better call them off," Ballantine said as he knelt and checked on Lake. The man was unconscious, but his pulse was strong. "There's a world of hurt waiting for them below deck."

***

Mike ducked around a corner as more shots rang out.

"Where the fuck are you going?" Gil shouted after him. "It's a ship! We'll catch up eventually!"

That's what I'm hoping, Mike thought.

He sprinted down the passageway and stopped just before he came to a set of steps. He waited until he saw Gil's face peek around the corner before he rushed down the stairs, his shoulders up to his ears as his pursuers opened fire once again. All he had to do was get to one more passageway and he'd be fine. He hoped.

His legs moved faster than he could think and he had to slow himself down to keep from overshooting his mark. He skidded to a stop and then took one of the biggest risks of his life.

He turned around, faced the direction where Gil and Lug were coming from, put his hands behind his head, and got down on his knees. Then just waited.

Only a minute later, Gil and Lug showed themselves, their rifles to their shoulders and aimed right at Mike.

"What the fuck?" Gil asked. "You really giving up?"

He quickly looked around as he walked forward.

"There're no doors in this passageway, nowhere up in the pipes to hide," Gil said. "If this is an ambush, it's a shitty one."

"Maybe," Mike smiled.

"What are you smiling at?" Lug said as he twitched behind Gil. "We're going to gut shoot you and leave you to bleed right where you are."

"Shut it, Lug," Gil said. "We're going to bring him up top and have Tank Top decide what to do." He nodded at the shiny prosthetics that Mike knelt on. "Those have to be worth something to someone."

"They're worth everything to Mike," Gunnar said from the two mercenaries' side as the wall became transparent. "So how about you put your guns down and we let him keep those legs?"

Gil spun about then went flying backwards as an arc of blue electricity slammed into his chest. He hit the wall and then collapsed into a pile of unconscious tan muscle. Gunnar turned the stun rifle on Lug and smiled.

"You want to set down the rifle or do I need to knock you out too?" Gunnar asked.

Lug carefully set the rifle down and then took up the position that Mike had just stood up from.

"Good boy," Gunnar said. "What's your name?"

"Lug," Lug replied, his head looking back and forth between Gunnar and Mike. "I give up. Don't shoot."

Mike walked over and slammed his elbow into the back of Lug's neck. The man fell forward onto his face, just as unconscious as his semi-scorched colleague behind him.

"Did you need to do that?" Gunnar asked. "I had him covered."

"It felt right," Mike said as he went over to Gil and started to drag him into the hidden back entrance of the Toyshop. "Sometimes, it's best to go with your gut feelings."

"Easy for you to say," Gunnar said as he set the stun rifle aside and tried to drag Lug inside as well. "Your upper body strength is a little better than mine. This would be way easier if the guy were awake and could just walk in on his own."

"The gut gets what the gut wants," Mike smiled as he dropped Gil and went back to help Gunnar.

As soon as both of the unconscious mercs were inside the Toyshop, Gunnar activated the controls and the wall became solid again, shielding them from sight.

"What did you do?" Carlos said as he showed up with two pairs of restraints. "You were just supposed to capture them, not kill them!"

"They aren't dead," Mike said, "and-"

"The gut gets what the gut wants," Gunnar said as he took a pair of restraints from Carlos and started to truss up Lug's hands and feet behind his back.

"What does that even mean?" Carlos asked.

"It means what it means," Mike shrugged as he took the other set of restraints and got to work on Gil.

"God, I hate people sometimes," Carlos huffed as he walked back into the shelves.

"Sometimes?" Gunnar called after him. "When do you not hate people?"

***

The knife pierced the man's heart as it was shoved between his ribs. He gasped once then his eyes glassed over as he fell, dead before he hit the ship's deck. Darby let the knife fall with the man and concentrated on spinning about and bending backwards as the machete came for her head. Her spine became an arch and her hands pressed against the deck then pushed off so her momentum brought her back up instantly.

She landed two quick shots to the machete man's solar plexus and he gasped as the air left him. Darby moved in close and lifted the man's arm that held the machete then brought it down on her leg, snapping it in half at the elbow. The man screamed and the machete clattered to the deck.

"On your nine!" Max yelled from his position by the railing.

The wound in his leg kept him from actively participating in the melee on the upper deck of the Monkey Balls, but he was a sniper and didn't need to be active to be effective. He fired from a rifle he'd snagged from one of the first men the Team had killed as they scaled and boarded the ship. The man that had been rushing towards Darby spun about, his neck spewing blood.

Darby gave Max a nod, then swept the bleeding man's legs out from under him, grabbed the pistol he held in his hand, jammed it under the man's chin, and pulled the trigger. Brains and skull fanned out across the deck, which Shane promptly slipped in as he sprinted past Darby to go help Kinsey.

"Son of a bitch!" Shane yelled as he corrected his fall, tucked his shoulder, and rolled back up to his feet. "Watch it!"

Just as Shane reached the man that had Kinsey by the throat, she managed to jam both thumbs into the pressure points in her attacker's armpits. He screamed, let go of Kinsey then stumbled back into Shane who wasted no time grabbing him by the head and snapping his neck.

Max fired several rounds at the two hatches where men kept trying to spill out of and join the fight. Those men thought better of it and retreated back inside, letting Max turn his attention to the shooter on the observation deck. He never got the chance to take that man down as he realized what type of rifle the man held and decided that rolling out of the way of the .300 caliber slugs was the best course of action.

"Hi," Darren said from the shooter's side just as he put a pistol to the man's head and fired. "Bye."

The man collapsed onto the observation deck and Darren put two shots in his back just to be sure, even though the man was missing most of his skull.

"Fuck!" Thorne yelled from outside the bridge just below Darren.

"You alright, Vinny?" Darren called down.

"They locked it tight," Thorne said as he slammed his fist against the hatch to the bridge. "We'll have to blow it if we want in there."

"We have any explosives?" Darren asked.

Thorne looked at the channel gun in his hand.

"In a way," Thorne said. "You think these rounds are strong enough to work?"

"Worth a try," Darren said, "but you'll want to be a little farther back."

"No shit. WHAT THE FUCK?" he screamed as Darren fired two shots just past his left ear. He whipped about to see two men tumble over the railing. "Oh, thanks."

"Any time," Darren nodded. He tucked the pistol in his belt and picked up the .300 Win Mag sniper rifle at his feet. "This'll come in handy."

He moved to the railing and steadied the rifle then zeroed in on a man running towards Darby. One squeeze of the trigger and the man's head turned to brainy mist. Darby looked over her shoulder and nodded to him, but Darren didn't have time to respond as he switched to another target that was about to shoot Kinsey while she fought off two men with fire axes.

Another trigger squeeze then another and another.

The man that was about to shoot Kinsey screamed as the bullet entered between his ribs then pierced his heart. The two men with fire axes fell with him as blood bloomed on their chests from two more shots.

"I had it under control, 'Ren!" Kinsey yelled up at him.

"Sure you did, 'Sey!" Darren yelled back. "I thought I'd lend a hand anyway!"

Darby gutted a man, dropped to her knees, spun about, gutted another man, and then jumped up and jammed her knife into the soft flesh under his chin. He choked and gurgled, but still stood upright as she pulled the knife out, turned and slammed the blade home into the first gutted man's eye socket. She tried to yank the knife free, but it was wedged too tight, so she just shoved the man away and turned back to the man still standing.

His eyes locked onto hers as blood dribbled from the corners of his mouth.

"You missed the brain," Shane said from her side.

"I wasn't aiming for the brain," Darby said as she reached out and slid her fingers into the slit under the man's chin, hooked them around his lower jaw, and then yanked as hard as she could.

The man's lower jaw ripped from his face and Darby spun it about and jammed the jagged ends into the man's eyes. He would have screamed if Darby had given him the chance, but she snapped his neck before a sound could come out of his mutilated mouth.

"You really scare the fuck out of me, you know that?" Shane said.

"I know," Darby replied, "it's part of my charm."

They looked around and saw no more men coming at them.

"Job well done," Shane said.

"Job is far from done," Thorne said as he joined them and pointed his channel gun at the bridge's hatch. "Hopefully this will finish it, though."

He put the channel gun to his shoulder and was about to squeeze the trigger when the hatch opened and two black hands reached out, their fingers spread wide.

"Hold on!" Bokeem yelled. "Don't shoot!"

"Why?" Thorne yelled back. "Give me one good reason!"

"Look over at your ship!" Bokeem shouted as he cautiously stepped from the bridge.

Everyone turned and looked at the B3 and was surprised to see Ballantine waving at them.

"Well, that's a sight for sore eyes," Shane said.

"Eye, dude," Max said as Kinsey helped him up and hobbled over to them. "You only have one eye, bro."

"Don't be mean," Kinsey scolded.

"Hello, Grendel!" Ballantine said, his voice suddenly coming from the coms in their ears. "I see you improvised and adjusted the mission accordingly."

"Big shark in water," Max said. "We get out of water."

"Yes, well that shark is what we need to talk about," Ballantine said. "Commander? If you'd stop pointing your weapon at Captain Bokeem that would be appreciated."

Thorne didn't stop pointing his weapon at Bokeem, but instead asked, "You want to give me a reason?"

"I do, Commander," Ballantine said, "but we don't have enough time. Let's just say that circumstances have changed our roles in today's drama. Instead of bitter enemies, it will be considerably more advantageous to become allies."

"We were set up!" Bokeem shouted down. "We're just as dead as you if we don't get out of here!"

"I think he's telling the truth," Darren said from the observation deck's railing. His pistol was aimed down at Bokeem, but his eyes were looking out at the ocean behind them. "Have a look, Vinny."

"Max? Shane?" Thorne asked.

"We've got the guy covered, Uncle Vinny," Shane said.

Thorne lowered the channel gun then turned his head. Only his years of training kept him from gasping.

"Holy shit," Thorne said.

They had all been so busy fighting for their lives that none of them had time to notice what had happened off the ship. Behind them was nothing but a swathe of destruction. Blood filled the water and coated the debris and remnants from the destroyers and the cutters. The only evidence of the ships' crews was the parts and pieces that floated like flotsam and jetsam.

Far off, the last cutter steamed away as it made a break for it in one last ditch effort of escape. Then the water exploded around it as the monster shark launched itself into the air. The beast's body rocketed over the upper deck of the ship, scooping men up in its mouth as it continued in an arc, and then fell back into the water on the other side.

Team Grendel stood with their mouths hanging open.

"The threat we need to worry about is not the men on the ship you have found yourselves on," Ballantine said, "but the beast that has been sent to kill us all."

"I'm going to have to agree with you for once, Ballantine," Thorne said, "but you better have a plan in mind, because I have no idea how to handle something that can do that."

"Oh, I have a plan, Commander," Ballantine laughed, "and the first part is we get the fuck out of here as fast as we can."

"I like that first part," Shane said.

"So far it's my favorite part," Max agreed.

Chapter Six- Paradise Found

"I'd apologize for Shabby Paul, Wonkers and...what was the other guy's name?" Ballantine asked.

"Bub," Tank Top said as he watched his men walk the planks set up from the Monkey Balls to the B3. "He'd just joined us."

"Yeah, him," Ballantine nodded, his eyes never leaving the line of mercs that hurried to escape the Monkey Balls and join his ship for a last ditch effort at outrunning the giant shark. "Yeah, I'd apologize for them having to die, especially Shabby Paul since I always liked his jokes, but any fool that follows you is bound to die sooner or later."

"I could say the same thing about you," Tank Top said as the last man hopped onto the B3's deck and raised his hands so Darby could search him. "Is that really necessary?"

"It is if you don't want your men to spend the rest of the trip in restraints below decks," Ballantine grinned then tapped the com in his ear. "Cougher? You ready?"

"I'm ready, Ballantine," Cougher replied, "but I'm not sure about this modification. The propeller shaft may not hold up to the extra strain."

"How long can it take the added power?" Ballantine asked.

"Six, maybe seven hours," Cougher responded, "maybe."

"We only need four," Ballantine said. "Keep the engines working that long and we're good."

"That your engineer you're talking to?" Tank Top asked, not privy to the other side of the conversation.

"It is," Ballantine nodded.

"You think he can juice this ship's engines so it will outrun that shark?" Tank Top asked.

They both looked out towards the horizon and the last cutter that was only a debris field of ship parts and dismembered bodies.

"We'll outrun the shark," Ballantine said confidently, "and once we reach where I'm taking us, then we won't have to worry anymore."

"That's a lie and you know it," Tank Top said. "You always have to worry."

Ballantine just smiled and stepped away from the man as Thorne's voice came on in his ear.

"Go ahead, Commander," Ballantine said.

"Charges are placed," Thorne said. "We're on our way back."

"Good," Ballantine smiled, "you'll want to hurry since I believe the shark is about to start looking for another target."

He waited by the railing until he saw Thorne, Kinsey, and Darren appear from a hatch leading to the lower decks of the Monkey Balls. They sprinted to the plank, balanced their way across, and then jumped onto the B3. Darren turned and shoved the plank over the side. He stood there for a second then shielded his eyes and looked out across the water at the bloody carnage.

"Thinking of Popeye?" Ballantine asked as he moved to Darren's side.

"Yeah," Darren said, "I can't believe the man is gone."

"But we aren't," Ballantine said, "keep that in mind, Mr. Chambers."

Darren nodded then looked over his shoulder at Tank Top.

"That the guy that killed him?" Darren asked.

"It is, but revenge isn't part of the plan just yet," Ballantine said. "Have patience and Popeye's death will be honored properly."

"He says one word to me and I rip his throat out. Got it?" Darren snarled.

"Fair enough," Ballantine said. "Now, get below, grab some food and rest. We're running now, there's nothing you can do to make that happen any faster."

"Not hungry," Darren said, "not tired."

"Bullshit," Kinsey said, "you have that tired and hungry look all over your face. I know it better than anyone."

"Except me," Gunnar said as he came up on deck. He glanced at the crew of the Monkey Balls and made sure to take a wide path around them. "Come on, D. We all need to eat, and talk."

"Oh?" Ballantine asked. "Anything I should sit in on?"

"No," Gunnar said.

"How's Max?" Kinsey asked.

"He's fine," Gunnar said. "I have him patched up and sleeping down in the infirmary."

"I want to check on him before we hit the galley," Kinsey said.

"Yeah, sure," Gunnar nodded.

The ship lurched and everyone grabbed what they could, even if it was another person, to keep from falling.

"That's new," Kinsey said.

"I have had Cougher apply some of Moshi's technology to our engines," Ballantine said, as they all felt the ship begin to move swiftly through the water. After a few seconds, the force of the momentum evened out and everyone was able to steady themselves again. "Excellent. We didn't explode."

"Was that a possibility?" Kinsey asked.

"It's always a possibility when you're around me," Ballantine smiled then turned and walked away. He nodded to Tank Top before he ascended the stairs up to the briefing room.

"That man is insane," Darren said.

"That's what we need to talk about," Gunnar said. "I've been chatting with Dr. Morganton and we both think something isn't adding up."

"When does it ever add up with Ballantine?" Kinsey asked.

"Never, but this adds up less than usual," Gunnar said. "That's why I need your input."

"Fine," Kinsey shrugged, "let's talk."

Shane and Gunnar started to move away, but stopped when Darren didn't follow.

"'Ren?" Kinsey asked. "You coming?"

She saw where he was looking and took his arm.

"Not yet," Kinsey said as she glared at Tank Top. "Let Ballantine do his voodoo then we'll gut this fuck and throw him overboard."

"I get to gut him," Darren stated.

"No problem," Kinsey replied, "But right now, Gunnar needs to talk with us."

Darren shook his head and nodded. "Sure. I'll be right down. I need to check in with Lake first."

He leaned in and kissed her on the cheek then took off for the stairs to the bridge.

"He's going to crack," Gunnar said.

"No shit," Kinsey nodded as she rubbed at the spot where he kissed her.

***

"How you holding up?" Darren asked Lake as he stepped onto the bridge.

"Oh, I'm great, man," Lake smirked as he sat in front of the wheel, his left leg in a heavy brace and propped on a stool next to him. "Plan on doing some jogging later."

"Marty, I'm sorry about your leg," Darren said, "and everything else that's happened since we lost the Hooyah and got mixed up with Ballantine."

"Popeye was the best of us," Lake said as he turned away from Darren and focused on the horizon. "That man was pure good inside."

"Yeah, he was," Darren said, "and when this is done we'll take care of the man that killed him. Our way. Not Ballantine's way, not Thorne's way, but our way. This is between the old crew and that fuck. This isn't Team Grendel business."

"I'm glad to hear you say that," Lake said, "because Team Grendel has enough business to deal with."

He nodded to the refugee crew that stood on the deck below then looked Darren in the eye.

"You sure they aren't going to be a problem?" he asked.

"I'm not sure of anything anymore," Darren said, "but Shane and Lucy are up top with eyes on the crowd. Ballantine said there's only a handful of mercs in there and the rest are just sailors hired to run their ship."

"Won't be a ship for long," Lake said as he looked down at the instruments in front of him. "It's going to be shrapnel in about five minutes."

"Will we be clear of the blast?" Darren asked.

Lake laughed and shook his head. "If the engines don't burn up, then we'll be well clear of the blast. We just hit seventy knots and we haven't leveled out yet."

Darren moved close and studied the same readings.

"We're going to burst into flames, aren't we?" he asked.

"More than likely," Lake nodded, "so go find me a beer and a sandwich so I don't die thirsty and hungry."

Darren laughed and patted his old friend on the shoulder. "Sure thing, Marty. I'm heading to the galley anyway." He moved to the doorway. "Has Ballantine told you where we're going?"

"Same coordinates as before," Lake said, "but that's as specific as he's been."

"Typical," Darren nodded.

"Know what else is typical? You standing there instead of getting me my beer," Lake grumbled.

"On it," Darren grinned as he took off out of the bridge.

***

"How many can you take in say, four seconds?" Shane asked Lucy as they sat up in the crow's nest, their sniper rifles trained on the men below. "I could probably hit six and kill five."

"I'd kill six," Lucy said. "That .338 doesn't quite have the same power as my .50."

"Like fuck it doesn't," Shane replied. "Okay, well, maybe not but it's fucking close."

"Fucking close doesn't win any cigars," Lucy said.

"That reminds me," Shane said as he pulled a joint from his pocket and sparked it. "Ahhhh, that's the stuff."

"Give me that," Lucy said, plucking the joint from Shane's fingers so she could take her own drag. He started to reach for it but she slapped his hand away as she took another drag.

"You've been hanging out with me and Max too much," Shane laughed when she finally gave it back.

"When in Rome," she smiled after exhaling, "especially when Rome is right and that shit does actually make you a better shot once you get used to it."

"Takes nerves right out of the equation," Shane said.

"Unless you count paranoia," Lucy said.

"Pshaw, paranoia is for sorority girls and high school kids," Shane said, "not seasoned professionals like us."

"Hey!" Lucy yelled down as two men moved closer together instead of keeping two feet between them as they'd been instructed to do by Darby. "Separate!"

"Do I need to handle it?" Darby asked over the com.

"Nope," Lucy replied, "all good from here. You keep having your reunion and we'll hold down the fort."

Darby, who was standing just outside of arms reach from Bokeem, turned and looked up at the crow's nest. Shane gave her a wave.

"Are you two stoned?" Darby asked.

"Are you a scary mother fucker that likes watching guts splash onto deck boards?" Shane replied.

Darby didn't answer.

"Yes, we're stoned," Shane said.

"Good," Darby replied, "you're easier to deal with when you're stoned. Just don't fall asleep. It's not the time for an adrenaline crash. Eyes open and alert."

"You're my brother's girlfriend, not mine," Shane smirked. "You can't tell me what to do."

"Want to test that?" Darby asked.

"No, ma'am," Shane replied quickly.

"Good," Darby said again then turned her attention back to Bokeem.

"Such a trusting, pleasant soul," Shane said.

"Like Mother Theresa if Mother Theresa had healed the sick with knives and bullets," Lucy added.

"Hallelujah," Shane laughed.

***

127

"Your snipers are high?" Bokeem asked Darby.

"They are," Darby said.

"The one with the patch is Shane Reynolds, right?" he asked.

"Yep," Darby responded.

Bokeem nodded then whistled and held his hand up. The men that stood on the deck all quit talking and looking around and focused their attention only on him. He pointed up at the crow's nest then shook his head. Darby waited as he made eye contact with each and every man.

"You still do that whistle thing, I see," Darby said. "Good idea to tell them not to fuck around while my people are up there."

"Who's to say I didn't give the signal to attack?" Bokeem smiled.

"Because if you wanted them to die then you would have left them on your ship," Darby said.

"True," Bokeem replied and the smile faded away. "Gonna miss that ship."

"There're always more ships," Darby said, "trust me."

"Yeah, but that was the first one where I was captain," Bokeem said. "Not sure if Tank will agree to that again."

"If you make it out of this alive," Darby said.

"You mean, if *we* make it out of this alive," Bokeem said.

Darby only nodded.

"Ballantine," Bokeem laughed, "he has this all under control, doesn't he?"

"I doubt that," Darby said.

"Really?" Bokeem asked, surprised. "Are the boss and the guard dog not getting along?"

"I haven't been the guard dog in a long time," Darby said.

"Right," Bokeem smirked.

Darby stared at him until the smirk faded away.

"Fine. Whatever you say, Darby," Bokeem said, "but we both know you owe that man more than just one lifetime. If I believed in reincarnation, I'd say you'll be paying your debt until you reach Nirvana."

"My debt is paid," Darby said. "If Ballantine doesn't think so, then that's his problem and not mine."

"His problem and not mine?" Bokeem echoed. "Wow, you really have gone off the Ballantine reservation, haven't you?"

"Hey!" Lucy shouted from above.

Darby whirled around and saw Tank Top stop with his hands held above his head.

"It's good," Darby said into the com then waved Tank Top over.

"You're not afraid we can take you?" Tank Top asked as he sidled up next to Bokeem. "Kind of reckless, Darby."

"Reckless would be for either of you to get close enough for me to grab you," Darby said, "or have you forgotten Taipei?"

Tank Top and Bokeem both crossed their arms and glared.

"No, I see you haven't forgotten Taipei," Darby said.

"What happened in Taipei?" Shane asked over the com.

"Yeah, I want to know too," Lucy added.

"Get off the com!" Darby snapped. "It's not cool to eavesdrop on a private conversation!"

"Geez, sorry," Lucy said.

"You're standing around a dozen men," Shane replied. "I'd hardly call that private."

"If I have to come up there, I'd hardly call you living," Darby growled.

"Right. Eavesdropping is bad," Shane said. "Com is off now."

"Sounds like a really disciplined Team," Tank Top smirked.

"More than you ever were," Darby replied.

"Ouch, that hurts," Tank Top said.

Darby kicked him in the balls, sending him to his knees.

"No. That hurts," Darby said. She looked at Bokeem and hooked her thumb over her shoulder. "I'm going to go sit in the shade over there and watch all of you assholes bake in the sun. You two have fun."

Bokeem waited until Darby was across the ship and sitting in the shade of the superstructure before he helped Tank Top stand up.

"I guess she hasn't stopped being a ball buster," Bokeem said.

"Fuck you," Tank Top squeaked. "You can kiss my-"

The Monkey Balls exploded into a massive fireball and everyone literally hit the deck.

"Shit," Bokeem said once the explosions subsided and he picked himself up. "Truly the end of an era."

He looked down and saw Tank Top just lying there.

"You alright, Tank?"

"Yeah, I'm good," Tank Top replied, "but I figure there's no reason to get up again since I'm sure something will just send me back down. You know, for a man without a dick, I sure get a lot of action down there."

"Oh, quit your bitching," Bokeem said, his eyes finding Darby again. "We aren't out of the game yet."

"Ballantine's pretty sure we were never in the game," Tank Top replied.

"Ballantine lives in his world," Bokeem said, "and we live in ours. We wipe out his world and we can make ours whatever we want it to be."

"Too philosophical for me right now," Tank Top replied. "My nuts hurt. Once they stop throbbing, then I'll have you run that by me again."

"No worries, brother," Bokeem said. "You just lay there and rest your nuts, but remember, we still have a job to do. The real job."

Tank Top closed his eyes and gave Bokeem a thumbs up.

***

The galley mess was empty except for Gunnar and Kinsey. They both gripped the edge of the table they sat at while they waited for the far off sounds of the explosions finally to be done.

"You think that will scare off the shark?" Kinsey asked Gunnar.

"The shock waves and sonic disruption it'll create should at the very least disorient the creature," Gunnar said. "Hopefully, that gives us enough time to get away."

"With how fast this ship is going now, I'd be surprised if we didn't," Kinsey said.

Gunnar only shrugged.

"What?" Kinsey asked.

"It's just a hunch I have," Gunnar said. Dr. Morganton came into the mess on shaky legs and Gunnar waved her over. "A hunch we both had."

"Should I get my dad?" Kinsey asked as Dr. Morganton sat down. "If this is about Ballantine then maybe he should hear it too."

"No, not yet," Gunnar said. "I want to talk this out before we go to Vincent."

"If we're wrong, then we could add to your father's already heavy suspicion of Ballantine for no reason," Dr. Morganton said. "I would have to guess that during a high stress time like this, it wouldn't be good for his performance as a leader or, well, considering his age, it wouldn't be good for his health."

"My dad is in great health," Kinsey argued.

"Your father is in his sixties," Dr. Morganton. "He may be in great health, but there is always added risk for man his age."

"What's an added risk for a man my age?" Thorne asked as he stepped into the mess. Everyone looked away. "Now I really need to know."

"Hey, I'm back, sorry," Darren said as he came jogging in then he saw Thorne and Dr. Morganton. "I thought this was just a chat for us three."

"Dr. Morganton knows Ballantine in a professional way we don't," Gunnar said. "I thought her perspective would be helpful."

"And mine wouldn't be?" Thorne asked.

"Uh-oh," Darren laughed as he took a seat at the table, "Vinny wasn't invited, was he?"

Thorne took a seat and glared at everyone.

"I just invited myself, so spill the fucking beans before I reach up your ass and pull them out of you," Thorne grumbled.

"Charming," Dr. Morganton said.

"Wasn't supposed to be," Thorne said.

"Here's how I see it," Gunnar started. "Ballantine hasn't told us anything about the company. We don't know a single fact other than a routing number to our bank accounts. I checked the routing number and it leads to another one and another one and so on."

"Which is typical of shadow organizations," Thorne said. "They wouldn't be very good if they just handed us their debit card."

"True," Gunnar said, "but what's really been bothering me is our first mission. Perry, Horace, and Longbottom were supposedly from the company, but they didn't act like it."

"They had gone rogue," Darren said, "except for that woman, Horace. She was on Ballantine's side."

"They had a relationship," Dr. Morganton confirmed, "but I'm not sure anyone is on Ballantine's side."

"Exactly," Gunnar said, "like you, Dr. Morganton, are you on his side?"

"Well, I guess," Dr. Morganton. "He's helped me out of a lot of trouble over the years."

"Because you work for the company," Gunnar nodded.

"Yes," Dr. Morganton agreed.

"How many of the company's executives have you met?" Gunnar asked.

"None that I know of," Dr. Morganton said.

"They'd insulate themselves," Thorne said.

"True," Gunnar nodded, "but you've at least met other scientists or division heads, right?"

"No," Dr. Morganton replied, "I've already told you this."

"Right, right, but you haven't told them," Gunnar said.

"Again, divisions may never have contact with each other," Thorne said. "With the type of company we're dealing with, they'd be smart to keep everyone separate."

"I'm not disagreeing with that," Gunnar said, "but here's the thing I don't get. Why is the company coming after Ballantine now? Why send a bunch of mercs, Somali pirates, and Mexican drug cartels to hunt him down? Why not just kill him when they see him next? Why not just cut off our funding, fire us all, and then pick us off one by one? Why not just hand us over to the Somalis, to the cartels, to the mercs? If a company like this is so powerful and so connected, then why aren't we already dead?"

Everyone at the table watched Gunnar for a minute, then they turned and looked at Thorne.

"What?" Thorne asked.

"You have the most experience with shadow organizations," Darren said.

"Yet, Gun didn't feel that I should be invited to this meeting," Thorne smirked.

"Sorry about that," Gunnar said, "but you're here now and I'd love your professional opinion."

"My opinion?" Thorne laughed. "I don't have one. I have a job and that's to run Grendel and make it the best Team it can be."

"Hooyah," Darren called out.

"Hooyah," Kinsey echoed.

Dr. Morganton cleared her throat. "Are you suggesting that Ballantine doesn't work for the company anymore?"

"Well, that's obvious since they're trying to kill him, and he said we'd been let go," Gunnar replied, "but I think it goes deeper than that."

"How so?" Kinsey asked. "That maybe he works for a different company?"

"That maybe there has never been a company," Gunnar said, "or something like that."

"There has been a company," Dr. Morganton argued. "I've sent in reports and my findings. I've had top level phone meetings with many of them."

"Not in person," Thorne said, "or even over video conferencing."

"Well...no," Dr. Morganton admitted.

"We need Darby," Darren said. "Darby knows Ballantine the best. She'll know what's real and what isn't."

"Will she tell us?" Gunnar asked.

"She will," Kinsey said, "or she'll tell me, at least."

Kinsey stood up and stretched.

"What? Now?" Darren asked.

"No time like the present," Kinsey said.

"Why will she talk to you?" Dr. Morganton asked.

"Because she loves my cousin," Kinsey said, "and we're almost family."

***

"Go away," Darby said as she sat in the shade of the superstructure, her eyes locked on Tank Top and Bokeem, "I'm not talking about this."

"But we're almost family!" Kinsey protested.

"Almost family and *actually* family are very different things," Darby said without looking at Kinsey, "and you are assuming I'd tell my actual family anything at all, which I wouldn't, even if they were alive."

"Your family is dead?" Kinsey asked. "All of them?"

"Yes," Darby replied.

"Wow, I'm sorry," Kinsey said. "So, I guess that means you need almost family more than ever."

"You are relentless," Darby stated.

"That's what I've been told," Kinsey smiled. "So, to keep me from hounding you, just tell me one thing about Ballantine that will put my mind at ease. Just one thing that assures me that I can trust the man. That's all I'm asking for. One thing."

Darby finally looked away from the two mercs and fixed her gaze on Kinsey. "You will learn everything when it's time and not before."

"That doesn't tell me shit, Darby," Kinsey frowned. "That only makes me question things more."

Darby sighed. "You can trust Ballantine. He is looking out for all of us and has it all under control. He's not the bad guy. He's a lying bastard, but he's not the bad guy."

"Is he the good guy?" Kinsey asked.

For a split second, Darby smiled, then it was gone and she shrugged and turned back to watching the mercs.

"Good talk," Kinsey said as she patted Darby on the shoulder. "We should do this more often."

"Probably not," Darby said and the split second smile came and went again.

"Yeah," Kinsey laughed as she got up and walked off, "probably not."

***

"You get the feeling that not everyone is in the know?" Tank Top asked Bokeem quietly.

"I always have that feeling," Bokeem said.

"Typical Ballantine to put together a top notch Team and leave them in the dark," Tank Top said. "We were this Team once."

"We were never this Team," Bokeem said. "We were skilled, but undisciplined. We were loyal, but untrustworthy. We could take orders, but none of us could follow." He nodded up at Shane and Lucy in the crow's nest. "Those two have been smoking it up all day, and yet, I haven't seen them waver one bit. I keep waiting for them to slip up, but the second I think I see them relax, that one-eyed freak is suddenly scoping me."

"Not seeing your point," Tank Top said.

"Would you let any of our crew, God rest their souls, smoke pot while on duty and watching over a dozen prisoners?" Bokeem asked.

"Not a chance in Hell," Tank Top replied.

"That's my point," Bokeem said, "yet, look, they're lighting up another spliff right now. That's like the fourth one. Ballantine hasn't come out to check on them once."

"That's because the beautiful Darby is supervising," Tank Top said and blew a kiss over to Darby. She flipped him off. "Isn't she lovely?"

"Darby is watching *us*," Bokeem said. "She could give a shit about our crew. She has complete trust in the two shooters getting stoned, just after having kicked the shit out of most of our best men."

"I don't think Darby has complete trust in anyone," Tank Top said.

"Fuck you, you know what I mean," Bokeem snapped.

"Only the one-eyed asshole was on the MB kicking shit," Tank Top said. "The chick sniper was over here putting holes in our shooters."

"My point exactly. I would have laid my fortune on our shooters to take out anyone, on any day, in any condition," Bokeem responded. "She popped them while they had scopes on her. Fuck that."

"Okay, okay," Tank Top sighed, "what the fuck is your real point?

"That we were never meant to succeed with Ballantine," Bokeem said. "Not as his true Team. Everything he's done has led to these people. They're better than we are. They have skills above the norm, and I'm talking above the SOF norm, not every day soldier norm."

"Yeah, well, we knew that was possible coming in," Tank Top said. "We heard the stories, we read the reports our employers sent us, and we've studied these fucks. They've killed giant sharks, giant snakes, something with spiders or squids or squid spiders or whatever. They have taken on the cartels and Somali pirates, plus cannibal tribes and even a weird mist. These guys have been working non-stop since Baja. If our employers didn't think we could handle the job, then they wouldn't have sent us."

"They didn't send just us," Bokeem said, "they sent the cartels and the Somalis."

"That was the smoke screen," Tank Top said. "The Somalis and cartels bankrolled this whole operation, our employers let them, knowing it would all get cleaned up in the end."

"So zero financial risk on our employers' part," Bokeem stated, "and zero witnesses if it all goes wrong."

Tank Top opened his mouth then closed it, and thought about what Bokeem had just said. He started to respond again then stopped. Started, and then stopped.

"Our employers had nothing to lose," Tank Top said finally. "We could fail and it makes no difference."

"We could fail and it makes all the difference," Bokeem said. "Somalis, cartels, us. The three biggest threats to Ballantine. The Somalis have had a bounty on him and his Team's heads since day one. The cartels have as well."

"They've had a bounty on the Thorne chick's head," Tank Top said.

"You think Ballantine didn't know that when she was recruited?" Bokeem said. "The man misses nothing."

"He wanted the cartels to get involved? Why?" Tank Top asked.

"I don't know," Bokeem said, "but how about us? The man has always been on our radar, and eventually we were going to take him down before he took us down, but this is what bothers me. His new Team. They obviously have the skills to wipe us out, so why did Ballantine have them hunt down sharks and snakes and all that other shit? Why not send them to take us out first? Then this whole mess would have been avoided."

Tank Top thought about it then frowned deeply.

"He wanted us to find him," Tank Top said. "The fucker set us up."

"He wanted us to chase him," Bokeem said, "not just find him, but chase him. Force him in a specific direction."

"While bringing the last of his major enemies along for the ride," Tank Top added. "The crazy fucker. Except he doesn't know why we're really here."

"I think he does," Bokeem sighed. "I think the fucking asshole wanted everything to happen exactly how it has happened from day one."

"Seriously? Why?" Tank Top asked.

"You said it," Bokeem replied, "he wanted the last of his major enemies all in one place."

"No, no, that's what our employers wanted," Tank Top replied.

"Who are our employers, really?" Bokeem asked. "We've never met them in person."

That one Tank Top didn't have an answer or counter argument for.

***

All the briefing room's video monitors were extended from the ceiling and actively streaming different views and conversations on the B3. Ballantine switched his attention from one to the other while he changed the audio feed in the com in his ear.

The galley mess and the conversation still going on with Gunnar, Darren, Dr. Morganton, and Thorne. Kinsey walked into view, shrugging her shoulders and Ballantine didn't need the audio to know what she was about to tell them.

A view of the crow's nest where Shane and Lucy had just finished another joint, and were busy playing Twenty Questions while they kept close watch on the men on deck.

Darby sitting in the shade of the superstructure, watching two men she had once fought side by side with. Ballantine smiled as he saw Darby's middle finger extend surreptitiously while her hand rested on her thigh. He had no doubt she knew he was watching her.

The Toyshop and his industrious elves- Pissy, Perky, and Mute. They were all busy working on projects he had just given them, especially Ingrid, who wanted to earn his trust back so badly. He did feel bad for what he put her through.

The engine room and Cougher. The poor guy looked so stressed out as he hurried from instrument reading to instrument reading. Ballantine knew the engines couldn't handle too much more of the strain of their modifications, but he had confidence they'd hold out long enough to get them where they needed to go.

That brought him to the bridge.

"Captain Lake?" Ballantine asked over the com.

"What do you want, Ballantine?" Lake asked.

"Just checking on our ETA," Ballantine replied.

"We're on schedule," Lake said. "Should be approaching the coordinates in less than an hour. Care to tell me what I'm looking for?"

"How do you mean?" Ballantine asked.

"You aren't just sending us into the middle of nowhere," Lake replied. "There's something important at these coordinates."

"I *am* sending us into the middle of nowhere," Ballantine said. "That is the point, and don't worry, Captain, you'll know it when you see it."

"Great," Lake grumbled.

"Call me as soon as you know what I mean," Ballantine said.

"Yeah, I'll be sure to do that," Lake said. "Now get out of my ear."

"Gladly," Ballantine replied as he switched his view to monitor that showed nothing but the murky deep. "Come on. Where are you?"

He pressed a button and a sonar ping rang out in his ear.

Slowly, then faster and faster, the shape of the shark emerged from the murk. Ballantine grinned and checked the readings, then did some quick calculations in his head. While he calculated, the shark grew closer and closer until its jaws opened wide and the remote camera was swallowed whole.

"Well, this just got fascinating," Ballantine said as he watched the camera make its way through the insides of the shark. "Unfortunately, I do not have time for this."

Ballantine switched back to the view of Lake. "Captain Lake? Do you see anything on the sonar?"

"Not a thing," Lake said, "which is weird. Shouldn't I see at least something? Even if it is smaller fish?"

"Not this close to our destination," Ballantine said. "The waters around this area tend to stay clear of sea life. It's in their best interest."

"Comforting," Lake smirked.

Ballantine stood and stretched as he watched Lake with amusement. The captain went to reach for a bottle of beer by the wheel and accidentally knocked it over, sending it falling to the floor where it shattered, spilling beer and glass everywhere.

"Not to worry, Captain," Ballantine said. "I am heading in your direction right now. I'll bring some towels and a fresh beer for you."

Lake visibly stiffened.

"Are you fucking watching me?" he asked.

"See you shortly," Ballantine laughed as he killed the feeds to all the monitors and sent them back up to nest in the ceiling of the briefing room.

***

"Oh...hello, everyone," Ballantine said as he stepped onto the bridge with a roll of paper towels in one hand and a six pack of beer in the other. "Looks like I should have brought more beer."

"Marty told me you were watching him up here," Darren said as he stood by the captain. Kinsey, Thorne, Gunnar, and Dr. Morganton stood behind him. "Any reason why you're spying on our captain?"

"I get bored," Ballantine replied as he set the towels and beers aside. "I hate being bored."

Lake looked at the beer and snapped his fingers. "I still need a fresh one."

"Right, of course," Ballantine said as he popped open a bottle and handed it to Lake. "My apologies."

"Endgame," Thorne said, "now."

"No," Ballantine responded.

"No?" Thorne asked. "Why the hell not?"

"Because it's not time," Ballantine shrugged.

"Time for what?" Thorne asked.

"Time for the endgame," Ballantine sighed. "Commander, the entire point of an endgame is that it isn't revealed until the very end. It's in the very name. End and game. If you point out your endgame before the end, then it's just a boring, old game, and as I just stated, I don't like being bored."

"I don't like having information withheld from me," Thorne said. "One of us is about to be disappointed."

"That would be you," Ballantine said, "it's my endgame."

"So, you admit you have an endgame beyond what you've told us?" Gunnar asked.

"First, as a general policy, I admit to nothing ever," Ballantine said as he opened his own beer and took a swig. "Second, what have I told you? As far as I can remember, I haven't really told any of you anything. A few vague references here or there, a little misdirection this way and a little misdirection that way, but when you think of it, do you even have the tiniest bit of real information as to what's going on?"

"We know a giant shark is on our ass," Kinsey said.

"Some of the men now on this ship were part of the first Team you had before Grendel," Darren said.

"Maybe that ship we just blew up was the original Beowulf," Gunnar added.

Ballantine sipped his beer again and looked at Dr. Morganton. "Anything to add?"

"No," Dr. Morganton replied, "I've been busy with the technological assignments you've given me."

Ballantine nodded and looked to Thorne. "Commander?"

"I know that you are running from the company because of something you've done," Thorne said. "That something has already gotten Popeye killed, which is really all I need to know."

For the first time since stepping onto the bridge, Ballantine's ubiquitous cocksure smile faltered.

"Yes, well that was unforeseen and a true tragedy," Ballantine said. "At no point did I intend for Popeye to be hurt or killed."

"How about the rest of us?" Kinsey asked. "You have no problem with Team Grendel going into the water without all the information. You have no problem with us trying to take out a ship that used to be yours without giving us all the information."

Ballantine walked forward until he was only an inch from Kinsey's face.

"You are right, Ms. Thorne," Ballantine replied. "I have no problem with any of that, because it is your job to do all of those things and without question. You are an elite tactical Team of highly trained operators. You knew what you were getting into when you signed up and you know what you could get into every time you go on a mission. I regret Popeye's death because he was a boatswain, not an operator. There was no expectation of death for him, but for you? Always."

"Back off, Ballantine," Darren said.

"I don't think Ms. Thorne needs you to protect or defend her," Ballantine replied, his eyes still fixed on Kinsey, his body still only an inch away.

"I'm not protecting or defending her," Darren replied. "I'm just being a friend to a woman I care for and asking a threat to unthreaten itself."

"Dethreaten," Gunnar said.

"I don't think either of those choices are actual words," Dr. Morganton said.

Ballantine backed off and looked pained. "You see me as a threat?"

"Well, duh," Kinsey said, "have you ever been around you?"

"Commander?" Ballantine asked Thorne.

"You don't threaten me, but you aren't exactly the comforting type," Thorne shrugged. "Not that I could give a shit." He looked at Darren and Kinsey. "He is right. You two have been hired to be operators. If you die on a mission, it is understood that you knew the risks going in." He switched focus to Gunnar and Dr. Morganton. "You were hired for your skills as scientists. It's not always your job to know, or see the big picture. Sometimes, you need to focus on one detail at a time."

"Thank you, Commander," Ballantine said.

The fist hit him fast and hard, and Ballantine fell back against a bank of equipment. Thorne closed on him quickly, snatched the beer out of his hands and cracked the bottle against the edge of the console. He jammed the broken glass up against Ballantine's throat, but kept it just short of slicing into the man's skin.

"My job, Ballantine?" Thorne growled. "My job *is* to keep everyone on my Team alive. When you withhold information from me, whether you think it is vital or not, you hamper my ability to do that. You hired me to do a job and when you then make it difficult for me to do that job because you are a secretive prick by nature, and then we have a problem."

Ballantine looked Thorne directly in the eyes.

"How do I extricate myself from this problem?" Ballantine asked.

"By being disappointed," Thorne grinned. "Time to 'fess up, Ballantine. I'm no longer affording you the luxury of your secrets."

"I didn't know you were affording me anyt-" Ballantine started, but stopped as Thorne let the glass nick him slightly. "Okay, okay, Commander, you win. You will get your information, but not just yet."

"Why not just yet?" Thorne asked.

"Because we're here," Lake said. "We've reached the coordinates."

"Holy shit," Gunnar said as he looked out the bridge windows.

"Is that an island?" Kinsey asked. "Where are the binoculars?"

"Here," Darren said as he fetched them from beside Lake.

"Hey!" Lake protested. "I'm going to need those!"

"You'll get them back," Darren said.

Thorne turned and looked over his shoulder, but didn't move the broken glass from Ballantine's throat a single millimeter.

"An island? You have been leading us to an island all this time?" Thorne asked as he slowly, very slowly eased his grip on Ballantine, and then stepped back exactly three paces. "I expect you to tell me exactly why you couldn't just say we were going to an island."

"Because that's not just an island," Ballantine said.

"Looks like an island to me," Lake said.

"Then what is it?" Darren asked.

"Paradise," Ballantine smiled. "I suggest everyone get ready to disembark. The clock is ticking and our foe will be here shortly. We'll want to be ready for it because now the endgame begins."

"I fucking hate you," Thorne said as he stared at the island that was getting closer and closer by the second.

***

"Can we trust them not to try to sink us?" Shane asked Lucy as he sat up in the crow's nest, watched the former crew of the Monkey Balls hurry about the deck of the B3, and get it ready for docking.

"Well, that's why we have these," Lucy said as she patted her rifle, "and that's why they have those."

She nodded down at Kinsey, Darby, Darren and Thorne, who all stood on the deck with their weapons trained on the captive men.

"Why would they try to sink us?" Lucy asked. "Where else are they going to go? Do you see any other ships docked there?"

Shane looked out at the fast approaching small bay that had one dock, and quite a nice looking white sand beach that bordered a tropical jungle tree line with a small mountain beyond. Other than the dock, there wasn't a single sign of civilization of any type.

"Yeah, I guess the B3 is the only game in town," Shane said. "Still, I'd rather we use our own crew."

"They're busy below decks," Lucy shrugged. "Without Popeye running their asses, it's a little chaotic."

"Whatever," Shane replied, "as long as I can get off this ship and onto dry land, I'm cool. That fucking shark is still coming and I'd rather not be on the water when it gets here."

"Who says it can't get you on land? It is a freak of nature," Lucy smiled. "Maybe it has legs tucked up its ass."

"Don't even fucking think that," Shane snapped. "I do not need that image in my head." He groaned. "Dammit! Now I've got that image in my head!"

"My job here is done," Lucy laughed.

***

"I never thought I'd see this place again," Tank Top said quietly to Bokeem. The two men were the exceptions to the Monkey Balls crew helping dock the B3. Both men had been bound and tied together and sat back to back only a few feet from Thorne. "Especially since I could never find this place."

"Good thing Ballantine led us right to it," Bokeem said. "Saved us the hassle of capturing and torturing him. He just drove us right up to the front door."

"Shut the fuck up," Thorne growled.

"Yes, Commander, right away, Commander," Tank Top joked.

"Fuck you, merc," Thorne snapped.

"Why you gotta be so hurtful, Commander?" Tank Top asked. "It's hard being a mercenary. Just no love in the world for men like us anymore."

"I'm not like you," Thorne said.

"No, no, I wasn't saying that," Tank Top replied. "I meant like Bokeem and myself."

He physically rocked his head back to indicate Bokeem and the two men ended up knocking skulls.

"Ow!" they both said.

"Fucking be careful, Tank," Bokeem grumbled.

"Sorry," Tank Top said. "I think I bit my tongue."

"Too fucking bad," Thorne said and turned his attention back to the dock that was only a few meters from the bow.

Tank Top ran his tongue across his back right molar and felt the fresh crack in the tooth. He would have smiled, but he didn't want to draw attention to the fact he'd used the head bonk as a distraction for intentionally cracking open his molar and activating a hidden homing device.

"All hands to the port side!" Lake called over the loudspeaker. "I've cut the engines and we are coasting in from here!"

The Monkey Balls' crew hurried to the port side and got ready to jump onto the dock as soon as they could so they could secure the ship immediately. It was obvious to all that they didn't want to be on the water with a giant shark chasing after them any more than anyone else did.

Chapter 7- Hostile Takeover

"Fucking watch the leg!" Max yelled as he was carried on a stretcher down the gangplank of the B3 and onto the dock. "Dude! Pain! Pain hurts! Pain in leg! Hurts! Pain bad!"

"Is fire bad?" Shane laughed as he held the end of the stretcher closest to Max's head.

"Fire bad too!" Max said. "Fire bring pain! Pain hurt! Pain bad! Fire bad! Max no like fire pain bad hurt!"

"Fire spark doobie," Shane said.

"Ooooh, fire spark doobie," Max said. "Fire good!"

"You two are cracking me up," Lucy said from the other end of the stretcher. "Which is not a good thing, since I lose strength when I laugh and if I lose strength, then I'll end up dumping your ass into that bay, Max."

"Dumping ass bad!" Max yelled. "Bay wet! Wet good? Mmmm, wet good! Where's Darby? Max like wet good!"

"Shut up," Darby scolded as she walked behind the line of captured crewmembers, her rifle trained on their backs. "I need to concentrate right now."

"Concentrate bad!" Max replied. "Concentrate work! Work hurt! Work bad!"

Lucy started laughing and almost dropped her end of the stretcher.

"See?" she giggled. "You are so going in that water."

"Yeah, I don't want that," Max said seriously. "That fucking shark is still in there."

"Shark bad," Shane said. "Shark hurt."

The three snipers laughed as Kinsey walked by.

"You guys are fucked up," she said as she hurried past them, Darby, the line of captives, and up to where Ballantine stood with Thorne, while Tank Top and Bokeem stood off to the side, still lashed together.

"This is a nice beach," Thorne said from the edge of the dock as it met the glittering white sand, "but we'll need more than an open beach that leads into a jungle. I'm thinking shelter, food, a source of fresh water, you know, the basics."

"If all you want are the basics then be prepared to be the disappointed again, Commander," Ballantine grinned, "because there is nothing basic about any of this."

He grinned and looked towards the jungle. Thorne turned and looked as well, waited, waited some more, then sighed and shook his head.

"I'm going to shoot you now, Ballantine," Thorne said.

"What?" Ballantine asked, looking genuinely hurt. "Can a man not gaze upon beauty without the impatient about him threatening acts of violence?"

"No," Thorne said.

"Okay, very well," Ballantine shrugged as he pulled a phone from his pocket. He dialed a number and waited. "It's ringing."

"I thought we got rid of all the phones in case they were being traced?" Kinsey asked.

"Oh, this is my personal phone," Ballantine said. "I would never get rid of this. Impossible to trace."

"No phone is impossible to trace," Thorne responded.

"Mine is," Ballantine said. "Oh, hello... Yes, we have arrived... That would be excellent... Thank you... I look forward to seeing you as well... Right... In just a second... You have to hang up first, Doctor... Yes... Okay. Goodbye."

He laughed and tucked the phone back into his pocket.

"Scientists," he said, "not always the best when it comes to social skills."

"Hey, I resent that," Gunnar said as he and Darren walked up behind everyone.

"Where're the rest?" Kinsey asked as she looked down the dock. "The elves?"

"They are remaining on the B3," Ballantine said and put his finger to his lips. "Shhhh, it's a secret plan of mine. Don't tell anyone."

"I am going to shoot you," Thorne said. "I really am if you don't knock this shit off."

"You really are going to have to learn to relax, Commander," Ballantine said. "Especially with all the added risk of health issues for a man your age."

"Were you listening in on us?" Darren asked.

"Yes," Ballantine said and help up a finger, "now be quiet and don't spoil this for me, it's my favorite part."

Before Darren could protest, part of the jungle began to shiver and it became quickly apparent to all of them that they weren't looking at just a jungle, but a projected image of one bookended by the real jungle.

"Son of a bitch," Tank Top whispered to Bokeem. "No wonder we were never allowed onto the beach."

"It's beautiful," Ballantine said as a massive metal wall was revealed that stretched at least forty feet into the air. "Now, let's get everyone inside before some stupid Google satellite takes a picture. I may have the pull to task every other damn satellite in the sky from this area, but even I can't make Google do what I want."

"You have got to be fucking kidding me," Gunnar said.

"Okay, I am," Ballantine laughed, "Google isn't outside my reach. Not by a long shot."

"What are we looking at?" Thorne asked.

"That little old thing?" Ballantine replied as he pointed at the wall. "Just the front door to one of the most advanced biological research facilities on the planet. Possibly in the galaxy, but I'd be a little presumptuous with that claim."

"Fucking be straight with me!" Thorne yelled.

"How about I just be honest?" Ballantine said as he turned to the Commander. "What is inside that building is science that you cannot wrap your mind around. You have done a fair job putting bullets in that science, but you haven't come close to touching it with your mind. I'm about to correct that."

Before them, at the base of the wall, were several massive bay doors with one small, normal door in the center between them all. The door opened and a man in a lab coat came hurrying out. He had a head of wild hair that billowed about him like salt and pepper colored electricity. His face was etched and lined with deep crags and furrows, showing him to be much older than any of the people he rushed to meet. He wore Bermuda shorts and a bright yellow t-shirt under the lab coat with only flip-flops on his feet. His feet kicked up sand as he went, then he stopped just as he got to the first plank of the dock.

"Mr. Ballantine!" the man asked. "It is an honor to see you again!"

The man hurried forward and offered his hand. Ballantine shook it enthusiastically.

"You are probably the very first person to say that," Ballantine said.

"Oh, I doubt that, I doubt that, yes I do!" the man said as he continued to shake Ballantine's hand.

"Folks, this is Dr. Boris Kelnichov," Ballantine said as he pulled his hand back. The man kept shaking his up and down for a second even after Ballantine's was no longer in its grasp. Then he blanched and tucked his hand into one of the pockets of his lab coat. Ballantine grinned and turned to everyone else. "Let me introduce everyone to you, Doctor."

"No need, no need," Boris replied. "Commander Vincent Thorne, his daughter Kinsey, her ex-husband Darren Chambers, their gay childhood friend, Dr. Gunnar Peterson, and..." He looked over at Tank Top and Bokeem, "they look familiar, but I don't know them."

"That's a good thing, Doctor," Ballantine said. "There is no need to know them and I'd be worried if you did."

"Why are they tied up?" Boris asked.

"Aren't we all tied up in some way, Boris?" Ballantine smiled.

The doctor pursed his lips at Ballantine's words then broke out laughing.

"Yes, yes, yes, I suppose we all are!" Boris said as he clapped his hands together. "This is going to be great! Wonderful! Finally, I can show you my triumphs and not just my failures!"

"Failures? Triumphs? What the fuck is he talking about and where the fuck are we, Ballantine?" Thorne asked.

Boris took a few steps back and held his hands to his chest. His eyes had been twinkling with delight, but that delight was quickly replaced by fear.

"I'm sorry, Mr. Ballantine," he exclaimed. "Have I said too much? I didn't think a simple statement like that would violate my non-disclosure agreement. If it has, then it was purely unintentional, I can assure you. Have I assured you? I do hope I have. I most certainly do hope I have."

"Stop," Ballantine said, "first, it's just Ballantine, we've been over that. Second, you haven't violated anything. If you had I would have been the first to know and the first to tell you so. Have I told you so?"

"No, Ballantine, you have not," Boris nodded.

"Good!" Ballantine replied and clapped. "Now, how about we get the tour? It's been a while since I've seen the facility, so most of this will be new to me, as well as to everyone else."

"What about them?" Thorne asked as he nodded towards Tank Top and Bokeem.

"Oh, please bring them along," Ballantine said. "I think they will be pleased with the tour as well. The rest of their crew can remain behind with the snipers, but these two will certainly need to join us."

***

They entered through the small door and walked for several minutes along a concrete hallway before they came to another door.

"Now, I have to warn you," Boris said, "the first time can be disorienting because of the open nature of the facility. Personally, I wouldn't have designed it this way, but it wasn't my money that built it and it wasn't my choice to make. No offense, Ballantine."

"None taken," Ballantine smiled as he gestured towards the keypad by the door. "If you will do the honors."

Boris typed in a series of eighteen numbers and the door clicked unlocked. A bright light filtered from the door as Boris grinned broadly and grabbed the knob, pulling the door all the way open.

"Ladies and gentlemen," Boris said, "I give you The Menagerie."

"The Menagerie?" Ballantine laughed. "You named it."

"I thought it needed a name," Boris replied. "I hope you don't mind."

"Not at all," Ballantine said and gestured for everyone to go through. "Don't be shy."

One by one they entered into an enormous atrium that stretched over two hundred feet into the air. Despite the height, there were only three levels to the space, but it quickly became apparent to everyone why that was.

"Are you fucking kidding me?" Gunnar said as he spun about and stared at what the levels held.

Made up of what looked like thick glass, each level was comprised of several cells. The cells were of various sizes, but instead of holding people, they held animals, many of which the stunned guests could not identify. Except for Gunnar.

"Is that a megatherium?" Gunnar asked, as he pointed at a cell on the ground level where a huge animal was busy standing up to reach the large leaves of some type of palm tree within its enclosure. "That can't be!"

He ran past that cell and pointed at the next, then the next and the next.

"Gigantopithecus! Deinotherium! Aepycamelus!" Gunnar exclaimed.

"Well, good to see someone did their assigned homework," Ballantine said.

"I thought, I thought, I thought," Gunnar stuttered.

"Did you?" Darren laughed.

"I thought you wanted me to study these creatures because we might have to fight them," Gunnar said to Ballantine.

"Fight them?" Boris asked, shocked. "Not these gentle giants. You'd more than likely scare them off. No, the ones you have to watch out for are this way."

"There're more?" Gunnar asked, his eyes wide like a child on Christmas morning. "Incredible."

"See how he thinks of the discovery first and forgets the part where the crazy haired guy with the Russian name, but no Russian accent, mentioned that we're about to see the ones that we have to watch out for?" Darren asked Kinsey. "Wasn't hard to get him to help hunt for *Livyatan Melville*."

"Hunt for it?" Boris asked. "Why would you hunt for it? We have one in the lagoon at the other end of the facility."

It was Darren's turn to stutter. "You, you, you, you what?"

Boris frowned and looked at everyone closely, and then at Ballantine. "You haven't told them anything about this place, have you?"

"I like surprises," Ballantine said.

"No shit," Thorne said.

"You said there are more this way, Boris?" Ballantine asked as he pointed at another door at the far end of the Menagerie. "This isn't all of them?"

"With the budget you gave me?" Boris laughed. "This is Atrium One of the Menagerie. As you can see, there are only mammals in here, and specifically non-predators, although some could be called scavengers, so they may have an inclination to hunt if the hunger is strong enough."

"What is housed in Atrium Two?" Ballantine asked.

"Predators," Boris beamed, "Mammalian predators. Atrium Three houses the reptilian predators. Atrium Four is avian predators, reptilian or not, and Atrium Five is the non-predatory avian species. Atrium Six was just completed and I haven't had a chance to fill it yet."

"How big is your staff?" Gunnar asked. "This is like the ultimate zoo! You must have hundreds of caretakers."

"Staff?" Boris frowned. "Do you mean human staff?"

"Of course they mean human, Doctor," Ballantine said, "but feel free to tell them about the robots."

"What about-"

"The robots, Doctor," Ballantine said, "that's the only other staff on the island, yes?"

"Yes," Boris smiled weakly. "There are over sixteen thousand robots of various sizes and designs, all programmed to do precise tasks when ordered. Between them and the animals, I haven't missed other humans at all. Not that I would have time, what with my work."

"What robots?" Kinsey asked. "If there are sixteen thousand, then shouldn't we see some?"

"Oh, no, no, no," Boris replied, "they are offline and out of sight whenever a human is present. It prevents accidents."

"There were unfortunate issues with the first staff," Ballantine said, "but we fixed those issues and brought the robots here to work."

"Brought them from where?" Darren asked.

As one, including Tank Top and Bokeem, they turned and looked at Ballantine.

"Marvelous, isn't it?" he grinned as he ignored the question and walked away towards the door at the other end of the atrium. He started humming and Kinsey grabbed Darren's arm.

"Ow, 'Sey," Darren snapped, "you just broke flesh with your nails. Trim those fuckers."

"Is he humming Pure Imagination from Willy Wonka?" Kinsey asked.

Darren listened then shook his head. "Yeah, I think he is."

"We are so fucked," Kinsey said as they started walking and hurried to catch up with Ballantine.

Thorne let everyone get ahead then nodded to Tank Top and Bokeem. "Walk," he ordered.

"You know Ballantine is insane, right?" Tank Top asked. "Look at this fucking place."

"Yeah, I know," Thorne said, "but I don't care. So far, in my experience, I have yet to meet a truly sane person anyway."

***

Lake looked out the bridge window at the beach and the captives, as Dr. Morganton sat next to him, a beer in her hand to match the one in Lake's hand.

"That is quite the sight," Dr. Morganton said, her eyes focused on the massive wall with the bay doors. "Looks just like the facility where I worked."

"What?" Lake asked, his attention pulled from the beach. "What do you mean? I thought you were undercover?"

"For only a year," Dr. Morganton replied. "Before that, I spent most of my career on an island just like this. All alone with no one to talk to but my creations."

"All alone?" Lake asked. "Why the hell were you all alone?"

"It's how Ballantine wanted it," Dr. Morganton said. "The first few months were hard, but after a while, I realized that's what the job needed. My total focus without distractions."

"I wouldn't call being around people a distraction," Lake shrugged, "more an annoyance."

"You're a sailor," Dr. Morganton replied, "you're used to being in close quarters with others and still do your job. I'm not made that way. The isolation was good for me. It helped me foster coldness to my personality that came in handy once I had to deal with the cartel."

"How'd that even work?" Lake asked. "Going from being around no one to being around killers and psychos?"

Dr. Morganton looked about the bridge, took a drink of her beer, and then smiled. "You tell me, Captain. You know killers and psychos better than I do."

Lake clinked his beer against hers and laughed.

"No shit, lady," Lake said.

"Lisa," she smiled.

"No shit, Lisa."

***

"Having us work in here non-stop while he's out on that island drinking his daiquiris and eating his coconuts," Carlos grumbled as he held a flexible sheet of metal in his hands. "I hate that man. I hate him so much."

Ingrid poked her head from around the corner of a set of shelves. "Island? What island?" she asked.

"Haven't you checked any of the security monitors?" Carlos scoffed. "You're supposed to check them regularly."

"No, that's Moshi's job," Ingrid said as a hand with a thumb extended poked out from around a different set of shelves. "See.

Moshi checks the security feeds. I'm on buoyancy while you're on shielding."

"Right," Carlos sneered, "there'd be no way Ballantine would put you on security after you betrayed us."

Ingrid stared at Carlos for a second then ducked behind the shelves. She came running back around with a cup of glowing multi-colored goo and dumped it over Carlos's head.

"What the fuck, Ingrid?" Carlos yelled as he tried to wipe the goo from his face, but only ended up smearing it around as it stuck to his skin. "This burns, you idiot!"

"Huh," Ingrid said as she threw the cup at Carlos. He ducked and it struck a shelf behind him, and then bounced to the floor. "I thought the gel would maybe keep your assholeness in check, but I guess you're just too much for it. My bad. At least it'll keep the pineapples in place."

"You stupid cow! Help me get this off…" he stopped and looked at Ingrid through half closed lids. "Did you say it will keep the pineapples in place? Are you already finished?"

"Yep," Ingrid said, "how's your shielding coming?"

She walked over, took the flexible sheet of metal from him, and then placed it on the workbench in front of the shelves. She studied it from different angles then looked at Carlos.

"You aren't even close to ready, are you?"

"Shut up," Carlos said, "it's not as easy as it looks, even with those notes that Ballantine gave me. I can get it to shield, but the second it has to stay in form, it goes rigid again, which defeats the purpose of the flexibility. It has to be able to cover every inch of equipment in this ship. Anything left exposed could be fried beyond repair."

"Yeah, I know the science," Ingrid said. "I may be a weapon smith like you, but I'm a really good one."

"We're more than just weapon smiths," Carlos said.

"I know, I know," Ingrid replied then saw Moshi peeking at them from behind her shelves. "Hey, Moshi. What's up?"

The small woman walked over and picked up the metal sheet.

"Be careful," Carlos warned.

Moshi frowned at him then went back to studying the sheet. She stared at it for a couple minutes then hurried away with it in her hands.

"Hey!" Carlos yelled as he and Ingrid followed her. "What the hell?"

The woman set the sheet on her workbench then picked up a large screwdriver. Before Carlos could stop her, she started jabbing the end of the screwdriver into the metal, creating a couple dozen holes.

"NO!" Carlos yelled when he finally was able to yank the screwdriver from Moshi's grasp.

The woman pushed him away, picked up the metal again and rushed over to a different workbench. She took down an instrument that looked like a cross between a vacuum cleaner and a TV. Moshi set the sheet of metal on the instrument and pointed.

"What, you nutjob?" Carlos asked.

"Activate it," Ingrid said.

"No," Carlos replied, "she's ruined it!"

"Activate it," Ingrid insisted.

Carlos sighed and took a small box from his pocket. He walked over and touched it to the metal. Instantly, the sheet became flexible and form fitted itself about the instrument.

"Doesn't matter," Carlos shrugged, "it won't hold when the pulse hits it."

"Move," Ingrid said as she pushed him out of the way and set a large battery down by the metal.

She hooked up three electrodes to the metal and flipped a switch on the battery. The sheet began to waver, but it didn't return to its sheet state or move from the instrument.

"There," Ingrid said, "flexible shielding that holds its shape thanks to Moshi."

"I hate you guys," Carlos said.

***

"You hungry?" Mike asked the two prisoners as they sat on the brig's cold metal bench behind steel bars three inches thick each. "I can grab you some chow from the mess."

Lug and Gil glared at Mike, their eyes filled with barely contained rage.

"Suit yourself," Mike shrugged. "I'm hungry and I am going to get something to eat."

"You're gonna just leave your post?" Gil asked. "That how you lost your legs? Doing something stupid like dereliction of duty."

"Stepped on a land mine," Mike said.

"That was dumb," Gil sneered.

"Tell me about it," Mike glared. "If I had it to do over, I probably wouldn't step on that mine."

"Hindsight and all that shit," Gil said.

Mike stood up to leave, but stopped and looked at Gil.

"You knew Ballantine from before?" he asked.

"Sorta. Yeah," Gil nodded, "what of it?"

"Was he a weird, crazy bastard back then?" Mike asked.

"That fucker was off his rocker," Gil snorted. "He sent us in some strange places to do some strange shit."

"How'd you end up taking the ship from him?" Mike asked. "That was the original Beowulf, right? How'd you get it away from him and Darby?"

"Darby," Gil laughed. "Don't get me started on that bitch."

"She's good people, so I'll let that slide," Mike said, "but don't call her that again, got it? Just tell me how you tricked Ballantine out of his ship."

"You'll have to ask him," Gil said.

"He doesn't talk about it," Mike said.

"Rightly so," Gil replied, "I wouldn't talk about it either."

"I got the feeling the ship sank," Mike said, "but obviously it didn't. Why the hell would he say it sank when you guys still had it?"

"Ask him," Gil smiled, "it's a great story."

"Like I said, he doesn't talk about it," Mike said, "and neither does Darby."

"What about the geeks?" Gil asked. "They still keeping things quiet?"

"The geeks?" Mike asked, puzzled.

"Carlos and the pigtailed chick," Gil said as he snapped his fingers. "What's her name?"

"Ingrid?" Mike asked. "You mean the elves?"

"The elves!" Lug laughed. "That's funny!"

"They hate being called that," Mike said.

"Nobody likes being called elves," Gil said. "You should ask them though. Go have a chat, but watch that Carlos guy. He lies like a fucking snake."

"Yeah, I may do that," Mike said. "I'll be back in a minute."

"Hey," Lug said, "you guys got any muffins?"

"What the fuck?" Gil asked as he frowned at his comrade. "A muffin?"

"I'm hungry," Lug said, "but I don't want anything heavy."

"Yeah, there're muffins," Mike said. "They taste like shit, though. We lost our Chief Steward a few months ago and he did all the cooking. The new cook sucks, in my opinion."

"Blueberry would be good," Lug smiled, "anything but banana nut. I hate bananas and nuts."

"You have got to be shitting me," Gil said as he leaned back against the wall. "Fucking muffins."

"Be right back," Mike nodded then hurried from the brig.

He closed the door and keyed in the lock code. If anyone tried to get in or out, he'd be alerted immediately over the com. He took one last glance through the heavy glass porthole in the door, saw Gil and Lug just sitting there, secured behind those thick bars, and turned and left.

He needed to hurry since Thorne's last words were for him to "watch those mother fuckers with your life, and never let them out of your sight," but he hadn't eaten since the day before and he was starving. He'd only be gone for a couple minutes.

He rushed down two passageways and was about to ascend the stairs that led up to the mess, but he stopped and looked down the passageway to his right.

The Toyshop was down that way.

"Get your food and get back," he said to himself. "Curiosity killed the cat and Thorne will kill you."

The mystery of the Beowulf I was too strong to ignore. He hated not having some rudimentary idea of what happened. It could have bearing on their current situation. He looked down at his prosthetic legs and frowned, knowing that it was a lack of solid intel that had led his Team into the mine field that ended up taking his legs, and the lives of five of his closest friends and Teammates.

"Fuck, Ballantine," Mike said, "he doesn't get to keep secrets."

Mike wound his way through the passageways until he came to the Toyshop.

"Hey? You guys in here?" he called out as he worked his way past the rows of shelves and towards where he thought he heard voices. "Guys?"

"What?" Carlos snapped as he and Ingrid looked out from behind a set of shelves. "We're busy. Go the fuck away."

"He could help," Ingrid said. "We need help getting the sheets on the equipment and instruments."

"Sheets?" Mike asked. "What sheets?"

Moshi peaked around the shelves as well and shook her head while she tapped Carlos on the shoulder.

"Right," Carlos nodded, "aren't you supposed to be in the brig with Gil and that other guy?"

"Lug," Mike said. "You didn't know him from before?"

"He's new," Carlos said, "but we know Gil."

Moshi gave a squeak and ducked away.

"Yeah, he was a dick," Ingrid said.

"What the hell happened on that ship?" Mike asked. "No one has said anything to me."

"We don't talk about it," Carlos said.

"Gunnar told me that the Beowulf I sank," Mike said. "That's what you had said at some point."

Carlos watched Mike for a full minute in silence. Mike just waited. Having gone through BUD/S training to become a SEAL, then through hell as an operator in the field, Mike was not intimidated by a weapons nerd trying to stare him down.

"Listen," Carlos said finally, "when you're with Ballantine, you learn to pick and choose the truth, and the best way to survive around that guy is to always pick *his* truth. It doesn't matter if it is the actual truth or not, you pick his. Keeps you breathing another day."

"That's fucked up," Mike said. "The truth is the truth. You can't just pick what you want to be true."

"Sure," Carlos nodded, "like I'm sure you didn't pick the truth of being heterosexual when you first joined the Navy, right? You told the truth about being gay?"

"That's different," Mike said.

"Not really," Carlos shrugged, "but tell yourself whatever you want, and do me a favor, okay? Tell it away from here. We're busy."

Mike's face grew red with anger and he started to step forward, but a loud buzzing in his ear stopped him short.

"Shit," he said, "the brig."

Carlos looked at him then pushed by and over to a bank of monitors. He tapped at the keyboard until a view of the brig popped up.

"Good one, Bionic Man," Carlos said. "You had one job."

"How the fuck could they get out?" Mike asked as he stared at the image on the screen. "I'm going to need a weapon."

"We got those," Carlos said. He took off then came right back with an M4 and three magazines. "Here. Now get the hell out and catch those guys."

Mike nodded and took off as Ingrid came up next to Carlos and looked at the monitor.

"They cut right through the bars," Ingrid stated. "How'd they do that?"

"Not with their teeth," Carlos said as he studied the image of the jail cell. All of the three inch thick bars had two feet missing out of their middle. "We don't have time to deal with this. Let's hope Mike can handle it."

Moshi rolled a cart next to them with a stack of metal sheets on it.

"We finish in here then head to the engine room," Carlos said.

***

With the Desert Eagle in one hand, Lake pushed Dr. Morganton out the hatch and onto the landing outside the bridge with his other. He glanced at the flashing red light on the control console and grimaced.

"They could be anywhere. Get your ass off this ship," Lake ordered. "Don't cry out until you get down to the beach and can tell Darby, Lucy and the boys what's going on. You hear me?"

"Why?" Dr. Morganton asked as she grabbed onto the railing and started down the stairs. "We should start yelling now."

"Because that may be part of the plan," Lake said.

"Plan? What plan?" she asked.

"I don't fucking know!" Lake snapped. "I'm just being cautious! Do what I say and get your ass down there, and then tell them!"

Dr. Morganton shook her head, but didn't argue. She descended the stairs two at a time then hurried to the gangplank and down to the dock. She wanted to run, to sprint, to get away from the ship as fast as possible while getting to the beach even faster, but she kept her pace to a casual hurry.

Down on the beach she could see Lucy and Shane standing on either side of the group of captives, while Darby stood over Max's stretcher, their attention turned towards the bay and the water beyond. Darby looked at Dr. Morganton as she rushed across the dock's planks, but she showed no emotion or alarm.

"They've escaped," Darby said as Dr. Morganton rushed across the sand to her.

"Yes. How did you know?" Dr. Morganton asked.

"Because it was about time," Darby said, "Gil doesn't like to be caged."

"You knew he would get out of the brig?" Dr. Morganton exclaimed.

"Keep your voice down," Darby snapped. "I don't know what their signal is, so you going off at the mouth does not help."

"Going off at the..." Dr. Morganton trailed off. "Are you nuts? There are mercenaries loose on the B3! You need to get up there and stop them!"

"I don't see anything," Max said from his stretcher on the sand, his rifle to his shoulder and scope to his eye. "I don't even see Lake on the bridge."

"Hopefully, he's hiding," Darby said. "I warned him about Gil. That Lug person I don't know, but Gil is not a man you take for granted."

"Everything cool?" Shane called out from several feet away.

"Good, bro," Max said. "Just testing my sight. Don't want the pain meds to hamper my perfect shooting record."

"Keep dreaming, dude," Shane said. "The only thing perfect about your shooting record is how awful it is."

"That's a blatant lie," Max cried out. "Oh, how you have wounded my ego, dear brother! For shame! For shame!"

"How can you two joke right now?" Dr. Morganton asked.

"I'm not joking," Darby said.

"No, I meant the boys," Dr. Morganton replied.

"I'm joking so we look natural," Max said. "I have no idea what's going on, but I trust Darby, so I'll let her take lead. If she says to be chill then I'm going to be chill."

"I never said to be chill," Darby said.

"It was inferred by your nonchalant attitude to the doctor telling us that the prisoners had escaped," Max replied.

"She didn't tell us," Darby responded, "I told her."

"Oh, my God!" Dr. Morganton snapped. "Will you shut up? The B3 is under siege!"

"It is not under siege," Darby said. Several gunshots rang out across the water. "Now it's under siege."

Darby activated her com, but never got the chance to hail Ballantine. She collapsed onto the beach and across Max's legs right before Dr. Morganton's eyes.

"What the fuck?" Max cried out then grabbed at the back of his neck and doubled over Darby's body.

"Oh, God!" Dr. Morganton shrieked. "Shane!"

She spun about, but Shane and Lucy were already down. Her eyes went from the fallen snipers to the group of captives in front of her. A short Indonesian man stepped out from the group with a huge hairy man in a foot brace right next to him.

"Howdy," John Bill grinned, "the name's John Bill and I'll be accompanying you inside the facility now."

"Be cool and you won't get hurt," Slaps said. "Just follow my buddy here and it'll all be good."

Dr. Morganton stood there, stunned, her eyes going from the fallen operators to the men in front of her and then back to her friends.

"How?" she asked.

"They did a lousy job searching us," John Bill said as he opened his hand to reveal a small tube. He opened his other hand and showed her several small darts. "Not very professional of them."

More shots rang out from the ship, but Slaps held up a hairy hand so Dr. Morganton would pay attention to him.

"Never mind that," Slaps said, "you're going with JB. You're going to go inside that facility and help our friends."

"I don't know the code," Dr. Morganton replied.

"Doesn't matter," John Bill said, "I have the code. I just need your warm finger to enter it in." He smiled as Dr. Morganton's eyes went wide. "Yes, we know about the biometrics protocol installed within the keys themselves."

"This isn't my facility," Dr. Morganton said, "it won't recognize me."

"Oh, it will," John Bill said as he took Dr. Morganton by the elbow. "Your signature is programmed into both facilities."

"How do you know that?" Dr. Morganton asked. "I didn't even know that!"

"Our employers were very thorough with their briefing package," John Bill replied. "They made sure to prepare for everything."

He reached into his pants.

"Oh, no, please," Dr. Morganton pleaded.

"What? Oh, gross, come on," John Bill said as he pulled out a short knife. "You're cute, but a little old for me and not my type." He tossed the blade to Slaps who caught it easily.

"Thanks," Slaps said as he started to cut the captive crew free from their bonds. He got the first man free and handed him the knife. "Get the others free then take the weapons off those fucks and get them loaded onto the ship. As soon as that's done, you get your butts back here. You don't want to be anywhere near that ship when it heads back out into the water."

The freed man nodded and took the knife. He cut the bonds on the man next to him then gave that man the knife so he could be freed. Slaps walked over and picked up Max's rifle then looked over at John Bill and smiled.

"I got this," Slaps said, "you go find Tank and Bokeem."

"Come on, Doc," John Bill said, "let's go say hello to Ballantine."

***

Everyone could see that Ballantine was impatient to get through the atriums, but they ignored him as they stared at the incredible sights held in the cells before them. Even Darren couldn't tear his eyes away, even though his life's obsession was housed in the lagoon just on the other side of a few more doors.

"What the hell is that?" Darren asked. "Looks like a Komodo Dragon on steroids."

"Megalania," Gunnar said.

"Yes, very good, Doctor," Boris said, "that's exactly what it is, and that there is-"

"Titanoboa," Kinsey said. "Yeah, we know what those fuckers look like."

"Oh, you've encountered one?" Boris asked, looking to Ballantine. "I was not aware there were any in the wild."

"Accidents happen," Ballantine said.

"That they do," Boris smiled, "that they do."

"Am I the only one creeped out by that interchange?" Darren whispered to Kinsey.

"No secrets in class, kids," Ballantine said. "Boris? Are we finished here with the tour of reptile predators? I'd really like Darren to see the *Livyatan Melville* before the day gets away from us."

"Oh, yes, of course," Boris said, "this way."

The man led them through a door at the far side of the atrium and into a corridor that led to the next atrium. Instead of going forward, the doctor pressed his hand to a square in the center of the corridor's blank wall. That wall slid back to reveal a spiral staircase that wound its way down several stories.

"Sorry about this," Boris said, "there are no elevators in the facility. It's safer that way."

"Then how do you move the animals around?" Tank Top asked. It was the first thing he'd said since entering the atriums. "Teleport them?"

He laughed, then let it die away as he saw the look on Boris's face.

"Fuck me," Bokeem whispered as he turned to Ballantine, the same realization hitting him as well. "How the holy fuck did you manage that, Ballantine?"

"It's not safe yet for humans," Ballantine said.

"Teleportation?" Thorne asked. "Seriously?"

Ballantine shrugged then started walking down the staircase. "Coming?"

Everyone followed him, with Darren right behind Boris and Ballantine while Thorne and Kinsey took the rear just behind Tank Top and Bokeem. Neither father nor daughter caught the quick glances that Tank Top and Bokeem gave each other. If they had, they may have seen what was to come next.

***

Lake lay on the floor of the bridge, his head bleeding and hands clamped to his leg.

"Where'd they go?" Mike asked as he rushed inside the bridge. "Did they leave the ship?"

Lake started to respond, but it was too late. Mike collapsed to his knees, then onto his face, the carbine skittering across the bridge as Gil stood over the man with a fire extinguisher in hand.

"Get the M4," Gil said to Lug who stepped over Mike's body and picked up the carbine immediately. "Get Tank Top on the horn."

Gil looked at Lake and shook his head.

"Man, you are getting the shit kicked out of you," he laughed. "I hope Ballantine pays you well."

"Suck my dick," Lake said.

"He pays you by sucking your dick?" Gil grinned. "You're getting the short end of that deal."

"Ha, short end!" Lug laughed. "Good one."

"What?" Gil asked then got his own unintentional pun. "Short. Like Ballantine's dick."

Lug flicked a switch on the com console.

"Tank? We've got the bridge and it looks like John Bill has things covered on the beach," he said into a mic. "You read me, Tank?"

"I read you, Lug," Tank Top responded. "We'll take care of things on our end."

"Good luck," Lug said.

"Thanks. Now kill the com and don't contact us again in case the nerds can listen. We're on autopilot from here on out."

"Copy that."

***

Before Thorne could ask who Tank Top was talking to, the man spun about and threw himself up the stairs at Thorne's legs, taking him out at the knees. The old SEAL fell over the top of Tank Top and into Bokeem, who tossed him aside like a bag of old laundry, sending him down into the rest of the group.

"Daddy!" Kinsey yelled as she put her carbine to her shoulder.

Tank Top was faster. He rolled to the side and slammed himself into Kinsey's lower legs, sending her down at Bokeem as well. Bokeem didn't send her down after her father; instead, he gripped her about the throat with his hands and leaned in close to her face.

"Nobody moves!" Bokeem yelled down at the stunned Boris, Ballantine, Gunnar and Darren, who were untangling themselves from Thorne. "If you think about coming at us, I'll snap her neck before that thought even makes it halfway across your brains! All weapons on the ground!"

Everyone complied.

"Uh-oh," Ballantine said from below, "I guess we better do what you say."

"God, I hate you, Ballantine," Tank Top said as he got up and pulled a knife from Kinsey's belt. He flipped it about and cut his bonds then pressed it against Kinsey's neck. "One flick and you're dead, junkie."

"Not a junkie anymore," Kinsey said.

"Once a junkie, always a junkie," Tank Top said, "which means I won't take you for granted."

He slammed his fist into her temple then slid his arm under her shoulders as she fell, unconscious.

"Stop right there!" he said as he put the knife to her throat again when Darren started to move.

Tank Top carefully set Kinsey onto the steps and placed a boot against her throat. He held out the knife and Bokeem took it and freed himself. The two men grinned down at Ballantine and ignored the rest.

"You have been a very bad man, Ballantine," Bokeem said, "and our employers would like a word with you. Since they had a feeling you might bring us here that word is going to have to wait."

"Who are your employers?" Ballantine asked. "No, let me guess, it was a blind drop and you never met face to face, right?"

"Of course," Tank Top said.

"They fed you a bunch of intel on me, on my Team, on this island, yes?" Ballantine continued. "Then they informed you that the cartels and Somalis would be joining you in the hunt, but didn't know the whole story. They were only muscle and once you handed them the Thorne's, you were supposed to get me to bring you here. Once you had access to the facility then you'd kill everyone and contact your employers. The rest of your money would then be wired to your accounts and you'd live the rest of your life in luxury."

"Something like that," Tank Top said, "those are some pretty good guesses."

"I wrote the book on most of this shit," Ballantine said, "or at least read all the books already written."

"I should read more," Tank Top said, "but who has the time?"

"Only one problem," Ballantine said. "There's a very large shark headed this way."

"Yeah, we know that," Bokeem said. "That's why we won't kill any of you right away. We're going to keep the junkie with us while the rest of you get on that ship of yours and go kill it for us."

"Are you nuts?" Gunnar asked.

"The shark is Ballantine's mess," Tank Top said, "which means it's his Team's mess. You're his Team, so go do Team things."

"When you said 'the rest of you', I assume that excludes me," Ballantine said. "You want me to stay right here since your employers hired you to capture me."

Tank Top and Bokeem only glared.

"Just crossing I's and dotting T's," Ballantine smiled. "I'd hate for you two to lose your reputations in the mercenary community."

"Fuck you," Tank Top said.

"Yes, well, no time for that," Ballantine said, "better let my Team get out there and kill that shark."

Bokeem shook his head. "You are the most fucked up dude I have ever met, Ballantine," he said. "How has no one put a bullet in your head yet?"

"I'm too valuable," Ballantine said, then put his hand to his mouth and said in a stage whisper. "I know where all the bodies are buried."

"That would make them want you dead even more," Tank Top said.

"Not if you want to find one of the bodies," Ballantine laughed as he tapped at his temple. "Think it through, Jason. You have to think all the angles through. That was one of your many flaws when we worked together. You never saw all the angles."

"Your new Team does?" Tank Top asked.

"Not all of them, no," Ballantine frowned, "but they will."

Bokeem pointed the knife at Darren. "You. Get the old man and the fag out of here. Ballantine, the Russian, and the junkie stay here. Kill that shark and then we'll talk about how you might get out of this alive."

"You hurt her and you won't live to have that talk," Darren snarled.

"I'm not Russian," Boris stated. "Why does everyone think I'm Russian? I was born in-"

"Not now, Doctor," Ballantine said.

"Sorry," Boris nodded.

"Move," Bokeem said to Darren. "I won't tell you again."

"Can you find your way out of here?" Ballantine asked Darren.

"Yeah, no problem," Darren said, "but won't we need codes to get from one atrium to the next?"

"Nope," Ballantine said.

"But-"

"Don't argue," Ballantine interrupted, "just go."

Darren and Gunnar helped a groggy Thorne to his feet then ascended the steps. Once they got to where Tank Top and Bokeem stood with Kinsey, it became a tight squeeze and the tension of sudden violence loomed in the air. Then they were past the mercs and headed back to the atrium levels.

Tank Top watched them reach the top. He smiled once they were gone and looked back down at Ballantine.

"Now we have some fun," Tank Top said. "Time to show me the goodies."

"The goodies?" Ballantine asked. "Not sure what you mean. Jason."

"The data," Tank Top said as he looked about the dark staircase. "You think I'm going to leave this place without the research files? That shit is worth a million times what our employers are paying us."

"But, he can't-" Boris began.

"Hush, now, Doctor," Ballantine said, "we better give him what he wants. He'll kill us if we don't."

Ballantine held his hands high and waited as Bokeem came down and picked up an M4.

"Which way?" Bokeem asked.

"Down," Ballantine said, "down, down, down."

"Lead the way then," Tank Top shouted as he yanked Kinsey to her feet and threw her over his shoulder. She was unconscious dead weight and he had to keep readjusting her body as he followed the other men down into the depths of the facility. "Oh, and Ballantine?"

"Yes, Jason?"

"You try anything and John Bill kills Dr. Morganton, got it?"

Ballantine looked over his shoulder and up at Tank Top.

"Well, I wouldn't want Dr. Morganton to be in any danger, now would I?" Ballantine replied.

Tank Top just frowned and nodded for them to keep moving.

***

"I can walk, I can walk!" Thorne growled as he pushed Darren and Gunnar's hands away. "I can fucking walk!"

"Fine," Gunnar said as they reached the last door that opened onto the corridor that led outside. "Then fucking walk."

Darren opened the door and they all jumped back.

"Son of a bitch," Darren said as they looked at the dead Indonesian man on the floor, his head ripped right from his neck and resting a few feet from him against the wall. "Who the fuck is this guy?"

"One of the crewmembers," Thorne said. "I recognize him from the beach."

"How the hell did he get his head torn off?" Gunnar asked. "Who did this? Do you know the strength it takes to tear a man's head off?"

"Yes," Thorne said, "I know exactly the strength it takes."

He knelt down and studied the blood that coated the floor everywhere.

"No foot prints," he said. "How can there be no footprints? The killer would be coated in blood from the arterial geyser."

He felt something wet drip down onto his ear and looked up to see a massive air vent above.

"There," he said as he pointed at the ceiling, "it went up there."

"It?" Darren and Gunnar asked.

"You think a man could rip this guy's head clean off and then not leave a single footprint?" Thorne asked. "While also climbing a smooth wall twenty feet up into the ventilation system?"

"Stupid place to put a ventilation system," Darren said. "That's a security breach waiting to happen."

"Or a way to prevent a breach," Gunnar said as he nodded down at the dead man, "but we don't have time to survey this place's security. We need to get on the B3 and go stop that shark, or Kinsey and Ballantine die."

"You think we can do it?" Darren asked as they started jogging down the corridor.

"Can we?" Thorne asked. "Yes. Will we? There's a lot of maybe in that answer."

They walked out of the facility and onto the beach where the hairy Slaps stood grinning from ear to ear, Max's sniper rifle pointed right at them.

"Your friends are already on board," Slaps said. "You should probably join them and get the fuck out into that water. You have a shark to kill."

All three of them wanted to respond, but the way Slaps gripped the rifle told them, even Gunnar that words were going to be used as an excuse to reply with bullets. They stayed quiet and walked slowly past Slaps, across the beach, onto the dock, and down to the B3.

Chapter Eight- Bigger Boat Ain't Gonna Cut It

The sonar beeped and Darren stared at the shape on the screen. He ground his teeth together as he watched it get closer and closer.

"While it's nice to have our ship," Darren said, "it sucks it's our prison as well.

"Relax," Gunnar said, "I just pumped Shane, Lucy, and Darby full of adrenaline. They are wide awake and getting suited up for battle. It won't be a prison for long."

"Suited up for battle?" Lake laughed from across the bridge. He sat in a chair with his leg propped up and an ice pack on his head. "This isn't a fucking jousting tournament. There's a giant, one hundred plus foot shark out there that is heading straight for us. Did you not see it take down three cutters and two destroyers?"

"I saw it," Gunnar snapped. "I also just had a chat with Carlos on my way back up to the bridge."

"Carlos?" Darren asked as he looked away from the sonar and back out the window of the bridge. He turned the ship's wheel and guided it all the way out of the island's bay and back into open waters. "What does Carlos have to do with this?"

"Apparently a lot," Gunnar said. "They wouldn't tell me much, just that we have to get around to the other side of the island and drop the Team off there."

"I'm part of the Team," Darren said.

"You're my bitch right now, is what you are, D," Lake said. "You drive this boat like I tell you to."

Darren flipped him off, but kept his eyes out on the water.

"Why are we going to the other side of the island?" Darren asked. "Why the hell would we drop our people there?"

Gunnar wouldn't look him in the eye.

"Gun? What are we going to do on the other side of the island?"

"There's a plan," Gunnar said, "that's all I know."

"Fuck," Darren growled, "Ballantine always has a fucking plan."

***

Ingrid leaned against the wall of the passageway and closed her eyes.

"Last one is done," Carlos said as he came out of the Toyshop. "Everything we can't live without is shielded."

"Will it hold?" Ingrid asked.

"Will what hold? The shielding?" Carlos asked. "I don't know. We didn't have much time to test it."

"We didn't have much time to test it? That's your excuse if we all die?" Ingrid snapped as she pushed away from the wall.

Moshi came hurrying out of the Toyshop and got between them as they came at each other.

"No," she said quietly.

Carlos and Ingrid looked down at the woman and both sighed.

"Sorry," Ingrid said.

"Yeah, me too," Carlos said.

They looked like they were going to hug, but neither moved forward. They just stood there awkwardly. Moshi grabbed them, pulled them in for a group hug, and then hurried back into the Toyshop.

"Where is she going?" Carlos asked, but then had his answer as she came out with a large metal case in hand. "Oh, right."

"The pineapples," Ingrid said. "We better get these up top to the Team."

***

Thorne looked around at what was left of Team Grendel. Darby, Shane, Lucy, and Mike. He frowned at what he saw.

"We're lucky we're only bait," Thorne said.

"Wait, what?" Shane asked. "Bait? I didn't volunteer to be bait."

"None of us did," Thorne said, "we were drafted."

"Those assholes," Mike snapped. "Why are we even bothering to listen to them? They're going to kill Kinsey, and Ballantine and Dr. Morganton anyway. We just need to get clear off this place."

"Leave them behind?" Darby growled. "Never."

"It's not like we can get away," Thorne said. "That shark is in the water and headed straight for us. We kill it or it kills us. This is our fight no matter what that fuckhead Tank Top says."

"Then tell us the plan," Darren said.

"We're here! We're here!" Ingrid said as she came up from one of the hatches. "Sorry!"

"What's in the cases?" Shane asked.

"Pineapples in one," she replied, "a surprise in the other."

"The sensory concussion grenades?" Lucy asked.

"Yep," Ingrid smiled, "Pineapples."

"No offense," Shane said, "and with all due respect to your skills as a tech elf, but we've seen this fucking shark. Poking it in the eye is not going to stop it."

"No, it's not," Carlos said as he made it up on deck. He was huffing and puffing from the exertion. "No one say a thing. We all can't have a twelve pack and perfect biceps."

"Yes, you can," Shane said. "Stick with me and in just thirty short days, I'll have you-"

"Shane, shut the fuck up," Thorne said.

Shane hung his head. "I miss my brother."

"He needs his rest," Darby said. "He was shot in the leg and then darted."

"We only need the four of you anyway," Ingrid said as she set the case down and opened it. "Three apiece. You'll set them at specific intervals, and then when we're ready, we'll set them off remotely."

"You can do that?" Shane asked. "That wasn't in the training the other day."

"Nothing ever is," Darby grumbled.

"Hey! We worked hard to get this shit to work, so back the hell off!" Carlos snapped. "It's brand new!"

"Watch," Ingrid said as she took one of the pineapples and then opened the second case.

There were exactly twelve jars of gel in the case and she took one out and opened it.

"I need a bucket," Ingrid said, "filled with water."

Everyone stood there then Shane rolled his eyes and said, "I got it."

He ran over to a pile of equipment by the helipad and grabbed a bucket. He stopped and looked at the empty helipad.

"Too bad we don't have a Wyrm IV yet," he said. "Having a bird in the air would be helpful. Wasn't Ballantine supposed to get us another helo?"

"When would he have had time to do that?" Thorne asked. "We've been on the run for a while."

"Just saying," Shane said as he took the bucket to a hose by the railing and filled it quickly. He jogged back to Ingrid. "Here ya go, pretty lady."

"Ugh," Carlos moaned.

Ingrid opened a jar and smeared the gel on a grenade then set it in the water. It floated at the top and didn't move even when she kicked the side of the bucket, causing some of the water to slosh out over the sides.

"Well, that's cool," Shane said.

"Watch this," she said and reached in and pushed the grenade to the bottom of the bucket. It stayed exactly where she pushed it. "It doesn't matter what the currents are or what turbulence is around it, the grenade will not budge from where you place it unless it is physically moved by hand."

"How is that possible?" Mike asked. "Force is force."

"No, it's not," Carlos said. "Ingrid calibrated the gel to react to only specific solid force. Liquid force means nothing to the gel."

"Nope," Mike said, "that isn't scientifically accurate."

"Yes, it is," Carlos said, "trust me, Tin Man, it's accurate. We know what we're doing."

"Back off," Thorne snapped at the tech, "don't insult my people."

"Don't worry about it," Mike said, "I've been called worse than Tin Man."

"So we place these in specific spots and then what?" Shane asked.

"*Why* is the better question," Darby said.

"Okay, then *why*?" Shane asked.

"We'll coordinate their activation so that the shark is driven in the direction we want it driven," Ingrid explained. "The ones closest to the ship will go off first, so the shark doesn't try to attack us. It will flee from the grenades towards the others, which will steer it into a huge lagoon at the back of the island."

"Which we are approaching now," Thorne said as he pointed towards the island.

The B3 came about and they all stared at the massive cliff face that presented itself. At the bottom of the cliff was a small beach, which looked out on a huge lagoon that had to be over half a mile wide. Filled with crystal clear water, the lagoon was ringed by a natural rock barrier, but the opening that led out into the ocean was obviously blocked by something man made.

"Uh...what's in the lagoon?" Mike asked.

"The answer to our shark problem," Carlos said.

"Hold on," Shane interrupted as he counted on his fingers then pointed at Ingrid. "You said three apiece. There are five of us, so that would be two apiece with two left over."

"Four of you will be setting the grenades," Ingrid said, "while one of you opens the gate."

"Opens the gate?" Shane asked. "Opens the gate to what?"

"The lagoon, moron," Carlos said. "We can't corral the shark in the lagoon if it isn't open, now can we?"

"We're going to trap it in there?" Mike asked. "Then what? Blow it up?"

"No, not blow it up," Ingrid frowned. "All the weapons in the armory are, well, wrapped up right now. No explosives to use, even if that was the plan."

"So, if we aren't going to blow it up, then what are we going to do?" Mike asked.

"Let nature take its course," Ingrid shrugged, "sorta."

***

"We're going to do what?" Darren snapped. "No fucking way!"

"It's what it's designed to do," Gunnar said. "It's not real. D. Ballantine had Boris create it just like he created the other creatures."

"You think he created the sharks?" Lake asked. "What about the rest of those fucking things we've dealt with? You don't think Ballantine has had us out chasing monsters just to clean up his mess, do you?"

Darren and Gunnar turned and looked at Lake, and then they looked at each other, then back at Lake.

"What?" Lake asked as he cracked open a beer and tipped it towards them. "You know Ballantine and his secrets. Makes more sense that we're his fucking janitors, not his Team for hire out doing the company's business, and who the fuck is this company? You know what I think?"

"You're fucking drunk?" Darren said and looked out the window as he slowed the throttle and steered the ship right where he wanted it. "Get off my bridge if you're gonna be a drunk pain in my ass."

"My bridge," Lake said, "my bridge."

"Shut up," Gunnar sighed, "both of you. We need to get prepared for what's coming."

The sonar beeped again and they turned their attention to the shark that raced towards the ship.

"It's less than five miles out," Darren said, "this shit better work."

***

Tank Top stared down at the decapitated body and severed head of John Bill, then looked up at Gil and Lug. The two men backed away from the body they'd just set down, neither of them wanting to look Tank Top in the eye.

"Just lying there? In the fucking corridor?" Tank Top asked.

"Just lying there," Gil said. "Those Grendel assholes told us we'd find him and we did when we came inside. Fucking weird, Tank. His head was ripped right off. Not twisted off, but ripped off." Gil nudged the open neck with his boot. "See? Look at the flesh. Something pulled his head off from above."

Tank Top turned and found Ballantine smiling at him.

"You know anything about this?" he asked Ballantine.

"Nope," Ballantine said, grinning wider.

"You do," Tank Top said as he stomped over to where the man stood, leaning against a bank of servers. "You know what did this to John Bill!"

"I don't, Jason, honest," Ballantine said as he held up his hands, "but you've seen what's on this island. Maybe something got loose and is hunting you all one by one right now."

"Fuck you," Tank Top said, "I'll get an answer. Bokeem!"

"What?" Bokeem asked as he stood next to Boris while the scientist sat at a terminal and oversaw the data transfer from the server bank to a case of flash drives at his feet. "I'm busy."

"Ask Dr. Moreau there what ripped John Bill's head off!" Tank Top yelled.

"I need to concentrate, please," Boris said. "This system was not designed for the rapid transfer of information. It would be much easier if you just took the backups stored in the vault."

Ballantine's smile fell. He shook his head as he pinched the bridge of his nose.

"Thank you for telling them that, Doctor," Ballantine said, "that was very helpful."

"What?" Boris asked as he looked up from the terminal. "What was helpful?"

"You telling us we can skip this bullshit and just jack the backups from the vault," Tank Top said. "Now, where's the vault?"

Boris looked from Tank Top to Ballantine. "Oh, dear. I've made a mistake, haven't I?"

"It appears so," Ballantine said.

"So, where's the vault?" Tank Top asked Ballantine as he walked over to the still unconscious form of Kinsey that lay tied up next to the door into the server room. "Tell me, Ballantine, or the junkie gets a kick to the head. Every second you hesitate she gets another kick. How many do you think that noggin of hers can take?"

Ballantine didn't say a word. Tank Top drew his foot back, looked at Ballantine one last time, then lashed out, nailing Kinsey just above her ear. The woman moaned and grunted, but didn't wake up. Tank Top kept his eyes on Ballantine then drew his foot back again.

"Fine," Ballantine said, "I'll show you where it is."

"Good," Tank Top said, "but let's keep the doctor here on his task until I know for sure that there actually is a backup." He looked at Gil and Lug. "Gil, you're with me and Ballantine. Lug? You stay here with Bokeem."

"Stay here and babysit?" Lug complained. "Bokeem can do that."

"Can I?" Bokeem grinned. "Is that what I'm doing? Babysitting? Or am I studying the codes the doctor is inputing to access the servers?"

"Uh, probably the last part," Lug said, "sorry."

"You're here to watch the door," Tank Top said. "You don't let anyone in except for me and Gil, you hear?"

"Don't let anyone in?" Lug laughed. "There's no one here. All the Grendel dipshits are on the ship and you'll have Ballantine with you."

Tank Top stared at Lug for a second then looked down at John Bill's corpse.

"Oh, right," Lug said, "whoever did that could be here."

"Don't forget about Dr. Morganton," Ballantine said, "she's somewhere loose, remember?"

"Come on, smart ass," Tank Top said as he pointed his carbine at the door, "move it. I want those backups now."

"Yes, sir, Jason, sir," Ballantine saluted then kick marched his way out the door.

"Fucking asshole," Tank Top growled as he followed with Gil right behind.

"Could you do that?" Lug asked Bokeem as he pointed at the corpse. "You're a big guy."

"You're a big guy too," Bokeem frowned. "Can you do that?"

"No fucking way," Lug said.

"Then neither could I," Bokeem said. "I'm not some fucking monster."

***

"We are in the water," Thorne said over the com, "getting to our positions now."

"Okay," Darren replied, "good luck, guys."

"Hey," Lucy said.

"That was a generic 'guys', Luce," Darren replied.

"I know, just busting balls," Lucy laughed.

"Keep busting them," Darby said.

"No ball busting during working hours," Shane said, "it leads to an unproductive and hostile work environment. Plus busted balls. Busted balls suck."

"Guys, focus please," Darren sighed, "this shit is going to be cut close."

He looked at the sonar reading as the shark raced towards the island. Then he looked at the dead space that was the island's lagoon. The sonar wouldn't penetrate that protected area and he ground his teeth with frustration at not getting even a glimpse of what he had been hunting for most of his adult life.

"Maybe it will live," Gunnar said. "The whale is supposed to be designed to kill this shark."

"I should be in that water," Darren grumbled.

"I should be piloting this ship," Lake said from his stool, "but every time I try, someone beats the shit out of me, and every time you try to find your whale, someone dies. I say we read the signs for what they are and cut our losses, D-Man."

"D-Man?" Darren frowned. "How many fucking beers have you had, Marty?"

"Not enough," Lake said as he looked about for another beer but they were all gone. "Or too many. Not sure."

"D, look at the sonar," Gunnar said. "How can it move that fast? It'll be here in minutes."

"Hey, Grendel, get your asses in place. That fucking shark must have a rocket up its ass because it's covered half the distance to us just since we've been talking."

"Fuck," Shane said.

"Shit," Lucy added.

"You're fucking shitting me?" Mike said.

Thorne just growled.

***

Thorne kicked his way to the massive underwater gate that protected the entrance to the lagoon. He swam hard and fast, knowing that if he wasn't in place in time, then there was no point to any part of the plan. Herding a shark the size of the one coming for them at an unopened gate would just piss it off.

Herding.

Thorne shook his head as he thought about what they were going to attempt. How the fuck does a massive shark the likes of which the world has never seen, get herded where it doesn't want to go?

The elves assured him the pineapples would work, but he'd been in the business long enough to know that relying on tech was a sure way to get yourself killed.

Yet, there was no choice. It wasn't as if he could wave his arms and scream at the creature to get it to go into the lagoon.

Thorne stopped swimming as he came to the gate controls. He opened the access hatch, using the codes that Carlos had given him, and just stared.

"Hey," he said, "all I see is a big, red button."

"That's all you should see," Carlos replied over the com.

"A big, red fucking button?" Thorne snarled. "That's the extent of the system to this gate? Push a big, red fucking button?"

"What were you thinking would be in there?" Ingrid asked. "An intricate number puzzle only solvable by the first full moon in October?"

"What the hell?" Carlos asked.

"Oh, sorry, I've been watching old adventure movies," Ingrid replied.

"When have you had time to do that?" Carlos asked. "I've been busting my ass getting shielding together for the-"

"Will you two shut up?" Thorne asked as he looked from the big, red button to the huge gate. "I need to know how fast this opens up and whether it opens inward or outward."

"Hold on," Carlos replied.

Thorne turned himself so he could see the other Team members. Shane had just set his last pineapple by the ship while Lucy, Darby, and Mike, were still setting theirs. He mentally calculated the spacing between and realized that unless the shark came from the specific direction they wanted it to, then there was no point to plan at all.

"Carlos?" Thorne asked when he still hadn't received an answer to his question.

"Hold on, I said," Carlos replied.

"I don't have time to fucking hold on!" Thorne roared. Normally, he would have regretted losing his temper so fast, but damn if he didn't hate that guy. "Tell me how fast it opens and in which direction."

"It opens at fifty feet per second," Carlos replied, his voice cold and impartial, "and it doesn't go any direction except in."

"In? You mean inward?" Thorne asked. "Towards the lagoon?"

"No, I mean it goes into the island," Carlos said. "It slides into the land at the opposite end from you. No inward, no outward, just in."

"The island has a pocket door," Shane laughed. "Damn, I hate pocket doors. That's just lazy architecture."

"Pocket doors can be very space saving," Ingrid chimed in. "Sometimes, you can't fit a regular door in the space you need."

"No, sir, don't like 'em," Shane replied, "don't like 'em at all."

"No one cares, Reynolds," Darby said.

"Everyone shut up about the pocket doors," Thorne said, "focus. If we fuck this up, and my daughter dies, because you fucktards refuse to pay attention, then I swear I will kill you all. If you happen already to be dead, then I will have a fucking psychic hunt down your ghosts and then I'll exorcise you from God's memory. Are we fucking clear on this?"

"Damn, Uncle Vinny," Shane said, "we got it covered, so chill, and don't say fucktards. You're way too old to say fucktards. Leave that for the kids, okay?"

"Shane?" Thorne growled.

"Shutting the fuck up now, sir," Shane replied.

"Here it comes," Darren said over the com. "Are the pineapples in place?"

"They are," Ingrid said.

"I was asking the Team," Darren responded.

"Oh, sorry, I thought you were asking me since I can see them on my tablet," Ingrid said.

"Team?" Darren sighed. "All set?"

"Set," Mike said.

"Set," Lucy said.

"Setarooni," Shane said.

"Set," Darby sighed.

"You people going to tell me when to hit the button?" Thorne asked. He turned his attention back to the big, red button. Then that attention was drawn to what was peering at him through the slats in the gate. "Holy ten kinds of fuck."

"Now, that I like," Shane said. "You should totally say shit like that more. Holy ten kinds of fuck. That's brilliant."

"Whale," Thorne said.

"Okay, you've lost me now," Shane said. "Is that like a hipster term you heard somewhere? Because I'm just not feeling it. Whale? Nope, just doesn't hold up."

"I am looking at the whale," Thorne said, "or it's looking at me. Considering the size of its eye, I think it wins."

Thorne continued to stare at the huge whale eye that watched him. Then the creature turned and swam back deeper into the lagoon. Thorne watched it go, its massive body undulating through the crystal blue water like it had no care in the world.

Thorne felt horrible for a brief second knowing that the poor thing's world was about to be torn apart. Probably literally.

"Give me plenty of warning," Thorne said as he placed his hand next to the big, red button.

"We will, Commander," Carlos said. "Get ready."

***

The sonar beeped several times then a loud claxon began to sound in the bridge. Darren and Gunnar stared at the shape of a shark on the screen as it came at the ship.

"You know, if this doesn't work we are going to be sunk in less than a minute, right?" Darren asked. "That is a two-hundred ton meat missile coming right at us."

"Meat missile," Lake snickered. "Bet Gun would like that."

"You're a dick when you get drunk," Gunnar said to Lake.

"Sorry," Lake burped, "bad day and blah, blah, blah."

"This will work," Ingrid said. "I just hope everything else does once we're done with this stupid shark."

"Everything else?" Darren asked then looked at Gunnar. "What's she talking about?"

"I don't know," Gunnar said.

"Dammit, Ingrid," Carlos snapped, "one piece of the puzzle at a time! Don't you ever listen to Ballantine?"

"Sorry," Ingrid said.

"What the hell is she talking about?" Darren asked again.

"Yes, what is she talking about?" Bokeem asked over the com.

"Shit," Darren said.

"Shit," Carlos said.

"Sorry," Ingrid said again.

***

"Tank? You hear that?" Bokeem asked.

"Yeah," Tank Top replied over the com, "switch to private."

Bokeem switched the channel on his com. "Read me?"

"Loud and clear," Tank Top said, "I'll try to get to the bottom of what's going on."

"You do that," Bokeem said then looked over at Kinsey as she started to stir. "Little girl is waking up. Want me to have Lug send her back to dreamland?"

"You think she can handle another smack to the head?" Tank Top asked.

"Probably not, she doesn't look so hot," Bokeem said.

"Why keep her around? We should just kill her and not deal with the hassle," Lug asked.

"We keep her because she has value to the trained killers out in the water and on that ship, and until we know that we're in the clear, we don't kill her," Tank Top responded.

"Okay," Lug said, "just wondering."

"Don't wonder," Bokeem said, "it makes your fucking face look stupid when you do."

Lug's features scrunched up.

"Yeah, like that," Bokeem said, "just stand there and watch her. If she fully comes to then we'll-"

Bokeem stopped and looked up at the ceiling high above them.

"What?" Lug asked, following his gaze. "You hear something?"

"Shhhh," Bokeem warned. He kept studying the ceiling, and a large air vent in the middle, then reached out and gripped Boris's shoulder.

"Ow," Boris said, "what did I do? Why are you hurting me?"

"The ventilation system in this facility is supposed to be sealed and unbreachable," Bokeem said, "even through the air vents themselves. They are laser protected, right?"

"Yeah, yeah, right. It keeps the more nimble and flexible of my creatures from moving about in an unwanted fashion," Boris said. "Can you let go of my shoulder? It's hard to type when you're pinching my nerve like that."

Bokeem let go of Boris's shoulder. He kept his eyes locked onto the air vent far above. For a second he could have sworn he saw something looking back at him.

"How big are those ventilation shafts?" Bokeem asked. "Can a person fit in them?"

Boris stopped typing and looked up at Bokeem.

"Oh, those shafts could hold something much larger than a person," Boris said, "much, much larger."

Bokeem popped the magazine out of the M4 he held and checked to make sure it was full. "Tank?"

"Hold on," Tank Top said, "we're here. I need to watch Ballantine's ass closely."

"I don't think we're alone," Bokeem said, "pretty sure we have company up in the ventila-"

He didn't finish as the air vent was kicked from the ceiling and came flying at him. He dove out of the way and barely got clear as the heavy vent slammed into the floor right where he had stood. Boris screeched and fell sideways out of his chair, the vent having just missed him by an inch.

There was a roar from above and Bokeem looked up in time to see a mass of brown fur falling at him.

"Holy fuck!" Bokeem shouted. "What the fuck is that?"

***

"Here it is!" Ingrid yelled. "Move, move, move!"

Mike, Lucy, Darby and Shane didn't have to be told twice as they swam as fast as they could back to the B3. They wanted to be on the safe sides of the pineapples before Ingrid did her thing.

Thorne, still by the big, red button, looked out at the open ocean and had to use all of his willpower not to gasp and swallow a fuck ton of seawater.

The shark was bigger than he could imagine. Even with the glimpses he had had of it before, he was still shocked by what he saw racing straight at the B3. The creature defied imagination. Hundreds of tons of killing power all wrapped up inside a sharkskin suit.

"Ingrid," Thorne said, "now."

The shark swam at the ship, its tail whipping left and right propelling it forward at a blinding speed.

"Ingrid!" Thorne shouted. "Now!"

There was no answer from the woman.

"Darren? What's happening?" Thorne asked.

There was still no answer.

"Fuck!" Thorne roared, as the shark was only about 100 yards from the B3. "FUCK!"

He slammed his hand against the big, red button and the gate slid away.

"Hey, whale!" Thorne yelled even though he knew the creature couldn't hear him. "Time to get to work!"

***

"What the fuck is going on?" Darren shouted as all instruments went dead on the bridge. "Did we just lose power?"

"We just lost power!" Ingrid shouted as she ran onto the bridge. "Someone killed the engines! There must be another one of the mercenaries on board!"

"Son of a bitch," Darren growled as he pulled his 9mm from his hip. "Gun? You up for a fight?"

"Who'll watch things up here?" Gunnar asked as he looked over at the passed out form of Lake slumped against a control console.

"I will," Ingrid said, waving her tablet at them. "I can activate the pineapples from here as soon as you get the power back up."

"Good," Darren said. "Come on, Gun."

He raced from the bridge with Gunnar right behind him. They sprinted through passageways, down stairs, through more passageways then came to a skidding halt.

"Max? What the fuck are you doing?" Gunnar asked as Max came limping out of the infirmary with a crutch under one arm and his sniper rifle in the other. "You need to be resting or you'll open those sutures and risk bleeding to death!"

Max waved his rifle up at the emergency lights that glowed faintly in the passageway.

"Lights went out," he said, "and the backups don't look so hot."

Darren and Gunnar both studied the emergency lights spaced throughout the passageway.

"The engines are out and now the backup power is draining," Darren said, "what the fuck is the going on?"

"Let's find out," Max smiled.

"No," Gunnar said, "you go lie the fuck down *now*. We'll go check on it." Max started to argue, but Gunnar jabbed him in the chest. "No arguing, Maxwell Reynolds. You are not coming with us. Do you hear me?"

"Yeah, yeah, I hear you," Max said, "I'm not coming with you."

"That's right," Gunnar said, "let us handle the engines. You go lie down. Now!"

"Yes, Doctor," Max said, "I'll go lie down."

"Good," Gunnar said.

"Come on," Darren said, "we're wasting time."

They took off down the passageway and neither of them bothered to look back at Max as they hit the stairs and rushed down to the next deck.

"You know he's not going to lie down, right?" Darren said.

"Yeah, I know," Gunnar replied. "Fucking Reynolds."

***

The creature came at him so fast that he barely had time to get the carbine up to block the swipe from the beast's claw.

"Mother fucker!" Bokeem screamed, as he lay flat on his back and stared up at the huge, white canines that gleamed inside the black mouth that loomed over him. "What the fuck are you?"

The beast snarled and tried to snap at Bokeem's face, but the man was able to get a knee up under it and shove with all his strength, sending the creature flying up over his head. Bokeem rolled over and tried to take aim with his M4, but the weapon was kicked from his hands and he had to scramble away to keep his face from being kicked from his head.

He crouched by the far wall, his eyes locked onto the creature as it stood up. It was close to nine feet tall, covered in brown fur, and looked very familiar.

"You were in the Menagerie," Bokeem said. "How the fuck did you get out?"

Shots rang out and Bokeem flattened himself against the floor as Lug ran towards the creature, his carbine barking fire. Not a single bullet hit the creature and for a split second, Bokeem wondered how the fuck he'd ever thought hiring Lug was a good idea.

"Die, you fucking-" Lug shouted then was cut off as the creature reached out and gripped him by the neck.

"Oh, fuck," Bokeem said as he watched Lug's face turn purple.

Then the man's head popped right off as the creature squeezed all the way through his neck.

"Holy fuck! Doctor!" Bokeem yelled as he got to his feet and then dove for his carbine. "Doctor! How do I stop this thing?"

The M4 was in his grasp then it wasn't as a hairy foot that must have been a size twenty slammed down on his hand. Bokeem screamed as every bone in his left hand was pulverized into dust and sharp shards that ripped up through his flesh.

"Stop him?" Boris asked as he got back in his seat at the terminal. He just sat there smiling down at the wounded merc. "You don't stop him. Boy, have I learned that over the years. When Ronald gets a goal in his head, he tends to be single minded until he moves on to the next goal. Right, Ronald?"

"Goal?" Bokeem screamed. "What are you talking about?"

The creature attached to the hairy foot crouched low and put its face right in Bokeem's.

"I'm a goal oriented being," the creature said. "I like to have my life planned out, step by step."

Bokeem was yanked to his feet as the creature grabbed him under the shoulders and lifted him up as if he was made of air. There was the faint smell of monkey mixed with something else.

"Are you wearing cologne?" Bokeem asked the creature then immediately shook his head and closed his eyes. "You've lost it, man. You think you're talking with a giant ape. You must have been hurt earlier and now you're hallucinating."

"While hallucinations can be associated with head trauma at times, they are not as common as intense headaches and dizziness," the creature said. "Are you experiencing any intense headaches or dizziness?"

Bokeem opened his eyes to the inquisitive gaze of the creature.

"I, uh, no," was all Bokeem could say.

"Oh," the creature responded, "then let me help you with that."

Bokeem suddenly found himself weightless as he flew through the air. Then his weight came rushing back as he slammed into the wall and crumpled to the floor. He tried to stand and scramble away, but he collapsed back to the floor when he put his weight on his crushed hand.

"You have hurt and scared my friend and colleague," the creature said. "I do not take kindly to intruders on my island and I certainly don't take kindly to violence. I am, by my nature, not a violent being."

The creature loomed over Bokeem.

"Please," Bokeem begged as he looked up at the creature, "please, I give up."

The creature bent down and took one of Bokeem's wrists in each hand then slowly stretched out the merc's arms to the side.

"Give up?" the creature asked. "I don't remember asking for, nor granting you the opportunity to surrender. You see, this is the problem with humans, you never see anything through. You are a species that gets easily distracted. Lord knows where our research would be if I left everything up to Boris there. That man cries squirrel more than a golden retriever."

"Well, that's hardly fair, Ronald," Boris pouted. "I just like to explore the tangents that our discoveries bring."

"Tangents," the creature laughed. "If that's what you want to call them."

Bokeem felt the tension in his shoulders and knew what was to come. He'd been a soldier of fortune for too long not to know what the creature intended to do.

"Listen to me, please," Bokeem said, "you can't kill me. A signal has been sent and if I don't activate my own corresponding signal, then this whole island will be swarmed down on by more men with guns, than you can even think of killing. You need me."

"Do you need your arms to activate the signal?" the creature asked.

"Yes!" Bokeem cried. "Yes, I do!"

"You are lying to me," the creature sighed. "Another human trait I could go the rest of my life without dealing with."

He pulled hard and Bokeem's arms tore from their sockets. Blood spurted left and right as the creature stepped back and admired his work.

"I enjoyed doing that," the creature said. "See? That's the truth. I don't lie and I don't distract easily. These are traits of my species."

Bokeem whimpered as his life quickly drained from him. He stared at the creature then whispered.

"What was that?" the creature asked as he bent down and put his ear to Bokeem's mouth.

"I wasn't lying about the signal," Bokeem said with his last breath. "You are all dead."

Then the life left his eyes and the creature stood up.

"Do you think we are in danger?" Boris asked. "More danger than we're already in?"

"Apparently so," the creature named Ronald replied, then looked up at the open ventilation shaft in the ceiling. Dr. Morganton stared down into the room, her eyes wide with shock and terror. "Oh, Doctor, sorry. I forgot you were up there."

She didn't respond, just kept staring. Ronald looked down at the arms he held in each hand. He let them fall to the floor.

"Oops," Ronald laughed, "forgot I was holding those. Do you remember the shaft ten meters back that we had to climb down?"

Dr. Morganton just kept staring.

"Doctor? Hello? Dr. Morganton?" Ronald asked. He snapped his enormous fingers. "Doctor!"

"Oh...," was all Dr. Morganton said.

"The shaft," Ronald said slowly like he was talking to a small child. "Go back to the shaft and wait there. I'll be right up and help you get down."

"Oh," Dr. Morganton said.

"I believe she's in shock, Ronald," Boris said. "Hardly unexpected."

"True," Ronald nodded as he turned his attention back to Bokeem, "but it is annoying. Yet another weakness of your species. How homo sapiens ever became the dominate hominid on this planet I will never figure out."

"Our procreation rate," Boris said. "We're worse than bunnies."

"Yes, well, that is true," Ronald sighed, "and to think what you could accomplish if you'd get that sex drive under control."

Boris just shrugged.

Kinsey stirred and Ronald walked over and cut through her bonds with a flick of a claw.

"Be careful when she comes to," Ronald said as he went to the stairs. "She's a trained killer and might go after you."

"Where are you going?" Boris asked.

"I have to help Dr. Morganton then go find Ballantine," Ronald said. "There's no way he can carry the backup drives all on his own."

"Those men are with him," Boris said.

"Not for long," Ronald smiled. "See you in a few minutes, friend."

***

The shark's mouth opened wide and it was about to chomp into the B3's hull when it felt excruciating pain in its tail. Its jaws clamped closed and it whipped its head about to find the source of the discomfort. For a brief second, it was honestly confused. Its mind had no way to comprehend the animal that had a hold of its tail.

Its killer nature took over and it no longer cared about comprehending the thing. Instead, it only wanted to destroy what it believed to be its new and greatest enemy.

A target. A true target. One that wouldn't just float in the water and let it tear it apart. No, the new target was an active foe.

The shark opened its mouth once again and twisted its body almost in half as it lunged at the attacker.

***

"What the fuck did this shit do to my ship?" Cougher yelled in Carlos's face. The two men stood in the middle of the engine room, only an inch apart. "I let you do this because you said it would protect us from whatever was coming."

"It will!" Carlos yelled.

"Well, does this look like protection?" Cougher yelled as he pointed a wrench at the cooling engines then at the dimming emergency lights. "This looks like a serious fucking problem to me!"

Darren and Gunnar raced into the engine room.

"What happened?" Darren asked.

"Tinker toy here fried my engines!" Cougher shouted. "He wrapped that metal shit over everything and now we are fucked! Look at the emergency lights! This shit is sucking the power from the battery banks!"

"What is this?" Gunnar asked as he stepped next to a metal shrouded piece of equipment. "Is this some sort of shielding?"

"Yes," Carlos said, "it's designed to absorb electromagnetic energy. We found deflection caused too many problems, so containment was the best option."

"Containment?" Darren asked. "Why the hell would we need to do that?"

"Yes, well, that's a question for Ballantine," Carlos said, "not for me."

"Contain this, mother fucker," Cougher said as he raised the wrench up over his head.

"Whoa!" Darren yelled as he lunged at Cougher and grabbed the Chief Engineer's arm before he could brain Carlos. "All friends here, Cougher!"

"Not friends with him!" Cougher shouted as Darren shoved him away from Carlos. "Fuck this guy!"

"Carlos, you have to be straight with us," Gunnar said. "Why did Ballantine ask you to do this?"

Carlos hesitated, but then slumped his shoulders and glared. "Because of the EMP coming."

"What EMP?' Gunnar prodded. "Why would there be an EMP? Is it part of the plan? Is there a device on the island that sends out an EMP? What does Ballantine need an EMP for?"

"He doesn't need it," Carlos said. "He just said it was coming. You know, when the nuke hits the island and goes off."

"Nuke?" Cougher and Darren asked at the same time.

"Yeah, a nuke," Carlos said then glared harder. "I am going to get my ass handed to me by Ballantine if I say anything more."

"What do you think we are going to do to you?" Gunnar asked.

"Whatever," Carlos said, "but if Ballantine asks, you say you tortured me, got it?"

"Not a problem," Gunnar said. "You're such a pussy that Ballantine will believe that easily."

"Nice," Carlos sneered.

"Tell us," Darren ordered.

"You know how we have been disowned by the US government?" Carlos asked.

"Disavowed," Darren corrected.

"Yeah, that," Carlos nodded. "Well, apparently they didn't just disavow us. They also sent these folks after us. You know, the folks we've been fighting and took us hostage and all that good stuff."

"The US government is behind these merc fucks?" Darren growled.

"Yeah, or some branch of it. Ballantine said it was all black cover stuff," Carlos shrugged.

"Black ops," Darren said. "The CIA and NSA's shadow organizations."

"Whatever," Carlos replied, "not that it matters. Crazy assholes are crazy assholes no matter who they are."

"What does this have to do with a nuke?" Gunnar asked.

"Ballantine believed there was a fail-safe in place," Carlos said. "He's pretty sure that we've been tracked to this island and if the mercenaries don't report in, then an ICBM is going to be headed right for us."

"ICBM?" Darren gasped. "Mother fucker. That'll wipe out the island and pretty much half the ocean around it."

"Yep," Carlos nodded as he pointed at the metal. "That's why I shielded all essential equipment. I just may not have calibrated it right. Instead of absorbing the energy from the EMP, it's started absorbing the energy from the engines and battery banks."

Darren looked at all the metal.

"How do we get it off?" he asked.

"Get it off? Why?" Carlos asked. "If the EMP hits, then it'll destroy every piece of electronic equipment on this ship."

Darren moved from Cougher and over to Carlos then tapped the tech on the forehead.

"You need to look up in your weapon smith brain just exactly the kilotons worth of damage an ICBM does," Darren said. "Then you need to tell us how to get this shit off so we can start up the engines and get the fuck away from this island as fast as possible."

"Oh, right," Carlos said as his eyes went wide.

"Did the calculations?" Darren asked.

"We need to be at least forty miles from here," Carlos said, "or we're toast."

"Nuked toast," Darren nodded.

"Wait a fucking minute, D," Gunnar said, "even if we get the engines up and running, we can't just leave everyone on the island!"

"I know," Darren smiled. "So I guess we better go get them then."

Gunnar smiled back. "Yeah, I guess we better."

***

"Hey there," Max said from the railing as Mike, Shane, Darby, and Lucy climbed up to him. "How's it going?"

"What the fuck are you doing?" Shane snapped. "You need to be resting!"

"Oh, you know me," Max said. "I rest better with a rifle in my hand and an eye on the danger."

The four teammates climbed up over the railing then turned and looked down into the water below. Except for Darby. She walked over to Max, grabbed him by the back of the head, kissed him hard then shoved him away and slapped his face even harder.

"Ow," Max smiled.

"You're an idiot," Darby said. "Get below and rest."

"With you up here all vulnerable and shit?" Max smiled as he rubbed his cheek. "Not a chance, sugar ass." Then Max noticed the others were busy studying the water and there was one person missing. "Uh, where's Uncle Vinny?"

"Still in the water," Shane said. "He was by the gate."

"He has a few hundred tons of sea monsters between him and this ship," Mike said.

"Oh, that's not good," Max said.

"What happened to the com?" Lucy asked. "We were trying to hail the elves forever, but they didn't respond. Why didn't they activate the pineapples?"

"Power's out," Max said. "Engines are offline and the batteries are borked."

"How the hell did that happen?" Shane asked.

"I can make a guess," Darby frowned.

"Carlos screwed up," Ingrid said as she ran up to them waving her tablet. "I think I have a fix. I just need one of you to go back in that water so you can activate the pineapples. You'll have to be about fifty feet out away from the ship for it to work, though."

"Back in the water?" Mike asked.

"With those fucking things?" Shane asked.

"Fifty feet? Fuck you," Lucy said.

"I'll do it," Max smiled. "I'm hopped up on painkillers and crap and could give a shit right now. I'll totally do it."

"No, you won't," Shane said, "I'll do it."

"Cool," Ingrid said. "Let me show you how it works. You have to activate them individually, one by one, or the whole network will collapse. That means there is more room for error, but it should still work as expected."

"More room for error," Shane frowned, "great."

Max pulled a joint from his pocket and lit it up. "Here. You'll need to focus up."

Shane took the joint and drew deeply.

"Uh, I think that's going to increase the chance for error further," Ingrid said.

"All these long months and you still haven't figured us out," Shane said as he handed the joint back to Max and exhaled.

"Yeah, get with the program, Ingrid Bobingrid," Max said as he took a hit from the joint and looked at Shane. "I'm going in with you. I'll cover your ass with a channel gun."

"No, you won't," Lucy said as she took the joint from him and smoked it down to a roach. "I'll cover him. You sit up here and watch the island. If the bad guys come for the ship, then send Mike down to get us."

"No need," Darren said as he stepped up on deck, fully geared out with Gunnar next to him. "We're going to the bad guys."

"There's the possibility of an ICBM coming to destroy the island," Gunnar said, "so we sort of need to get on the road and get the fuck out of here."

Darby just shook her head. "I'll go in the water. Max can stay up here and be my spotter."

"Don't you want to come rescue the others?" Darren asked. "We could probably use your help."

"You'll be fine," Darby said. "Ballantine has it all under control like the ass always does. Kinsey is a survivor and the facility isn't without its own protection."

"What does that mean?" Shane asked. "What protection?"

"Ronald," Darby said.

"Who the fuck is Ronald?" Darren asked.

"Bigfoot," Darby said without any hint of irony.

Everyone stared at her and didn't move until Max pulled out another joint, lit that one, and passed it down the line. Even Ingrid had a hit that time. Darby rolled her eyes.

"I'll help get the Zodiac in the water," she said as she walked off.

"Dude," Shane said to Max.

"I know," Max nodded. "Totally."

Chapter Nine- Race The Boom

Thorne decided the best thing for him to do was to swim into the lagoon and away from the thrashing, gnashing giants of the sea. He had no idea what was in the lagoon, but he knew it was better than being anywhere near the teeth and blood of the battle that raged before him.

He pumped his arms and legs with all his strength as he swam through the lagoon's opening and into its main body. The water was so clear that if it wasn't for the weight of his body he would have thought he was flying through open air. Open air that had a small coral reef below it and a multitude of bright colored fish swimming about.

Thorne wondered how the massive whale survived in a space that was obviously too small for its size. A creature like that needed the open ocean to live, not a glorified water cage that was the lagoon. Not to mention the amount of food it would need daily. There was no way the lagoon was its permanent home. Every instinct in Thorne's body knew that much.

Those questions and musings had to wait while Thorne focused on getting himself to the beach that he could see was about a quarter mile from his position. Unfortunately, he was so focused on getting to safety and up out of the water that he didn't pay attention to the fight that had followed him.

Thorne's world became one of swirling water and clouds of bubbles as he was knocked aside by an errant tail swipe. As he rolled and tumbled through the crystal blue, he knew the attack hadn't been directed at him, just that he hadn't been watching his back as he should have. When he was finally able to slow and right himself, he stared in horror as two monsters of the deep locked in mortal combat blocked his way out of the lagoon.

***

"Jesus Christ!" Shane said as the Zodiac bounced over the waves away from the B3 and around the island. As the sight of the lagoon was lost to him, he turned to look at the others in the raft. "Did you fucking see that?"

"Yeah," Lucy shouted over the sound of the Zodiac's motor. "Was that the whale or the shark?"

"Whale," Darren said, a far off look in his eyes. "It breached."

"Going for the whale body slam," Shane said. "Off the top rope, mother fuckers!"

"More like trying to evade a bite," Darren said.

"You can keep your sciencey nerd speak for when you and Gunnar are geeking out over your fish friends," Shane said. "Me? I prefer to think in terms of professional wrestling. It's simpler that way."

"I know you're smart, Shane," Gunnar said, "but sometimes I have a hard time believing it."

"I'm a simple, complex person," Shane said.

"You're an oxymoron," Lucy said.

"How have we ever beaten anything?" Mike wondered out loud, as he steered the Zodiac around the island and towards the dock in the front bay.

"No dock," Darren said as he pointed at the Monkey Balls crew that stood on the sand and milled about the dock. "We're beaching it. Just run it up there and get ready to roll and fire, kids."

"Beach it?" Gunnar asked as he watched the others rack the slides on their M4s. "What the fuck does beach it mean?"

"Just follow our leads!" Shane said as he put his rifle to his shoulder and started firing at the men on the dock. "Remember, once we hit the beach you get the fuck off this raft and run straight for the wall! Do not stop or look back! Run your fucking ass off!"

"Wait...you're going to run this up onto the sand?" Gunnar exclaimed. "Without slowing down?"

"That's the plan, Gun," Darren said opening up with his carbine. "Don't worry, you'll be fine! Just do what Shane said!"

Gunnar watched as men's heads, chests, arms, legs, were ripped apart by semi-automatic gunfire. Some tried to return fire, but Lucy and Shane picked them off easily with their sniper rifles. Gunnar looked down at the M4 in his hands then over at Mike as the man pushed the motor's throttle to the limit.

"Why the fuck did I agree to come with?" Gunnar shouted.

"You said you wanted to try to save the animals," Mike shrugged. "How's that plan sound now?"

"Pretty fucking shitty!" Gunnar said as a bullet hit the water by the Zodiac's side. "Stupid! Really, really stupid!"

"All in the name of science, right?" Mike grinned.

Gunnar grimaced then looked at the rest of the Team. They all had the same grin on their faces.

"You people are so fucked up," he said. "Totally fucked up."

***

"Bokeem?" Tank Top asked as he tapped the com in his ear. "Bokeem? Come in, man!"

"It's the vault," Ballantine said as he waited just inside the massive steel encased room. "The entire place is shielded. I doubt a nuclear warhead could penetrate this place, but that's not a theory I want to prove. Shall we retrieve the backups and get back to the ship so you can call in to your employers?"

Tank Top was about to respond then he stopped and closed his mouth. He ran his tongue over his teeth for a minute or so, not saying a word as he studied Ballantine.

"How much of all of this shit is your doing? I mean, really?" Tank Top finally asked. "Be honest for once. Am I working for you or against you?"

"Oh, you are working against me, that's for sure," Ballantine said. "I would have taken things in a very different direction if it wasn't for you being employed by whatever stupid, self-important, lazy black ops, hide in the shadows and go pew pew, US government agency that you're employed by."

"How the fuck do you know that?" Tank Top asked. "None of my Team even knows that except for Bokeem."

"So he must be the one with the second beacon embedded," Ballantine said. "Good. When we get back to the others you can have him activate it so we don't have to worry about the ICBM."

"Worry about the what?" Tank Top laughed. "Damn, you have gotten even more paranoid over the years than you used to be. There's no ICBM coming, that's just crazy. If Bokeem doesn't activate his half of the beacon then an entire platoon of men will come down on you so hard you'll be begging for mercy. God, would I love to see that, but, if that happens, then I lose my bonus."

Ballantine studied his former employee then shook his head in disappointment.

"You honestly believe that," Ballantine said, "and to think I had put way more faith in you, Jason."

"Shut the fuck up, Ballantine," Tank Top said. "I'm not going to let you mind fuck me. Just point me to the backups so we can get the hell out of here and I can finish the job I was sent to do."

"Which is to take me back to some people that will lock me away for the rest of my life," Ballantine said. "While also pumping me full of drugs and using interrogation techniques that even they don't know that I was the one that developed them."

"If that's what happens then that's what happens," Tank Top said. "I could care less what they do to you once I drop you off."

"And the Thornes? What will you do with them now that the cartels and Somalis have been taken off the board?" Ballantine asked as he crouched by the bottom of a perfectly smooth wall. He ran his finger along the junction of the wall and the floor then stopped. "I guess you probably didn't think that all the way through."

"I don't give a fuck about Mexican cartels and Somali pirates," Tank Top said. "All I have to do is hand the Thornes over to my employers. They can deal with who gets them. That's not my job anymore."

Ballantine pressed his finger into a soft spot at the bottom of the wall and the sound of motorized gears filled the room. Tank Top jammed his M4 into the back of Ballantine's head.

"If you just triggered a trap, then you have about one second to live," Tank Top snarled.

A drawer about three feet wide by one foot high popped out from the wall and Ballantine slowly turned to look at Tank Top and the barrel of the carbine.

"The backups," he said, "all there for the taking."

Tank Top stepped back and let Ballantine stand.

"Then take them," Tank Top said, his carbine still pointed at Ballantine. "You're my mule."

"Am I?" Ballantine asked as he stepped to the drawer. "Here I thought *you* were the jackass." He looked inside and frowned. "It's going to take both of us to carry these."

"Are you joking?" Tank Top laughed. "That drawer isn't big enough to hold anything that's too heavy for you to carry."

"Except that's not quite true," Ballantine said as he struggled to lift out a box that was no bigger than one foot square. "Did you think I could backup all of this facility's data on a couple of thumb drives? Hardly. These drives are made of an insanely dense material I had developed."

"Of course you did," Tank Top replied. "What'd you use? Dark matter?" Ballantine didn't respond. "No shit. You used dark matter?"

"Dark matter is a theoretical substance that has never been able to be truly identified, let alone isolated into a form that could be used for any type of technological application," Ballantine replied. "This is more like, semi-dark matter."

"Jesus," Tank Top said, "you are something else."

"Oh, hello, there you are."

Tank Top turned and looked at the nine-foot creature standing in the entrance to the vault.

"Fuck me," Tank Top said as he lifted his M4. "It's fucking sasquatch."

Before Tank Top could pull the trigger, Ronald was inside the vault and ripping the weapon from the man's hands. He was about to rip the head from the man's neck as well, but Ballantine cleared his throat.

"We need him alive," Ballantine said, "or I would have killed him myself."

"I already killed his partner," Ronald said, "so I figured I'd kill him as well. You know how I like symmetry."

"You killed Bokeem?" Ballantine asked.

"Bokeem is dead?" Tank Top choked.

"Be quiet," Ronald said as he squeezed Tank Top's throat. "We are having a conversation that you are not invited to participate in."

"With Bokeem dead then that means the ICBM will certainly be launched," Ballantine said as he set the box back inside the drawer. "I'm no longer sure we have the luxury of the time it will take to remove the backups from this vault."

"Here," Ronald said as he tossed Tank Top at Ballantine's feet, "you handle him and I'll carry the backups."

Tank Top tried to get up, but Ballantine stomped on his back and sent him down to the floor again.

"Did you run into Gil on your way down?" Ballantine asked Ronald as the creature lifted out four boxes from the drawer.

"No, I did not," Ronald replied as he barely struggled with the weight of the boxes. "These are deceptively heavy, Ballantine. You should really work on their design. A person could hurt their back or shoulders trying to lift these."

"Are they too much for you to handle?" Ballantine asked.

"Hardly," Ronald smiled, his massive canines showing prominently in his huge mouth. "I'm a gigantopithecus, not a person, Ballantine. I said a person could get hurt. My kind are a different matter."

"So is that," Ballantine smiled as he pointed at the boxes in Ronald's hands.

"Oh, that is a good one," Ronald laughed. It was a booming, gravely guffaw that echoed off the sterile walls of the vault. "I have missed our happy interactions."

"What the fuck is going on?" Tank Top asked.

"Oh, Jason, that seems to be your life's motto," Ballantine said. "It is truly a pity that a person of your skill set and intelligence is so pitifully clueless."

"He's coming with?" Ronald asked.

"With Gil still at large?" Ballantine replied. "I think not. We'll leave him in here." Tank Top started to protest, but Ballantine slammed a fist into the back of his head and stunned him into silence. He knelt next to the wounded merc and put his lips close to the man's ear.

"Remember how I said this vault could withstand a nuclear blast?" Ballantine said quietly. "Well, now is your chance to find out. There is plenty of food, water, and even a cot and extra clothing in here, if you can figure out how to find them. It'll give you something to do. If the place isn't too radioactive, then I may come back for you in a year or two. That can be the hope that gets you through the long nights and endless days. Because once the lights go out, you won't be able to tell the difference."

Tank Top mumbled something, but Ballantine couldn't make sense of it. He just patted the man on the shoulder, went and retrieved the M4, then nodded towards the vault's entrance.

"I have no idea how long we have until the missile strike," Ballantine said. "Have you found Dr. Morganton?"

"She is safe and secure," Ronald said. "We'll retrieve her on our way to Boris and that young woman."

"Kinsey Thorne," Ballantine said. "A wonderful girl. You'll like her once you've had a chance to get to know her."

"I look forward to that," Ronald said as they left the vault. "So, what is the plan, Ballantine? How are we escaping doom this time?"

"I have a ship," Ballantine said.

"You always do," Ronald chuckled.

"Yes, I always do," Ballantine said. "Let's just hope the modifications have been made that will shield it from any EMP we might encounter."

"Oh, yes, let us hope for that," Ronald said.

***

"No!" Cougher yelled at Carlos. "Not that one! The other one! Have you ever been in an engine room, you fucking moron?"

"Do not yell at me!" Carlos shouted. "I have more advanced degrees than you could even imagine!"

"Lot of good they did you considering how totally fucked up these engines are!" Cougher replied. "You never thought that the shielding would absorb energy from what it was designed to protect? How many degrees did it take to fuck that up?"

"I have been under a lot of stress!" Carlos said. "I don't have the luxury of sitting down here and dealing with equipment that was invented over a century ago! I am busy inventing new equipment that keeps us all from dying!"

He stopped and looked about the engine room.

"What?" Cougher asked. "What are you looking for?"

"Don't dismantle the shielding," Carlos barked. "That isn't the issue. The engines themselves are the issue. I'm so stupid. How did I not think of this first?"

He started moving about the engine room in an almost random pattern.

"What the hell are you looking for?" Cougher shouted. "Just fucking tell me!"

"The modifications, where are they?" Carlos asked.

"Right there," Cougher said as he pointed to an already unshielded portion of the engines.

Carlos rushed over to the equipment and reached for a large, bright orange tube that rested against the engine.

"Whoa, dude!" Cougher shouted. "Moshi said not to touch that! Ever!"

"She said that?" Carlos asked.

"Well, she didn't really say it, but I sure got the impression that touching it would not be a good idea."

"We need Moshi," Carlos said as he looked at Cougher.

"Yeah, okay," Cougher replied.

"Go get her," Carlos said.

"Me? Oh, fuck that," Cougher said. "Where'd I put that wrench? Now I am going to crack your fucking skull open."

"Fine," Carlos snarled as he jogged towards the door. "I'll go get her. Don't touch that tube!"

"I was the one that told you not to touch it!" Cougher yelled after the man. "Asshole!"

***

The giant whale's teeth ground down on the equally as giant shark's dorsal fin. The shark turned on its side and went for the whale's belly, but the ocean mammal was too fast and it rolled with the shark, keeping the serrated teeth from ripping into its flesh.

The impossible shark thrashed and tried to free its fin from the clamp of the whale's jaw, but all it did was tear more of itself. Blood poured from the wound and the shark became incensed at the smell of it. Despite the blood coming from its own body, the scent built the shark's hunger and rage higher and higher until, in a frenzy of violence, the shark ripped free of the whale.

The severed dorsal fin fell from the whale's mouth and floated down to the bottom of the lagoon. Without the monster in its grip, the whale was forced to dive quickly in order to avoid the shark's lunging attack. Pain ripped through the whale's body as the shark turned the tables and bit through one of its fins.

The warm, heavy mammal blood filled the shark's mouth and it drew strength in the fury that the liquid produced. A bloodlust beyond anything it had felt before overtook it and was so intense that even the whale could smell the difference in chemicals the shark excreted into the crystal blue water.

The tide had turned for the whale and it pumped its tale in order to get free of the shark, but the other beast was too focused, too driven to be put off. There was no escaping the shark. The whale knew it, felt it, and believed it. It had to hold its position and fight or it would certainly lose. Fleeing was no longer an option.

The whale sacrificed its right fin and let the shark swallow it down in one gulp. That one motion was enough distraction for the whale to flips its entire body around, sending its tail rocketing towards the shark's head.

The collision shattered part of the shark's jaw, shoving teeth out through the flesh of its mouth. As it thrashed its head, the now external teeth tore strips off the whale's tail, flaying it open like a choice cut of meat.

Both wounded, the giants swam apart then turned almost as one and faced each other. There was a moment of hesitation, a brief respite from the carnage and brutality. That respite could not last, not with the natures of the beasts modified, warped, and amped up to levels that made them the most deadly and dangerous creatures in the water.

They came at each other, jaws wide, wounds just as wide, and blood spilling everywhere.

***

Gunnar opened fire with the M4, strafing the beach wildly as the kick of the carbine nearly ripped it out of his hands.

"Fucking A, Gun!" Shane yelled as he dove, rolled, and came up next to the doctor. He grabbed the carbine and tore it from Gunnar's grip. "You nearly killed everyone!"

"I suck with rifles!" Gunnar snapped. "That's why I'm a knife guy!"

"Then here," Darren said as he took a heavy blade from a dead man's belt and tossed it to Gunnar, "use this."

Gunnar caught it easily and smiled at the blade. "Now we're talking."

"Down!" Shane yelled as he shoved Gunnar to the sand.

Bullets flew around them as a group of men came running from the shadows of the jungle. Slaps was in the lead, despite his foot.

"Where the fuck did they come from?" Mike yelled as he knelt, aimed, and opened fire.

"Fuck if I care!" Darren replied, kneeling as well.

They made short order of the men, but Slaps made it through and lunged for Shane, a knife aimed right for the sniper's remaining eye. Shane ducked and twisted his body, letting the knife slice past him then he stomped down as hard as he could on Slaps' foot. The man screamed in pain and tried to correct his body, but the momentum from the knife attack plus the stomp to the foot was too much physics for the hairy man to overcome.

He fell to the sand and immediately flipped himself over, but he wasn't fast enough to get out of the way of the rifle butt to the face that hammered down on him again and again. In second, Slaps' head was pulp almost as fine as the sand it was melding with.

"Fuck and you," Shane said and smiled at everyone else as they got to their feet. Then he gasped. "Oh, shit! Lucy!"

Gunnar pushed up from the sand and looked over his shoulder. "Oh, fuck!"

Lucy sat on the beach, her hands against the spreading red stain on her belly.

"Ow," she said as Gunnar got up and ran to her. "That fucking hurt."

Gunnar nearly fell on her as he dropped to his knees and took her hands in his.

"Let me see," he said. "Lucy? Let go and let me see."

Lucy reluctantly let go of her stomach and the blood gushed freely.

"Fuck!" Gunnar said as he put Lucy's hands back in place. "Press down as hard as you can!"

Shane stood over them as he turned from target to target; expertly putting the remaining men down before they could get shots off.

"Almost clear, Gun," Shane said. "Should we move her inside? They have to have medical supplies in that place!"

"I'm afraid if we move her she'll bleed out," Gunnar said. He pressed his hands on Lucy's and she gasped. "Sorry."

"We'll find what you need," Darren said as he came up to them, his eyes and carbine sweeping back and forth, ready for the next attack.

"You have to save Kins," Gunnar said.

"We can do both," Darren said as he risked a glance away from the jungle and down at Lucy. The sand around her was coated in dark blood. "Looks like we have too."

"What about her compression suit?" Mike asked. "Can't it be set to press in and stop the bleeding?"

"If I could figure out how to alter and control it," Gunnar said, "or get Ingrid to do it remotely, but I don't know how it works and we have no com with the ship."

"We'll make it work," Darren said. "Shane? You stay here and cover them. Got it?"

"Got it," Shane nodded. "You two going to be alright?"

"We'll handle this," Darren said then looked at Mike. "Right, frogman?"

"Right," Mike nodded. "Hooyah."

"Hooyah," Darren and Shane said together in response.

"Fucking hooyah," Lucy groaned. "Now go. Kill some bad guys and get our people."

"And get you help," Darren said as he and Mike ran off.

Shane looked down at Gunnar and they both shared a look that said they knew the reality of Lucy getting the help she needed in time.

***

Dr. Morganton marveled at the sight of all the exotic, and thought to be extinct, creatures that filled the cells as she, Ballantine, Boris, and Ronald made their way through the Menagerie and towards the exit. Ronald not only carried the backups in his arms, but he had Kinsey thrown over his huge, hairy shoulder.

"Last atrium," Boris said. "Phew. I always forget how large this facility is. I rarely have to go from bottom to top and then one end to the other in a single day. I could use a rest, if you all do not mind."

"We don't have time to rest," Ballantine said. "We need to get clear of this island as fast as possible. Every second will count as we race to be free of the blast radius."

They made it to the end of the atrium and Boris opened the door to the corridor that would lead them outside.

"What about these creatures?" Dr. Morganton asked. "We can't leave them."

"We must," Ronald said. "It is sad, and my heart is heavy because of it, but there is no way to bring them with us." He looked down at the backups he carried. "We can begin again."

"How can you say that?" Dr. Morganton asked. "How would you feel if it was you in there? These creatures are living, breathing animals that have every right to live as you do!"

"They are creations, not born of nature," Ronald said. "Whereas I am born of nature. I should exist and they should not.

There was a moral element ignored when they were created and that means there is a moral element ignored as they face destruction."

"Born of nature?" Dr. Morganton asked, looking at Ballantine. "You didn't have him made?"

"Me? Oh, God no," Ballantine laughed. "Not that we didn't try to create more of his kind. Unfortunately, gigantopithecus is not an easily reproducible species. The few we managed to clone went mad within weeks of their awakening."

"It takes time to develop minds as deep and keen as my species are known for," Ronald said. "I mean, we have kept ourselves hidden for centuries while remaining close to heavily populated areas all across North America and other parts of the world. You don't just recreate that kind of intelligence."

"Not if sanity and stability is your goal," Boris said as the door clicked open. "Oh, dear me!"

Darren and Mike burst through the door, their carbines swinging left to right, right to left.

"Down! Down! Down!" Darren yelled. "Put your weapons down!"

Nobody got down or put their weapons down.

"Darren," Ballantine nodded, "it is good to see you."

Darren and Mike stared at Ronald, their jaws dropping.

"Uh, why does that thing have Kinsey over its shoulder?" Darren asked.

"Thing?" Ronald frowned. "How rude."

"Oh, fuck me running," Mike whispered.

"Darren Chambers, Mike Pearlman? This is Ronald," Ballantine said. "Please do not refer to him as a thing."

"It is nice to meet you," Ronald nodded. "I'd shake hands, but they are occupied."

"Uh...okay," Darren said then looked at Ballantine. "We'll talk later?"

"Will we?" Ballantine smirked. "I can't see why."

Darren glared at Ballantine for a second then scanned the atrium. He lowered his M4. "Where the fuck are the assholes?"

"They have been dealt with," Ballantine said. "Except for one. You didn't happen to encounter Gil, did you?" Ballantine looked over his shoulder then about the Atrium. "We seem to have misplaced a foe."

"Great," Darren said. "That's just what I want to hear."

"Lucy," Mike said, "we need medical supplies for her."

"What has happened to Lucy?" Dr. Morganton asked.

"Gut shot," Darren said. "She's bleeding out quickly."

"I thought we could use her compression suit to stop the bleeding, but none of us know how to work it," Mike said.

"Compression suit?" Ronald asked. "Oh, I am a wiz with those. I am sure I can assist with saving this Lucy's life. If you'll please move, I should hurry."

"Want me to take that?" Mike asked as he reached for the backups.

"That would not be wise," Ballantine said. "Ronald is more equipped to carry the backups."

"Show me to your wounded comrade," Ronald said to Darren.

"Yeah, sure, this way," Darren said as he turned back to the entrance corridor.

***

"That's a lot of blood," Max said from the railing, his sniper rifle trained on the darkening water below, "and you know what happens when there is blood in the water."

Darby looked up at him from the rope ladder hanging over the side of the ship. "I'll be fine."

"Oh, I know that," Max laughed, "just making an observation."

Darby sighed and a small smile played across her lips. "Max? I'll be fine. Do you hear me? I am going to be just fine."

"Yeah, of course," Max said, "you always are."

Darby put her mustache in place, winked at him then let go of the ladder and dropped the rest of the way into the water. Max watched her go under then bob back to the surface a second later. He gave her a thumbs up and she returned it just before she dove under and was lost from sight.

"She'll be fine," Ingrid said. "I've known her longer than you and I can say that no one knows how to survive better than Darby. Well, except for maybe Ballantine."

"That guy is a human cockroach," Max said, "and by that, I mean he is fucking hard to kill. I'm not saying he's a pest that needs to be stomped on with a heavy boot. Although, sometimes, I wouldn't mind if I could grind his ass under me heel now and again."

"Max?" Ingrid asked.

"Yeah?" he replied.

"Darby will be fine," she smiled.

He started to reply then only smiled back and nodded.

***

Thorne pulled himself up onto the lagoon's small beach and then collapsed onto his back and closed his eyes for a second. He quickly opened his eyes as a shadow fell across his face. He barely rolled out of the way, as a boot came down right where his head had been.

"You're gonna be my way off this piece of shit island," Gil snarled as he chased the rolling Thorne across the sand, one boot stomp at a time. "Now hold the fuck still!"

Thorne stopped rolling and flipped his legs around, taking Gil out at the knees. The big merc fell to the ground and Thorne started to lunge at him, but the rifle barrel that was shoved in his face stopped him cold.

"I should squeeze a round into your brain," Gil said. "Then take that silly suit you have and swim over to that ship of yours. I'll be up on deck before they know I'm not you and then the fun will really start."

"Then why don't you?" Thorne asked.

"Because I still need something," Gil said. "I need Ballantine, and knowing that prick, I'm betting your Team will trade the crazy fuck for you in a heartbeat. Ballantine doesn't exactly instill loyalty."

"You'd be surprised," Thorne said as he glanced over at the B3. "You're basing your assumption on your time with the man. Our time with him has been vastly different."

"Vastly?" Gil laughed. "I fucking doubt that. Anyone that spends any amount of time with the man knows-"

Half of Gil's head vaporized into a mist of blood and brains. Thorne didn't even flinch as he wiped some of the goop from his cheek and stood up. Gil's corpse slumped over and Thorne bent down to pick up the M4 when Max's voice exploded in his ear.

"You see that, Ingrid? I fucking nailed that bitch in mid-sentence. That's how you take out a bad guy. You don't wait until their monologue is done. You use the monologue as a natural distraction."

"Max? The coms are back up," Thorne said.

"Uncle Vinny? Well, son of a bitch, they are," Max replied. "How'd you like that shot?"

"It was one of my personal favorites," Thorne said, "but forget the fucking shot for now. How about you figure out a way to get me off this fucking beach."

Thorne looked out at the water and the churning chaos of the battle that still waged.

"I'm sure as fuck not swimming my way over there," Thorne said.

"True," Max said. "I'll get a Zodiac and come get ya."

"The fuck you will," Darby interrupted over the com. "You can barely walk. No way you can climb into a Zodiac and pilot it over there."

"But you can, Darby!" Ingrid said. "The power is back on! I can remotely activate the pineapples again! You get up here and take the Zodiac to go get the commander!"

"On my way," Darby said.

Thorne watched as the waters suddenly went still.

"Better hurry," he said.

***

"That does it!" Carlos said. "It's fixed!"

"Thanks to Moshi," Cougher said. "So don't even try to take her glory."

"Yes, well, if she had calibrated her device properly then it wouldn't have shut down the engines," Carlos said.

"Shut up," Cougher said, "and get out of my engine room."

"I can't," Carlos said as he looked at all the metal sheeting that had been removed from the power equipment. "We need to reshield everything."

"Are you insane?" Cougher said. "After what just happened?"

"Cougher?" Lake slurred over the com. "Good work."

"Thanks," Cougher said. "What's going on up there?"

There was no answer.

"Lake?" Cougher asked.

Still no answer. Then a long, loud snore filled the com.

"Fuck," Cougher said as he looked at Moshi and Carlos. "Can you two handle it down here? I better get on the bridge and relieve Lake, or there's no one driving this boat."

"Yeah, get out," Carlos snapped then backed up as Cougher jammed a finger in his face.

"Do not break my engines again," Cougher said. "If you do, then you get fed to the monster shark. Got me?"

"Yes, yes, whatever," Carlos said. Cougher ran off and Carlos turned to Moshi. "Like I could break any of this primitive equipment."

Moshi raised her eyebrows.

"Oh, shut up and get to work," he snapped at her.

***

Ingrid helped get the last Zodiac lowered into the water, watched Darby speed off across the light waves, and then turned her attention back to her tablet.

"Darby? Do you read me?" Ingrid asked.

"Loud and clear," Darby replied.

"We may not have much time," Ingrid said. "I don't see the shark anywhere. As soon as you get Thorne, then race back here so I can activate the- Holy shit!"

The ship shuddered.

214

"Ingrid?" Darby asked over the com. "What's wrong?"

"I don't know," Ingrid replied. "Something hit the ship."

"Shark," Max said as he looked over the side of the ship and into the water below. "Big, fucking shark." He straightened up and grimaced at Ingrid. "I'd say we need a bigger boat, but I don't think a bigger boat would make a fucking difference. We're totally fucked if that thing breaches the hull."

"Darby?" Ingrid said.

"I heard," Darby replied. "Moving as fast as I can."

"I'm swimming to you," Thorne said over the com.

"No, stay put!" Max shouted as he focused his scope on his uncle. "You get back in that water and you're shark food!"

"No time to argue," Thorne said. "Ingrid needs to activate the pineapples. She can't do that while I'm in this lagoon. I'm swimming out to Darby."

The ship shuddered once more.

"What the fuck is happening?" Cougher asked as he came up on deck.

"Shark," Max and Ingrid replied together.

"Great," Cougher said. "I better take the wheel and get us the fuck out of here."

"We wait for my uncle and Darby," Max said.

"Like fuck we do," Cougher said as he took the steps up to the bridge two at a time. "We move this fucking ship, is what we do."

Max was about to respond when the ship was rocked so hard that he tumbled from his stool and cracked his head on the deck.

"Ow," he said.

"You okay?" Ingrid asked.

"Yeah," Max said. "I just hope everyone else is. I hate it when we split up."

"Me too," Ingrid replied then went back to checking her tablet. "Max?"

"I know, I know," he said as he sat up, ignoring the pain in his leg and his head. "You do what you have to do to save the ship."

Ingrid smiled weakly and nodded. "Okay. I'm going up with Cougher so I can watch the sonar. I'm sorry, Max."

"Don't be," he said. "They'll make it."

***

Gunnar stared as Ronald knelt and carefully rolled Lucy over.

"Uh," was all Gunnar could say as he stared at the fur-covered creature.

"Yes, he is the gigantopithecus you saw in the atrium, Doctor," Ballantine smiled. "How very perceptive of you."

"Uh," Gunnar replied, "he isn't wearing pants."

"Leave it to you to look right at his wang," Mike said.

"And you didn't?" Gunnar asked.

"'Sey? 'Sey, can you hear me?" Darren asked as he cradled Kinsey's head on his lap. "Jesus. Look at the bruising on her temple. If I get a hold of the asshole that did this, he's going to live a very, very long time."

"I think you have that wrong," Shane said as he stood over everyone and watched for any stray crewmembers that they may have missed during their first assault. "Pretty sure you're supposed to shorten the guy's life."

"Not with the amount of torture I have planned," Darren replied.

"Oh, right. Good call," Shane responded.

"'Ren?" Kinsey asked as she tried to open her eyes. "'Ren?"

Darren leaned in and kissed her then pulled back and smiled as he stroked the hair from her face.

"Hey there," he said, "how you feeling?"

Kinsey's eyes opened then she closed them quickly and turned her head to puke all over the sand.

"Concussion," Gunnar said. "Keep her still."

"Don't move, 'Sey," Darren said.

"Not going to," she whispered.

"You guys hear that?" Shane asked as he put a finger to his ear. "Are the coms back on?"

"It sounds like it," Ballantine said then glanced back at the small mountain that lay between them and the other side of the island. "The terrain is blocking the signal."

"There we go," Ronald said as he rolled Lucy back again. " have adjusted the compression suit's setting so that it is holding her blood pressure in check and also slowing the bleeding in he abdomen. She is not out of the woods, but she should live long enough for us to get her back to the ship."

"Then let's load up," Shane said as he tried hard to listen to the garbled voices that cut through the static on the com. "It's not sounding good."

***

Darby brought the Zodiac around as she reached Thorne. She let the motor idle and reached over the side of the raft to help the commander in.

"We have to wait at the gate," Thorne said, "or there's no point in setting those pineapples off."

"Understood," Darby nodded.

"Uncle Vinny?" Max asked over the com. "You think you two could hurry it up?"

"We'll do our best," Thorne replied as Darby took the throttle again and gunned the motor.

She swung the Zodiac around and aimed it towards the gate. As soon as they were outside the lagoon, she slowed the raft and steered it off to the side.

"Hey!" Max yelled. "Where the fuck are you going? Why aren't you coming this way?"

"Someone has to close the gate," Thorne replied. "We can't come right back to the ship. Is Ingrid there?"

"Yes, Commander," Ingrid replied, "I'm on the bridge."

"Good," Thorne said. "Fire off those pineapples and send the thing into lagoon. I'm getting back in the water and I'll make sure that the gate shuts it in."

"There's a problem with that," Ingrid said. "The shark isn't headed this way! I don't know where it's headed. I can't find it on the sonar!"

"What?" Max, Darby and Thorne exclaimed just before the Zodiac was launched into the air as the giant shark attacked from below.

***

Mike piloted the burdened Zodiac around the island. With everyone inside, plus the weight of the backups, it was a miracle the raft hadn't sunk as soon as they pushed off from the beach.

"Oh, shit," Shane gasped as they all watched the massive shark fall back into the water with the other Zodiac gripped in its jaws. "That's not fucking good!"

"Marty?" Darren called out on the com. "Do you read me, Lake?"

"Yeah, Lake's passed out," Cougher replied. "I've got the helm right now."

"What the fuck did we just see?" Darren asked.

"Thorne and Darby were in the raft," Ingrid interrupted. "They were waiting to shut the gate after I activate the pineapples, but the shark got to them first instead of coming back at the ship."

"Back at the ship?" Ballantine asked. "Is there much damage?"

"We don't know," Cougher said. "I sent some of the crew down below to look for breaches, but they haven't reported any yet."

"Good," Ballantine said, "because we need the ship in working order. I don't know how much time we have." Ballantine looked up at the sky and noted how the sun was slowly dipping towards the horizon. "The strike will come while it's still daylight so the blast can't be seen miles away."

"Awesome," Max replied sarcastically, "thanks for the nuke update. Now, how about someone go get my fucking uncle and love of my life, please!"

"Take us to the ship," Ballantine said to Mike. "Then we go get them."

"Will do," Mike said.

"Hey!" Max shouted over the com. "You're wasting time! Just go get them!"

"Dude," Shane said, "we saw what just happened. We don't even know if they're still alive. Lucy is bleeding out and Sis has a concussion. We're bringing them and the civilians back to the ship, then I swear I'll get in that water myself and grab that shark by the fucking tail if I have to."

"They're still alive," was all Max said. "They have to be."

***

The Zodiac was crushed easily and Darby had just managed to get free of it before the shark's jaws closed fully and swallowed the raft whole.

"Commander!" she called out. "Thorne!"

"Here," Thorne replied from below her in the water. "Come on."

He tapped her ankle and pointed towards the gate controls that were about a hundred yards away. Darby nodded and swam as fast and hard as she could after Thorne. She never looked back, knowing that she didn't have the luxury of time to check on the shark's location.

She was about halfway to the gate controls when she felt herself start to tire. Then the throbbing began and she looked down to see the gash across her right thigh.

"Fuck," she said, "I got nicked."

Thorne reached the big, red button then turned and looked back at Darby.

"That's more than a nick," he said. "Ingrid? Can you hear me?"

"Yes," Ingrid replied, "I see her vitals and I'm adjusting the suit to help."

Darby moaned as the compression suit tightened about her right leg and hip. Thorne swam out to her and helped get her to the gate controls.

"You going to make it?" he asked.

"I think so," Darby said then shook her head back and forth. "Yeah. I'll make it."

"Good," Thorne said, "because we have a job to do."

They both looked at the massive shark that had finished with the Zodiac and was swimming back and forth between the lagoon and the B3.

"What's it doing?" Darby asked.

"It's your blood," Thorne said. "Its instincts tell it to follow the scent trail to you, but its programming says to go after the ship."

"It's stuck in a loop," Darby said.

"Yes," Thorne replied. "It doesn't know which way to go."

***

Ballantine stepped onto the bridge with Dr. Morganton and Boris while Ronald stood outside on the landing.

"Hello there, Ingrid," Ballantine said. "This is Boris and our hairy guest there is Ronald."

Ingrid stared with her mouth hanging open.

"Yes, that's generally the reaction," Ballantine said as he snapped his fingers in front of her face, "but you're going to have to save being stunned for later. Right now, we need you to send that shark into the lagoon so we can be on our way before the ICBM turns this area into a radioactive mess."

"Yeah, sure," Ingrid said as she had to force herself to look away from Ronald and down at her tablet. "Right. Shark. Send shark."

"Good girl," Ballantine said. "Now, if my ear heard right, the shark doesn't know whether it wants to eat Darby or attack the ship, yes?"

"Yes," Ingrid nodded.

"Is that Bigfoot?" Cougher asked, not having to turn his attention away from Ronald at all. "That's a fucking bigfoot, isn't it?"

"I am not a fucking anything," Ronald frowned and he leaned down so he could look through the bridge's hatch at Cougher. "I am a gigantopithecus, an ancient and noble line of hominids."

"Wow," Cougher stared. "Bigfoot."

"Well, you're a rude one," Ronald said and left the landing to walk up to the observation deck.

"Did I piss it off? Is it going to eat me?" Cougher asked.

"Yes, to both questions," Ballantine said with a smirk. "Now, call down to the galley and have them bring up every bit of meat we have, will you?"

"Meat?" Cougher asked.

"Meat," Ballantine nodded.

***

"Set her there!" Gunnar yelled as Shane and Darren carried Lucy into the infirmary. "Scrub up, because I'll need your help!"

"I need to go and help Uncle Vinny and Darby," Shane said.

"I have to go get Kinsey," Darren said, "she's still up on deck."

"Fine," Gunnar said. "Shane, you go get your uncle and Darby. Darren, you're staying here. Kinsey will be fine, but Lucy may not be."

Darren started to argue, but Gunnar held up a bloody hand.

"Do what I fucking say, D!" Gunnar snapped. "I'm Chief Medical Officer on this ship and during a medical emergency. You do what the fuck I tell you to do!"

"Yeah, right," Darren nodded as he hurried over to the sink. "Sorry."

Gunnar looked over at Shane. "Go. We have this. Bring Vincent and Darby back to us."

Shane nodded and took off out of the infirmary.

***

Blood, the ever pulling call.

The shark swung its head about and began to swim towards Darby and her irresistible wound. Its tail whipped back and forth, as it built up speed and came at the woman in a frenzy of evolutionary instinct and pure will.

Then the splashing began and the scent of more blood, more meat, and more food. There was no longer a decision to be made. Meat, blood, and a target were right behind it. The scent of the meat and blood wasn't as fresh as it was coming from the other way, but it was still the scent of blood.

The shark turned itself quickly and shot towards the B3.

***

"Here it comes!" Ingrid cried. "Get ready, everybody! If the pineapples don't work then it's going to hit us hard!"

"Great," Cougher said, "just great."

Ingrid watched the shark approach as it moved at a speed she really never thought possible. Just before it reached the pineapples closest to the ship, she pressed the button on her tablet and waited.

Everyone waited.

"What's happening?" Darby asked over the com.

"Is it turning back to you?" Ingrid asked.

"No!" Darby said.

"Shit," Ingrid replied, "shit, shit, shit."

"Hold on," Darby said. "Wait. Oh, wow…"

"That's high praise indeed," Ballantine said. "A Darby 'oh, wow' means quite a lot."

***

The sensory assault was beyond torture for the massive creature. It felt as if its own teeth had punctured its brain, sending bolts of pain shooting through every nerve ending. The shark turned and fled, forgetting the lure of the meat, forgetting the lure of the blood, forgetting the target that waited in the water, ripe and ready for destruction.

All the shark wanted to do was escape the agony that threatened to overwhelm it.

Then the agony built and built. Every direction it went it was tormented by its own senses; senses that had never let it down before, never betrayed it in such a way that all it wanted to do was dive down to the bottom of the ocean and die.

Then the pain leveled off and the shark found a window of relief just ahead. A sanctuary where it could retreat from the brutal torture that the open ocean hammered down on it.

The shark aimed itself for the lagoon and put every ounce of energy it had into getting away from the never-ending sensory overload.

***

"There it goes!" Ingrid cried over the com. "It's coming for you!"

"We see it," Thorne said. "Trust me, we see it."

Thorne looked over at Darby and was alarmed to see the woman barely conscious. She floated in the water, her legs and arms moving just enough to keep her in place. At that moment, Thorne's respect for the woman as a warrior grew. Not that he needed to see anything more to prove that Darby was the most skilled and determined on his Team. The fact that she refused to succumb to her wound and situation made him smile.

If he could smile around the rebreather mustache.

The shark rocketed towards the lagoon.

Thorne watched it rush at him and for a split second, he almost lost his resolve. The beast didn't look like it was headed for the lagoon's opening, but right for him and Darby. Maybe the blood was what it wanted most after all.

"Darby," Thorne said, "we may need to move."

"Fuck...that," Darby said as she reached out and placed her hand on Thorne's as it rested on the bug, red button. "It'll turn."

The shark came at them, its mouth open wide. Thorne pulled his channel pistol and took aim, knowing that the weapon would do almost nothing against a creature that size.

Then the monster seemed to shudder and suddenly adjusted course. It aimed itself directly into the lagoon and before Thorne knew it, the creature had passed him and Darby and it was through the gate.

Darby's hand weakly pushed down on Thorne's and they both pressed the button, activating the lagoon's containment gate. Before the gate was even closed, Thorne had one arm under Darby and was swimming them both away from the lagoon and up to the surface.

"Hold on," Thorne said. "You stay with me. We'll get you on board and Gunnar will fix you up."

There was no reply and Thorne looked over at the woman. Her eyes were closed and her head bobbed loosely in the water.

"Oh, fuck," Thorne said as they broke the surface.

Hands grabbed at him and he started to fight, and he then saw the Zodiac and his nephew Shane above him.

"I don't know if she's breathing!" Thorne yelled as he pulled the rebreather from his mouth. "She's lost too much blood!"

"I got her," Shane said as he pulled Darby up into the Zodiac. "Get your ass in now, Uncle Vinny."

Thorne grabbed onto the side of the Zodiac and hauled himself up just as Mike swung the raft around and gunned it back to the B3. He slumped into the raft and looked over at Darby's sheet white face.

"Somebody better tell Max," Thorne said.

"He's listening," Shane replied as he put pressure on Darby's wound. "He'll be waiting for us."

Thorne leaned back against the Zodiac and closed his eyes for just a second. He needed to catch his breath, to get just a small respite from the chaos of the moment. He was getting too old for the Team shit and the old SEAL adage of "sleep when you can" was no longer going to be enough for his body.

When they got back to the B3, no matter what Darby's outcome, Thorne was going to make a few changes.

Chapter Ten- Under Their Own Power

Ballantine stood on the upper deck next to Thorne as they watched Darby be carried through the hatch and down into the ship.

"She'll make it," Thorne said.

"Yes, I am sure she will," Ballantine replied.

"She's strong," Thorne said.

"The strongest person I have ever known," Ballantine responded.

"You going to be okay?" Thorne asked.

"I'll be fine," Ballantine said.

There was a sharp ringing from Ballantine's pocket and he pulled out a sleek, black sat phone.

"Is that a different phone?" Thorne asked as he looked at the phone. "How many of those do you have?"

Ballantine gave him a sly grin. "As many as I need."

"Of course," Thorne nodded. "You better get that before they hang up."

"Oh, this person would never hang up on me," Ballantine said, "but if you'll excuse me."

Ballantine walked a few feet away and took a deep breath.

"William," he said as he answered the call, "what do you have for me?"

Thorne didn't bother to pretend he wasn't listening as he watched Ballantine closely. Nor did Ballantine pretend he was been listened to.

"That close? Right, no, I see... No, the ship is crippled... Yes, I understand and I appreciate it. You've risked everything to help me out and it won't be forgotten... We can try, but I'm not sure the facility's vaults will be enough to save us... Yes, quite unfortunate. Has Protocol Fifty-four been fully implemented? Good. The company is liquidated? Excellent. Thank you for overseeing that part... Yes, yes, I know... I can't say it hasn't been fun, William. Give my best to your wife and little Kristi and thank you again for everything... Hey, hey, cheer up, man. I've had a great run and the people I'm with are professionals. When you watch the satellite feed, be sure to say a prayer for us."

Ballantine gave Thorne a wide grin then wiped it from his mouth so it wouldn't be reflected in his voice.

"Right, how stupid of me, of course the satellites have been retasked. Can't have any record of an illegal nuclear detonation anywhere on the servers. The international shitstorm that would happen if those records were leaked would be catastrophic to the United States' intelligence community. God knows those people don't need more of that."

Thorne furrowed his brow with worry, but Ballantine gave him a wink and a thumbs up.

"William, again, thank you," Ballantine said. "I wish you all the luck in life. Goodbye, friend."

Ballantine ended the call then threw the phone over the side of the ship.

"I'm sure you have another one," Thorne said. Ballantine shrugged.

"We have about an hour before the ICBM reaches the island," Ballantine said to Thorne. "Not much time to get away, but it should be enough with Moshi's modifications."

"What the fuck was that all about?" Thorne asked. "We are not on the island and the ship is not without power."

"Well, duh," Ballantine replied, "but they don't know that. I just provided all the cover we need for our deaths."

"For our what?" Thorne exclaimed. "Our deaths?"

"It's the only way to get governments and certain organizations to leave us alone," Ballantine shrugged. "We have to die in order to be free. They will hound us to the ends of the Earth if we don't take ourselves off the board."

"So we fake our deaths and then what?" Thorne asked. "We spend the rest of our lives in hiding on this ship?"

"What? No, don't be stupid," Ballantine said. "Do you know how valuable we'll be as an outfit when we become ghosts? I have more than a few aliases I can use to secure us employment when needed. We'll be active and alive, just the only people that will know it."

"You're insane," Thorne said. "This should have been something we discussed before you pulled the trigger. You had no right to do this to everyone, Ballantine."

"Bullshit, Vincent," Ballantine replied as he turned and looked out at the island. "I had every right. This is what you signed up for back at that cabin on the California coast all that time ago. You knew who I was then and you know who I am now. I'm the man that kills us all, but makes us more alive than any of us have ever been before."

Thorne started to respond then just shook his head.

"You'll see," Ballantine said, "it'll all work out just fine."

Far off, in the island's lagoon, the massive shark surfaced for a second then disappeared below the water once more.

"I will miss the sharks, though," Ballantine said. "That baby is the last of her kind. We're done with the things from here on out. When this island is obliterated, that shark will be as well. Pretty much anything within a mile radius will be vaporized. Oh well, sharks aren't the only adventures out there, as you well know."

"You crazy fuck," Thorne said. "I'm going to go check on my daughter."

"Good thing to do," Ballantine said. "I'm going to make sure we turn this ship around and get away from this doomed island as fast as possible."

"Yeah, you do that," Thorne responded as he walked off.

Ballantine watched the man go then turned and hurried to the steps and up to the bridge.

***

Sweat dripped from Gunnar's forehead as he finished suturing Darby's leg. He'd managed to stop the bleeding, but she'd lost so much blood that keeping her stable was the real trick.

"Can you dress that?" Gunnar asked Darren as he stepped back from the table. "My eyes are about to cross."

"Yeah, I got it," Darren said. "Check on Lucy, then sit your ass down."

Gunnar gave him a weak smile then started to move over to the table that Lucy lay on, but shouting from out in the passageway got his attention and he turned towards the door.

"That was something you should have accounted for, Carlos!" Ballantine roared. "That is why you are still employed by me! So that you can predict technological issues like this and fix them before we have to escape nuclear destruction! Is that too much to fucking ask? Is it?"

Carlos and Ballantine hurried past the door just as Gunnar got there. He looked into the passageway and saw Shane and Mike rushing towards him along with several members of the support crew.

"What is going on?" Gunnar asked.

"That device of Moshi's that makes the engines go way faster won't work if the engines are shielded with Carlos's metal shit," Shane said as he skidded to a stop. "We're all heading down to the engine room to strip off the shielding so Moshi can get her thing running again."

"The engines are running fine now," Gunnar said, "what's the problem?"

"The problem is we have an ICBM headed straight for the island and if we don't get clear we'll be crispy critters in about forty-five minutes," Shane said.

"Plus the surge from the blast," Mike added. "These waters are about to be hell. The nuke could produce fifty foot waves easy."

Shane looked in at Darby and Lucy. "You better secure them and do what you can now while we have power," he said, "because even if we get clear of the blast radius, we're going to be dead in the water as soon as the EMP hits us. Ballantine doesn't think we can outrun that."

"Fuck," Gunnar said then waved at Shane and Mike. "Go help. Do whatever you can."

The two men nodded and sprinted away. Gunnar was about to turn his attention back to his patients when he heard Max call out.

"Care if I sit with you guys?" Max asked as he limped down the passageway. "I'm not going to be much use to anyone else. I'd rather hang in the infirmary with you and the ladies."

"How's Kinsey?" Gunnar asked as Max hobbled through the door. "Do I need to go up there and check on her?"

"There's no one up there," Max said. "Ballantine had all the upper decks cleared. Hatches are being battened and shit secured. Even if we live, things aren't going to be fun."

"Have they ever?" Gunnar asked.

Max looked from Gunnar to Darren and couldn't help but smile. "Well, yeah. I've never had more fun in my life. Haven't you guys been having a total blast?"

"Nope," Darren said.

Gunnar sighed. "No."

"Alright then," Max said and pointed at a stool. "Set that by my lady friend, will ya? I need to take a load off this leg. Hey! Darby and I will have matching leg wounds!"

"Not quite," Gunnar said. "Yours wasn't nearly as life threatening as Darby's."

"Do me a favor and don't tell her that, okay?" Max said. "I want to milk the whole wounded together thing for as long as I can."

"Jesus, Max," Gunnar said, "you really have no idea what you're doing, do you?"

"What? What do you mean?" Max asked.

"Never mind," Gunnar said as he plopped a stool next to Darby's table. "Just sit down and rest that leg, and rest that brain. You may have overloaded it today."

"You're the doctor," Max smiled as he sat down.

***

Carlos's shielding was torn free of the engine equipment and tossed out into the passageway. Men hauled it as far away from the room while Moshi squatted inside, her hands working as fast as possible to get her device hooked back up.

"You can't blame me," Carlos snapped at Ballantine as they stood over Moshi and watched her work. "I did what you said and created shielding for the engines. You never said it had to work with Moshi's booster. Not once did you mention that."

"We are done discussing it, Carlos," Ballantine replied, "not another word on the subject."

"There," Moshi said quietly.

"It's finished?" Ballantine asked. Moshi nodded. "Excellent. Thank you for doing your job, Moshi. It's greatly appreciated."

He tapped at the com in his ear.

"Cougher? You set up in the auxiliary bridge?"

"Yeah, I'm set up," Cougher said.

"Then push this ship to its limits," Ballantine ordered. "You red line these engines as much as you can and get us as far as you can, do you hear me?"

"Yes, I hear you," Cougher said. "You're talking in my ear. All ahead, full steam."

"Thank you," Ballantine said, "now, patch me through to the ship's PA, will you?"

"I'm not the communications officer," Cougher said.

"Just do it," Ballantine snapped then looked at Moshi again. "Why can't everyone be as agreeably silent like you?"

Moshi just shrugged.

***

"Attention crew of the Beowulf III," Ballantine's voice rang throughout the ship. "As all of you have heard by now, there is a nuclear missile coming to destroy the island we were just by. While I had intended to use the missile as a way to fake our deaths and free us from the pursuit of our enemies, there have been some unforeseen technical issues that could derail that plan and it may lead to our actual deaths. For this, I apologize.

"Now, let me just say before everyone panics that my gut is telling me we will survive. Unfortunately, my gut is also telling me that we will not survive unscathed. The ship's engines have been modified and we are currently moving at sixty knots. That should get us clear of the blast radius, and hopefully, any dangerous waves that are produced by the blast, but it will not get us clear of the EMP that the blast will produce.

"Carlos has been working hard to shield what equipment he can, but in order for the engines to work at the capacity we need them, they cannot be shielded. That means once the EMP reaches us, it is highly likely that our engines will be fried. Will they be too damaged to repair? That I do not know, but let me assure you that I have the utmost confidence in this crew that we have the skills and expertise needed to get us up, and going as soon as possible.

"Until that time, I ask that you remain at your stations or in your cabins. Strap yourselves in and hang on. If you thought life with me was bumpy before, it's about to get a whole lot worse.

"Thank you for listening. Ballantine out."

***

"Well, that was a bunch of crap," Thorne muttered as he sat next to Kinsey's bunk and held her hand. She muttered something back, but he couldn't make it out so he just leaned in and kissed her brow. "I think you could have done a better job at a rally speech than that."

He leaned back in his chair and closed his eyes. All there was left to do was wait.

***

The missile soared above the ocean, racing at over 15,000 miles per hour. The water that was only twenty feet below it, spread out in a wide fan in the wake of its passage.

The island, its target, lay before it, thirty miles away, then five, and then none.

The missile impacted on the beach that connected with the dock. Both beach and dock were gone in less than .05 seconds after impact. The entire island was gone in less than .1 seconds.

All that was left was a massive fireball and mushroom cloud that reached far up into the late afternoon sky.

The shockwave from the blast nearly carved out the ocean around it, peeling back the water all the way down to the ocean floor. What water that wasn't vaporized instantly was pushed out at a rate of several hundred miles per hour.

A wave began to grow from the force and it too climbed up into the late afternoon sky. When it reached its crest, it was over one hundred feet tall, and it carried something with it.

***

"Hold on!" Shane shouted as he sat on the infirmary floor, having decided to join his brother, Mike, Gunnar, and Darren as they watched over Lucy and Darby. "Here it comes!"

"Dude," Max said. "We aren't going to feel the EMP. It's not like it's made of rock or something. We'll probably get a little nauseous and then the lights will go out."

"I know," Shane said. "I just wanted to yell something dramatic."

"Well, that's okay then," Max said and opened his mouth wide. "We're all going to die!"

"You two are not helping," Gunnar said.

"We aren't hurting," Shane smiled.

***

Ingrid, Carlos, and Moshi sat on the floor of the Toyshop, all wearing harnesses that clipped into rings in the floor.

"Will the armory make it?" Ingrid asked. "Did you shield it well enough?"

"I hope so," Carlos said, "but I'd be a moron to say I'm certain."

"Wow," Ingrid laughed, "never thought I'd hear you admit that."

"Never thought I'd admit it," Carlos said. "Don't tell Ballantine."

***

Ballantine sat up in the briefing room, his sunglasses on and his head turned towards the huge nuclear fireball off in the distance. He did some quick calculations then took a drink from the glass of scotch he held. He began to mentally countdown as he watched the horizon. When his mental countdown hit zero, he drained his glass and stood up.

He grimaced just as the lights went out and he felt the engines die from deep within the ship.

"Sorry, everyone," he said to himself, "but now we really get to work."

***

The days went by slowly as the ship languished in the open waters.

The three women watched from the observation deck as Lake and Cougher stood below the improvised sails and argued over the proper way to secure the rigging to the helipads.

"How many times have we had to listen to this shit?" Lucy asked as she shifted her position in the lounge chair. She winced as the wound in her belly stretched, but she didn't worry about the pain. Gunnar had said she was out of the woods over a week before. "Why are they still fighting about the sails?"

"They have nothing better to do," Kinsey said as she closed her eyes and leaned her head back into her chair. Her body was roasting from the bright sun, but it felt good to soak up the rays. It made her feel alive and considering how many times in her life she almost didn't have that luxury, she didn't intend to take a single second for granted. "Let them bicker. It keeps them occupied and out of our hair."

"Three weeks straight," Darby said as she adjusted her bikini top and then reached for her water bottle that sat next to her chair on the deck. "Three fucking weeks. I'm going to kill them both if they don't shut up by tomorrow."

"You're giving them a deadline?" Lucy laughed. "I think you're softening, Darby."

"Hardly," Darby replied then turned her head and shielded her eyes as someone came up the steps from the lower deck. "Woman time."

"Is that code?" Max grinned as he stepped onto the deck, a cane in his hand. "You left this in our cabin."

"I don't need a cane," Darby said. "It will only slow me down and make me dependent. I'll heal faster if I put as much weight on my leg as possible to get it back to full strength."

"You realize that goes against all modern medical wisdom, right?" Max said as he set the cane by her chair then pulled up one of his own. "Don't make me tell Gunnar."

"Woman time," Lucy said as she lifted her sunglasses and glared at Max.

"What?" Max asked. "You're serious?"

"Woman time," Kinsey said. "Not Max time. Go play with your brother or find something else to do. We have the observation deck for the next hour."

"You have to be joking," Max said. "You can't just call dibs on the observation deck."

"Yes, we can," Lucy said, "and if you have a problem with it then go talk to Thorne. He's the one that put the sign-up sheet in the mess."

"Wait, what sign-up sheet?" Max asked, looking at Darby. "What did I miss?"

"You missed your chance to sign up," Darby said. "You shouldn't have overslept this morning."

"Overslept? You told me to sleep in! You said that whatever Thorne had to say you'd fill me in on!" Max protested then arrowed his eyes. "Hold on...did you know this was going down? Did you block me out on purpose?"

"Hey!" Shane shouted as he climbed the stairs and stormed onto the observation deck. "What the fuck is this shit about a sign-up sheet?"

"Oh, did you miss the meeting too?" Lucy asked. "Bummer."

"Bummer?" Shane snapped. "You said it had been cancelled!"

"Did I?" Lucy shrugged. "I guess I was wrong."

"Dude, we got screwed," Max said. "They had inside info and totally blocked us out. The observation deck is booked for another hour for 'woman time'."

"Woman time? What the fuck is that?" Shane growled.

"That is us sitting up here without worrying about all the men staring at our tits and asses," Kinsey said. "You think it's fun being on a ship full of men, stranded out at sea?"

"It kind of is," Lucy said, "but mostly, it kinda isn't."

"Woman time," Darby said. "Leave."

Max sputtered and fumed then just shook his head and walked over to his brother.

"Are we just going to take this?" Shane asked.

"Let's talk to Uncle Vinny," Max said, then growled as he saw Ingrid and Moshi in their swimsuits with towels and sunscreen in hand come up the steps. "Not you guys, too."

"Sorry we're late," Ingrid said as she and Moshi pushed past the brothers. "Hope we still have some time left."

"Yeah, but not much," Max snapped, "only an hour."

"Only an hour of woman time," Kinsey smiled, "but then there's two hours blocked off after that for book club."

"Oh, good," Ingrid said. "Although I don't think my skin can take three hours out here in the sun."

"Take whatever time you want," Lucy said. "The deck is ours for the next three hours."

"Book club? Book club!" Max shouted. "What fucking book are you reading?"

Kinsey lowered her sunglasses and looked at Max like he was a small, simple child. "Come on, Max, everyone knows book clubs have nothing to do with books. Stop whining and take off, will ya? Or we'll have to tack on more time at the end of book club."

Even with his wounded leg, Max still had to be dragged away by Shane.

"Come on," Shane said, "we're getting this worked out right now."

***

Ballantine, Darren, and Thorne, all studied the map that was laid out on the briefing room table.

"You're saying it's here?" Darren asked as he pointed to a spot on the map that held nothing but open water. "How is it possible for there to be an uncharted, secret island in the 21st century?"

"Easy," Ballantine said, "you don't let it get charted. It's not on any shipping lanes, it's in a permanent satellite blind spot, and there is no other land for nearly a five thousand square miles. No one in their right mind would go there."

"Which is obviously why we're going there," Thorne said.

"Obviously," Ballantine laughed. "Trust me, gentlemen, it is our only option, and I assure you that you won't be disappointed when we get there."

"It's just like the other uncharted island?" Darren asked. "With the same type of facility?"

"In a way," Ballantine said, "this island's facility is much larger due to the nature of the work done there, but yes, it is the same. We'll have more than enough supplies to keep us fed and in relative comfort while we repair the ship. Once the Beowulf III is back in action, then we can decide what to do from there."

"Fresh water?" Thorne asked.

"An almost infinite amount," Ballantine said. "Almost. Trust me-"

"Stop saying that," Thorne interrupted. "I don't trust you. No one trusts you. You want me to trust you? Then make good on what you are saying here and now. We get to that island and I find it's all that you say it is, and then we'll be on the road to trust."

"Of course," Ballantine nodded. "I understand."

"So, if it's there," Darren said as he tapped at the empty space on the map. "Then we should arrive in the next day or two as long as we have the wind with us."

"Exactly," Ballantine said. "I'm sure everyone will-"

"What the fuck is this about a sign-up sheet?" Max snarled as he came into the briefing room. "When the hell did that happen?"

"This morning," Thorne replied. "You missed it. Deal. Go away."

Shane pulled his brother back and held up his hands. "Uncle Vinny, you have to be joking. Why do we need a sign-up sheet for the observation deck?"

"Because we have all been in close quarters and under a lot of stress," Thorne replied. "A little space is good. Now, like I just said, deal and go away." Max started to argue, but Thorne held up a finger and he closed his mouth. "Good. Go away."

Max shook with anger then turned and stormed back out of the briefing room with Shane right behind.

"What was that about?" Darren asked. "A sign-up sheet?"

Thorne waited a few seconds to make sure the Reynolds were gone then grinned from ear to ear at Darren.

"It's all bullshit," Thorne said. "Darby was bored and wanted to push some buttons so she came up with the fake sign-up sheet to fuck with the boys. It worked. I haven't seen them this bent out of shape for a long time."

"That's because they are out of weed," Darren replied.

"Are they?" Thorne said. "Huh."

"It is always fun to see how people choose to amuse themselves," Ballantine said, "but I guess you must in times like these."

"That's what I've learned over the years," Thorne said. "If people don't have a chance to let off steam, then they'll snap and kill each other."

"We wouldn't want that," Ballantine nodded.

"No, we wouldn't," Thorne agreed.

***

"Hey, 'Ren," Kinsey said as she stepped from the shower and found Darren waiting there with a towel in hand. "I could have gotten that myself."

"We have to talk, 'Sey," Darren said.

"Can I put some clothes on first?" she asked as she started drying off.

"No," Darren said. "This is the only way I can keep you from dodging me. I have to catch you naked coming from the shower."

"You just wanted to do a little ogling," Kinsey smiled. "Don't make me have Darby create a sign-up sheet for the showers too."

"That was pretty funny," Darren smiled. "The boys are still pissed."

"They'll get over it as soon as they find out it was a practical joke," Kinsey said as she wrapped the towel around herself and walked over to a bench by the wall where her clothes lay folded. "They love practical jokes."

"They love playing them on others," Darren said, "not when they're played on them."

"Oh, well," Kinsey said as she got dressed.

Darren reached out and lightly touched her temple. She didn't shy away.

"What are we doing, 'Sey?" Darren asked.

"I don't know, 'Ren," Kinsey replied. "Honestly, I don't. I love you more than anything in the world, but I don't know if I can risk getting hurt by you again."

"You did some hurting there as well," Darren said, "but, you're right, I fucked it all up. I have no illusions that this isn't all on me."

"It's not all on you," Kinsey said as she pulled a t-shirt on. "Only ninety-nine percent."

"So?" he asked.

"So, we keep going," Kinsey said. "We keep talking and we see what happens."

"That's what we've been doing," Darren said. "I need more, 'Sey. I need to know if we have a chance to be together again."

Kinsey didn't reply as she pulled on a pair of shorts, put on her socks then laced up her shoes. Finished getting dressed, she moved in close to Darren, put her hands on his cheeks, and kissed him.

"We'll be together again," she said, "I promise. Just let it happen, okay?"

"I'm not good with-"

"I know," Kinsey interrupted. "You never have been, but if we are going to avoid repeating our previous disaster, then you're going to have to let go and wait. It's not as if it'll be forever. I mean, I'm pretty fucking horny right now and it's taking all my willpower not to fuck your brains out." She patted his cheeks. "Hey, a little anticipation never killed anyone."

She turned and walked from the showers, leaving Darren just to stare after her.

***

The island was twice the size of the one that had been nuked only a few weeks earlier, but that wasn't the only difference. Instead of a long dock leading to a beach, nothing was there but cliffs, huge, sheer cliffs that reached for hundreds of feet into the air. Far off, there could be seen the cloud shrouded peak of a massive mountain.

"That's not the same as the other island," Thorne said as he stood at the railing next to Ballantine. "Where have you taken us?"

"Not to worry, Commander," Ballantine said. "It will all be fine."

"Should we lower the sails and drop anchor?" Lake asked from Ballantine's other side. "Or do we need to sail around to a different spot?"

"No, no, this will do," Ballantine said as he pointed at a dark spot at the base of cliffs. "We can take the Zodiac in through that cave. Once I've disengaged the security protocols, then we can bring the ship in to dry dock."

"Dry dock?" Darren asked. "What do you mean?"

Ballantine turned and looked at the rest of the crew as they stood up on deck and stared at the island. His eyes rested on Ronald's for a second, who was standing off to the side with Boris, still not exactly accepted by any of the crew. Ronald met Ballantine's gaze, looked out at the island, and then returned his attention to Ballantine and nodded slightly.

"You see cliffs, I know," Ballantine said to everyone, "but part of those cliffs open up. We'll be able to tow the Beowulf III inside for repairs."

"Tow?" Max asked. "Is there a tug boat or something?"

"Or something," Ballantine smiled. "Now, I'll be going in, as well as Commander Thorne, Mr. Chambers, Mr. Reynolds, the one not still nursing a leg wound, and Ms. Thorne. I don't believe we need more than that. The rest of you will remain on the ship and get your gear together. We'll return with a couple more rafts to haul everyone over. I say it'll be no more than an hour, tops."

No one argued and Ballantine smiled.

***

The cliff loomed over them, casting the Zodiac into a deep, dark shadow.

"What's through there?" Thorne shouted over the motor noise. "Is that how you get into the facility?"

"It's how you get into the island," Ballantine replied, as he adjusted their speed and direction so they were pointed directly at the cave before them. "The facility is up river a bit."

Before Thorne could ask about the river, they were in the cave and plunged into darkness. Darren and Kinsey cracked large glow sticks and held them over their heads to light their way, while Shane kept a tight grip on his sniper rifle.

They rode in silence for several minutes before they saw light up ahead. Ballantine slowed the motor even more and they basically drifted from the cave and into sunlight that was filtered through tall trees and thick foliage.

"Holy jungle boat ride," Shane said. "This place is crazy."

"It is," Ballantine said, "but a good crazy. You will be amazed at what this island has to offer. I called the other one paradise, but I was exaggerating. This island. This island is true paradise. In so many ways."

The motor purred as Ballantine moved them up the wide river. The sounds of jungle life filled the air and Kinsey pointed as she saw a group of monkeys sitting in a tree.

"Are they real?" she asked.

"They are," Ballantine said, "and thank you for checking. It's always good to ask around here."

"More experiments?" Thorne asked as he turned and focused on Ballantine. "Do we need to be worried?"

"Not particularly," Ballantine said. "The staff will have everything well in hand."

"Staff?" Darren asked. "You didn't say there would be other people here."

"Didn't I?" Ballantine smirked. "Oops."

"Not helping with the trust issue, Ballantine," Thorne growled.

"Relax, Commander," Ballantine chuckled. "You are about to see what trust is. These people are quite possibly the loyalist folks that I have ever had...the...pleasure..."

Ballantine trailed off and his face went white as the Zodiac motored around a bend in the river and came to a scorched ruin of what looked to have been an immense facility made up of several buildings. All that remained were a few blackened walls and some steel beams.

"No," Ballantine whispered, "no, no, no."

"Ballantine?" Shane asked. "Is this part of the illusion?"

"No," Ballantine replied.

"Yeah, you said no already," Kinsey said. "What the hell happened?"

Ballantine gunned the motor and sped the Zodiac over to a splintered dock that stuck out into the river. When they were only a few feet from the dock, he killed the motor and stood up. As soon as they were within reach, he grabbed onto a ladder and hauled himself up.

"Hey!" Thorne shouted as the Zodiac kept floating past the dock. "What the fuck?"

"Stay in the raft," Ballantine ordered. "Bring it back around and wait for me."

He took off at a jog and was quickly lost from sight as he stepped into the ruined buildings.

"That's not cool," Shane said as Thorne took Ballantine's place at the motor. "Nope, totally not cool. Not cool at all."

"What do you think happened?" Kinsey asked, as Thorne turned them around and positioned them by the dock's ladder. "What was this place?"

Before anyone could respond, there was a loud roar from deep in the jungle. The sound sent chills up and down everyone's spines and they all turned to look at each other.

"That was either something close or it was something very big a long ways off," Shane said. "I'm hoping for close. Not that I want whatever just roared to be close, but it would be better than-"

"Shane? Shut the fuck up," Thorne said quietly. "Just shut up and listen."

They all listened and soon realized that the jungle sounds weren't exactly ones they recognized. Another roar, this time much closer, made them jump and Thorne pointed at Shane.

"Get up there," he said. "I want eyes on this place. We can't see shit with this dock in the way."

Shane didn't argue. He strapped his rifle to his back and grabbed onto the ladder. He barely had time to get onto the dock and stand up straight before he saw Ballantine running towards him, his eyes wide with fear.

"Go!" Ballantine shouted as he waved his hands. "Go, go, go! Get back in the raft! We have to get out of here now!"

Shane didn't have to be told twice and he quickly got his ass back into the Zodiac, with Ballantine right behind him.

"Get us back to the Beowulf now, Commander!" Ballantine yelled. "Do not slow down for anything!"

There were the sounds of trees snapping in half and something very large stomping its way towards the river.

"GO!" Ballantine yelled. He was answered by a roar that made everyone clamp their hands over their ears.

Thorne gunned the motor and sped away from the dock. He aimed them back the way they had come then looked over his shoulder.

"Fuck me," he whispered as he saw what had made the roars come tearing from the jungle and into the ruins. "Ballantine, what have you done? Where did you bring us?"

They all watched as a creature that could only be described as a dinosaur, and looked eerily similar to a Tyrannosaurus Rex, but much, much larger, stopped by the edge of the river, opened its mouth wide, and roared again.

"Holy fucking shit," Shane said. "You asshole. You brought us to Jurassic Park! What the fuck were you thinking?"

"They weren't supposed to be this far along!" Ballantine cried, looking more shaken than any of them had ever seen him before. "This is years ahead of schedule!"

"What is going on," Thorne snarled. "What was that thing?"

"It was a fucking dinosaur," Darren said. "How the hell do we deal with something like that?"

"We'll figure it out," Kinsey said as she looked at Ballantine. "We can take that thing out if we need to. We're Team fucking Grendel. We'll fuck that up and anything else that comes at us."

"If it were only that simple," Ballantine said as they approached the mouth of the cave. "That creature is nothing compared to what else was being developed here. That's a puppy dog. It's the full grown wolves we have to worry about."

"Wolves?" Shane asked as they entered the darkness of the cave once again. "That's a metaphor, right Ballantine?" The man didn't respond. "Ballantine? That's a metaphor, right?"

"I don't know," Ballantine replied, barely louder than the motor. "I fucking don't know."

***

"Welcome back to the land of the living, Mr. De Bruhl."

Popeye's eyes opened slowly and painfully. He tried to turn his head, but found he was restrained and couldn't move a single muscle. All he could do was stare at the face that loomed over him. He didn't recognize the face, but he recognized the attitude.

Clean cut, young, ambitious. It was everything he loathed and a major reason he liked being a sailor on the open sea. The man glanced up at something out of Popeye's line of sight.

"You're thinking of the ocean," Clean Cut said. "Perfect. That's what I need you to think about. Now, let's try for ships."

Clean Cut kept his eyes averted from Popeye.

"Where am I?" Popeye asked. "Who the fuck are you?"

"No, no, Mr. De Bruhl, I ask the questions," Clean Cut replied. "You don't even have to answer them out loud. All I need you to do is think about the answers. Let that subconscious do the work for you."

"I don't know what the fuck you're talking about," Popeye replied as he tried to resist the restraints. "Let me go, asshole!"

There was a sharp beep and then a low trilling from a machine out of Popeye's sight. Popeye wanted to see what was going on when he heard a door open and several feet come running inside.

"You were supposed to alert me the second he woke up," a woman said. "Interrogating him now could kill him. Get out, Jowarski. I'll get him stabilized and tell you when he's ready for questioning."

Clean Cut smiled down at Popeye. "Very well, Doctor," he said, "but get him stabilized ASAP. Ballantine will not be out there resting. All of us are dead if he decides to come looking."

"I understand the implications," the woman replied. "Now get out."

Clean Cut nodded and then patted Popeye on the cheek. He left quickly and was replaced by the face of a beautiful woman dressed in scrubs and a lab coat.

"Hello, Mr. De Bruhl," she said. "I apologize for Mr. Jowarski's actions. I can assure you that despite what you heard, your health and well-being is the number one priority here. Now, can you tell me how you are feeling?"

"Where am I?" Popeye asked. "I'm not telling you anything until you tell me where I am and who you are."

"I can't tell you where you are," the woman smiled, "but I can tell you who I am. My name is Dr. Dana Ballantine and once we get you back to the peak of health, you're going to help us find my husband. How does that sound?"

Popeye just gaped at her; he had no idea how that sounded.

The End

CHECK OUT OTHER GREAT DEEP SEA THRILLERS

MEGA
by Jake Bible

There is something in the deep. Something large. Something hungry. Something prehistoric.
And Team Grendel must find it, fight it, and kill it.
Kinsey Thorne, the first female US Navy SEAL candidate has hit rock bottom. Having washed out of the Navy, she turned to every drink and drug she could get her hands on. Until her father and cousins, all ex-Navy SEALS themselves, offer her a way back into the life: as part of a private, elite combat Team being put together to find and hunt down an impossible monster in the Indian Ocean. Kinsey has a second chance, but can she live through it?

THE BLACK
by Paul E Cooley

Under 30,000 feet of water, the exploration rig Leaguer has discovered an oil field larger than Saudi Arabia, with oil so sweet and pure, nations would go to war for the rights to it. But as the team starts drilling exploration well after exploration well in their race to claim the sweet crude, a deep rumbling beneath the ocean floor shakes them all to their core. Something has been living in the oil and it's about to give birth to the greatest threat humanity has ever seen.

"The Black" is a techno/horror-thriller that puts the horror and action of movies such as Leviathan and The Thing right into readers' hands. Ocean exploration will never be the same."

CHECK OUT OTHER GREAT DEEP SEA THRILLERS

PREDATOR X
by C.J Waller

When deep level oil fracking uncovers a vast subterranean sea, a crack team of cavers and scientists are sent down to investigate. Upon their arrival, they disappear without a trace. A second team, including sedimentologist Dr Megan Stoker, are ordered to seek out Alpha Team and report back their findings. But Alpha team are nowhere to be found – instead, they are faced with something unexpected in the depths. Something ancient. Something huge. Something dangerous. Predator X

DEAD BAIT
by Tim Curran

A husband hell-bent on revenge hunts a Wereshark...A Russian mail order bride with a fishy secret...Crabs with a collective consciousness...A vampire who transforms into a Candiru...Zombie piranha...Bait that will have you crawling out of your skin and more. Drawing on horror, humor with a helping of dark fantasy and a touch of deviance, these 19 contemporary stories pay homage to the monsters that lurk in the murky waters of our imaginations. If you thought it was safe to go back in the water...Think Again!

CHECK OUT OTHER GREAT
DEEP SEA THRILLERS

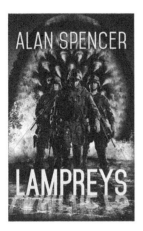

LAMPREYS
by Alan Spencer

A secret government tactical team is sent to perform a clean sweep of a private research installation. Horrible atrocities lurk within the abandoned corridors. Mutated sea creatures with insane killing abilities are waiting to suck the blood and meat from their prey.

Unemployed college professor Conrad Garfield is forced to assist and is soon separated from the team. Alone and afraid, Conrad must use his wits to battle mutated lampreys, infected scientists and go head-to-head with the biggest monstrosity of all.

Can Conrad survive, or will the deadly monsters suck the very life from his body?

DEEP DEVOTION
by M.C. Norris

Rising from the depths, a mind-bending monster unleashes a wave of terror across the American heartland. Kate Browning, a Kansas City EMT confronts her paralyzing fear of water when she traces the source of a deadly parasitic affliction to the Gulf of Mexico. Cooperating with a marine biologist, she travels to Florida in an effort to save the life of one very special patient, but the source of the epidemic happens to be the nest of a terrifying monster, one that last rose from the depths to annihilate the lost continent of Atlantis.

Leviathan, destroyer, devoted lifemate and parent, the abomination is not going to take the extermination of its brood well.

Made in United States
North Haven, CT
29 September 2023

42145735R00137